Never say never. You'd think I'd kr ___

Cross, the fourth in the Noughts and ___

That's it. The series is finished. Excep ___

or we'd soon run out of things to write about. The results of the UK Brexit referendum and the US presidential election in 2016 brought home to me just how potent the politics of fear and division can be. The food we eat, where we live, how we're educated, the job opportunities open to us, the healthcare we receive, how we're treated by the judicial system, the life opportunities afforded to us – every aspect of our lives is governed by politics.

I wrote *Double Cross*, the fourth in the Noughts and Crosses series, because Tobey Durbridge, a minor character in *Checkmate* (the third in the series), began to whisper his story into my ear, and he wouldn't leave me alone until I got it all down. After the events of 2016, Tobey started whispering in my ear again – but he'd changed. He was an adult now, a politician and ruthlessly ambitious. Hell, let's face it. He was just ruthless! It was interesting to explore just what had changed him over the years, and the consequences of that for the next generation.

Crossfire presents the third generation of Noughts and Crosses inhabiting the world I created almost two decades previously. Has life for Noughts improved? Is there more inclusion in society? Less division? I do believe in hope, in two steps forward for every one step back. But sometimes hope is hard to find and harder to hold on to. But hold on to it we must. I wanted to set up a situation for my two younger protagonists, Libby and Troy, which would place them in a predicament where hope was perhaps all they had. A

predicament where they would have to work together and finally *see* each other, otherwise they would both fail. And, as for the older generation of Callie and Tobey, they are in a situation where they need each other but both make mistakes. *Crossfire* is about the guilty, the innocent, motives and consequences.

There is an old proverb that goes, 'Get what you want, and pay for it,' meaning ambition and ruthlessness may serve you in the short term but they come at a price. Sometimes it's those we love who may have to pay that price as they get caught in the crossfire.

It's been such fun revisiting the world I created so many years ago. Fun and daunting. But, like *Noughts and Crosses*, it's a story I *needed* to tell.

I hope you enjoy it.

Malorie Blackman

CROSS FIRE

CROSS FIRE

MALORIE BLACKMAN

PENGUIN BOOKS

PENGUIN BOOKS

UK | USA | Canada | Ireland | Australia
India | New Zealand | South Africa

Penguin Books is part of the Penguin Random House group of companies
whose addresses can be found at global.penguinrandomhouse.com.

www.penguin.co.uk
www.puffin.co.uk
www.ladybird.co.uk

First published 2019

001

Text copyright © Oneta Malorie Blackman, 2019
Cover illustration by Fruzsina Czech

The moral right of the author and illustrator has been asserted

Typeset in 12.04/14.44 pt Bembo Std by Jouve (UK), Milton Keynes
Printed and bound in Great Britain by Clays Ltd, Elcograf S.p.A.

A CIP catalogue record for this book is available from the British Library

HARDBACK ISBN: 978–0–241–38843–3
PAPERBACK ISBN: 978–0–241–38844–0

All correspondence to:
Penguin Books
Penguin Random House Children's
80 Strand, London WC2R 0RL

Malorie Blackman has written over seventy books for children and young adults, including the Noughts & Crosses series, *Thief, Cloud Busting* and a science-fiction thriller, *Chasing the Stars*. Many of her books have also been adapted for stage and television, including a BAFTA-award-winning BBC production of *Pig-Heart Boy* and a Pilot Theatre stage adaptation by Sabrina Mahfouz of *Noughts & Crosses*. There is also a major BBC production of *Noughts & Crosses*, with Roc Nation (Jay-Z's entertainment company) curating and releasing the soundtrack as executive music producer.

In 2005 Malorie was honoured with the Eleanor Farjeon Award in recognition of her distinguished contribution to the world of children's books. In 2008 she received an OBE for her services to children's literature, and between 2013 and 2015 she was the Children's Laureate. Most recently, Malorie co-wrote the *Doctor Who* episode 'Rosa' on BBC One.

You can find Malorie online:
www.malorieblackman.co.uk
@malorieblackman

For Neil and Liz, with love as always

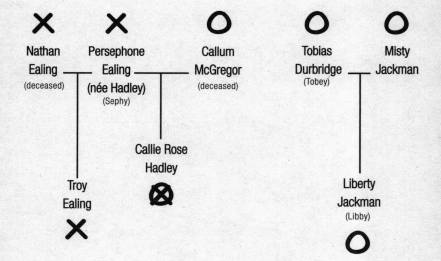

Nathan Ealing (deceased)

Persephone Ealing (née Hadley) (Sephy)

Callum McGregor (deceased)

Tobias Durbridge (Tobey)

Misty Jackman

Callie Rose Hadley

Troy Ealing

Liberty Jackman (Libby)

PROLOGUE

The Catalyst

one. Callie

A Nought woman, no doubt some poor jobbing actress desperate to pay her rent, knelt down in the middle of a stylized pigsty. She held twelve leads attached to a number of decorated sculptures of life-sized pink pigs that surrounded her like the petals of a flower, all looking out at the audience. Some of the pigs wore clothes – one a military uniform, another a flowery straw hat and gold-coloured high-heeled shoes. One sported a gaudy sapphire and diamond necklace, the stones as big as plums. Two of them were simulating copulation. The Nought woman at their centre wore a bodysuit that at first glance made her appear naked. She was kneeling, her head down. At random intervals, she looked up to stare at the person directly in front of her for a few seconds before slowly bowing her head again. Now it was my turn to receive her numb stare. My lips twisted in distaste. Blinking rapidly, the 'exhibit' lowered her head, her cheeks reddening.

Embarrassed for both of us, I said quietly, 'The look on my face wasn't aimed at you. It was aimed at this ridiculous so-called art installation.'

The woman's head remained bent, the slight tensing of her shoulders and reddened face the only indications that she'd heard my words. Whether or not she believed them was another matter.

I shook my head, sighing inwardly. It had taken me years to cultivate a poker face, but there were moments − like now − when the mask inadvertently slipped. After glancing at my watch, I took a seat at one end of the gallery. A huge sign hanging above all the exhibits declared: ALBION − LESSONS LEARNED: A 21ST-CENTURY RETROSPECTIVE. Talk about the chieftain's new robes. This was supposed to be the most avant-garde, exciting art exhibition currently in the capital. Nought actors and actresses adorned the various works of art, a few of them naked, some covered from head to toe in body paint of various hues. They sat in, on or among the various exhibits, seldom moving. The whole thing had a melancholy air of crass awkwardness to it.

If I were an art critic, I knew how my review would read: *Dubious style and precious little substance.* The few articles I'd read about this so-called exhibition described it as 'daring', 'innovative', 'a fresh take' − blah-blah.

Yeah, right.

Sauley J'Hara, the Cross artist responsible for this hot mess, had been all over the news during the last two weeks, responding to the very vocal criticism of his art stylings.

'It's a challenging, forward-thinking look at how we used to regard and treat Noughts, juxtaposed with how they are regarded now,' he'd argued. 'This isn't a museum's historical installation; this is art.'

What a steaming pile of horse manure. An exploiter, seeking to define and monetize the exploited. If it really was art, why not use Crosses and other ethnicities in his exhibition? The whole thing was nothing more than a self-congratulatory exercise in nostalgia for the backward thinkers who still wished – or still believed – they lived in the past.

I looked up at the ceiling and cornices. Now *there* was real art. Panels depicting Zafrika's history – some carved from wood, some from marble, some just painted, but all exquisitely beautiful. I glanced down at my watch again. It hadn't been my choice to meet here and I was burning to leave. The ceiling, which was part of the fabric of the building, I admired. The rest of the exhibition in this gallery was making my skin itch. I drank in the artwork on the ceiling, closing my eyes to imprint it on my memory as I lowered my head. A sudden frisson of awareness crackled through me like a static shock.

'Hello, Callie. What's what?'

The baritone voice made my head snap up.

Tobey Durbridge.

Damn it! My heart jumped at the sight of him, dragging me to my feet. God, it had been so long. Too long. When did the air get so thin in here? There was no other explanation for feeling this light-headed.

Oh, come on! You're a grown woman for God's sake. Get a grip, Callie Rose!

It had been such a long time since Tobey and I last met. A lifetime ago. What had I been expecting? Certainly not this. Over the years, just like the rest of the country, I'd seen Tobey on the TV countless times as he rose in prominence to become the first elected Nought Mayor of Meadowview, then a Member of Parliament, but seeing him in person was so different. Tobey had moved on and up – the only directions he was ever interested in. He was now the country's first publicly elected Nought Prime Minister and there wasn't a single soul in the country and beyond who didn't know his name. As Solomon Camden, the head of my law chambers, had put it, 'Only a fool would bet against Tobey Durbridge.'

And how had I voted in the recent general election?

Well, I was nobody's fool.

Over the last twelve years, during each general election, the public had had the chance not just to vote for the person they wanted to represent their constituency, but also to choose between two or three candidates from each of the main political parties who would run the country should that party win the majority vote. After the scandal that hit the Liberal Traditionalists a decade ago, it had been judged a more democratic way of electing our country's leader, rather than just relying on each political party to select candidates who may have bought or bribed their way to the top. Over the last couple of years, not a week passed without Tobey making the news headlines, and, when it was announced he was running for Prime Minister, I understood why. Publicity. Publicity. Publicity. The lifeblood of the ambitious.

But, even without all the TV coverage, I would've known this man anywhere. The Tobey of old with his chestnut-brown hair and darker brown eyes still stood in front of me, but his face was harder, and his lips were thinner, and the gleam he'd always had in his eyes – like he was constantly on the verge of a smile – well, that had all but vanished. Something told me it would take a lot to make Tobey smile these days. And he'd filled out. He was not just taller but broader. He made me feel like I was slacking on the body-conscious front. Which I was, I admit. I enjoyed my food! I hit the treadmill regularly, but only so I wouldn't have to buy a whole new wardrobe every six months. Tobey, on the other hand, wore his charcoal-grey suit like a second skin. That hadn't come off a hanger in a department store. His suit screamed bespoke from the rooftops. His black shoes didn't have a scuff mark on them; his white shirt was spotless, as was his purple silk tie. Damn! He was wearing the hell out of every stitch he had on. Instead of looking staid and boring, he managed to make the whole ensemble look . . . dangerous. Like this guy could quite easily hand you your head if you messed with him, and still look fine doing it.

Suddenly aware that I was staring, I mock sighed. 'For Shaka's sake! I see you're still taller than me.'

A shared smile – and just like that the tension between us lifted.

We grinned at each other as the years began to fall away, but then reality rudely shoved its way between us. Another moment, as we regarded each other. My mind was racing. Should we kiss? Hug? What? I moved forward at the same time as Tobey. A brief, awkward kiss on the lips was followed by a long hug. The warmth of his body and the subtle smell of his aftershave enveloped me. I stepped back. The moment for anything deeper, anything more, came and went and faded away unclaimed.

'It's so good to see you, Tobey.' I felt faintly foolish that I'd had such a visceral reaction to him. 'How are you?'

Tobey opened his mouth, only to close it without saying a word. An eyebrow quirked, followed by that wry smile of his — there it was! 'I was going to say, *All the better for seeing you*, but you deserve more than cheesy lines and platitudes.'

Momentarily thrown, I wondered how exactly I was meant to respond to that.

Tobey indicated the seat behind us. He waited for me to sit before parking himself next to me, his thigh pressed lightly against mine. His warmth was unsettling in its familiarity. I should've moved my leg slightly so that we were no longer touching — but I didn't.

Time for a change of subject. 'You and Misty — I guess things didn't work out between you?'

'No. We tried for a while but — no. Does that please you?' said Tobey.

Stung, I said, 'D'you think I'm so petty that I'll jump up and down with glee at the news of your break-up? Seriously?'

Thanks a lot.

'You did warn me that I was making a mistake.' Tobey shrugged. 'And more than once.'

My cheeks burned. Not some of my finer moments. 'I was wrong to do that. One of my many regrets when it comes to you — and us.'

'Oh? What else d'you regret?' Tobey asked quietly.

I might have known he'd leap all over that one. No way was I going there.

'How's your family?' I asked.

'They're fine. Jessica is doing a masters at uni now and Mum is enjoying her retirement. How's Troy?' said Tobey.

I shrugged. 'Same as ever. He manages to work my last nerve every time we meet.'

Tobey smiled. 'Isn't that what all brothers are meant to do to their sisters? I know I have that effect on Jess.'

'Troy works extra hard at it. He's seventeen so he's at the age when he knows *everything*. I love my brother, but he's hard work.'

'And your mum? How's Sephy?'

'She's fine. Still running the restaurant,' I replied.

Tobey nodded. 'I was sorry to hear about what happened to Nathan.'

'Thanks.'

'I mean it. I meant to get in touch, but . . . you know how it is.'

Yeah, I knew exactly how it was. We were old friends who shared painful memories – and a great deal of hurt. How much easier then to let our friendship simmer at a distance rather than boil away to nothing or, worse still, turn to ice between us.

'Is it worth me apologizing again for what happened?' asked Tobey, not looking at me but at the people milling about the gallery.

'Tobey, let it go. I have.' Which wasn't quite true, but it would do. 'Is that why you asked me to meet you here? To rehash old times?'

'God, no. That's the last thing I want.' Tobey now looked directly at me.

As we regarded each other, I felt yet another crack ripple through my heart for what might have been.

So many wasted years. So much wasted time.

'Why did you want to meet here of all places?' I had to ask as I took another look around.

'Restaurant tables can be bugged. Outdoor listening devices have a range of one hundred metres and more; some can pick up conversations through walls. Museums and art galleries tend to have scanner jammers and disruptors built into the fabric of the building so that no one can bypass their security. When I want a truly private conversation, this is where I come. And it's close to my office.'

'Oh, I see.'

Nothing to do with the current exhibition then, I realized.

'I'm surprised to see you alone. Don't you have minders?' I couldn't quite believe that Tobey wandered the streets and went where he liked without bodyguards and security up to his armpits. God knows, there'd been enough threats against his life from the headbangers who believed that being Prime Minister and a Nought should be mutually exclusive. There were even some Nought nutjobs who considered Tobey a traitor for engaging in what they considered 'Cross politics'.

'They're here, don't worry.' Tobey gave a faint smile.

Ah! I should've known. There had to be upwards of fifty people in the gallery, but Tobey didn't seem at all concerned. That meant his security detail had to be top-drawer. So good in fact that, as I looked around the room, I had to work at guessing who they might be – there had to be more than one. A Cross woman with braided hair and glasses studiously examined the painting to my right. I'd put money on her being one of Tobey's bodyguards – or close-protection officers, as they preferred to be known. I continued to look around. A suited Nought man by one of the middle installations kept throwing careless glances in our direction. He wore wireless earbuds like he was listening to music, but I knew better. He was definitely another of Tobey's close-protection officers. I had a nose for them, like I had a nose for undercover cops, guilty clients and bullshit.

And that nose didn't lie or steer me wrong.

Tobey and I were getting some curious glances – Tobey more than me. He was instantly recognizable. Famous and powerful – a killer combination. In the years since school, any doors that hadn't opened for him automatically, Tobey had kicked in. Hard. A couple of people, when they recognized him, immediately tried to make their way over, but they were diverted by a tall, beefy Cross wearing a suit, sunglasses – indoors! – and earbuds. The sunglasses indoors were a dead giveaway.

'So why did you want to see me after all this time?' I asked. 'Shouldn't you be off somewhere being interviewed to within a millimetre of your sanity?'

'I should but I need you, Callie. Look, I'd love to play catch-up and then honey-coat this, but I don't have the time.' Tobey sighed. He took a deep breath, looking into my eyes. 'The thing is . . . I . . . Well, I need your help.'

I bit the inside of my cheek to suppress a grin. 'Wow. Those are obviously some rusty words.'

'Huh?'

'You're not used to asking for help, are you?' I teased.

Tobey's smile faded as quickly as it had arrived. 'You're right, but I really do need you. The thing is – within the next week to ten days, I'm going to be arrested for murder and I require a good lawyer. The best. And that's you.'

What?

Well, damn! Whatever I'd been expecting, that wasn't it. I stared. 'Who are you supposed to have killed?'

Tobey didn't flinch, didn't look away. He didn't even blink. 'Daniel Jeavons.'

My eyes were starting to hurt from staring so hard. A super-surreal conversation in an unconventional setting. Come to think of it, there was no better place for this revelation.

'Dan? Dan is dead?'

Tobey nodded.

Daniel Jeavons, 'ex' criminal and shady AF kingmaker, was dead. Stunned, I tried to process what I'd just heard.

Dan was dead.

'Did you do it?' I asked, the words falling out of nowhere.

The art gallery, the capital, the country, the whole world fell away until there was just Tobey and me watching each other – and the question pushing, pulsing, between us.

NOW

two. Troy

OW! A cascade of pain volley-punches me awake. With a groan, I slowly open my eyes. Damn it! My wrists, my shins, knees, neck, even my backside ache. The jabs and stabs of pain overlap and keep coming. And my head . . . That hurts worst of all. My head is in a vice and, with each beat of my heart, the vice tightens – gripping, squeezing. I stare up at the ceiling, its sickly yellow-brown colour telling me nothing, before closing my eyes again.

Where the hell am I?

I remember walking back to school—

'Troy! Wake up, damn it. Troy—'

I try to sit up, only to groan again as the vice tightens its grip on my skull in response. The pain is now so acute I feel physically sick from it. I lie back again and, swallowing down the bile now filling my mouth, concentrate on my breathing. *In. Out. Rinse. Repeat.* Rolling in the direction of the voice, I try to focus on the person lying on the ground over a metre away.

'Libby?' I whisper, stunned.

A juggernaut of memories slams into me. A dusty, dirty grey van . . . The doors at the back bursting open . . . Two men wearing animal masks – a rabbit and a tiger – jumping out . . . an arm round my throat . . . struggling for air . . . wrists cable-tied behind me, the plastic biting into my skin . . . a filthy cloth pushed into my mouth, a canvas bag pulled over my face . . . being dragged backwards and thrown into the rear of the van . . . my head hitting something hard. Pain ricocheting around my skull as the van pulls away at speed.

I stare at Libby as more jarring memories crash through my mind. I relive them all.

Being dragged out of the van by my feet, the canvas bag pulled further down my face so I can't see where we are. I try to run, though I can barely make out shapes through the bag over my face. A crippling punch to the side of my head comes like an explosion inside my skull. I drop to my knees. Flashing lights strobe before my eyes. While I'm dazed and doubled over, my phone is removed from my trouser pocket, my smart watch from my wrist. I'm half hauled, half carried into this place – wherever and whatever this place might be. Though my face is still covered, I know I'm being taken inside some kind of building. Sounds echo differently. The very air around me morphs into something stale and rank. I buck and kick and twist like a snake shedding its skin, but the two men carrying me never loosen their grip.

Moments later, I'm dragged down a couple of steps. The canvas bag is pulled off me, then there's a brief feeling of weightlessness as I'm pushed and fall the rest of the way down the stairs. The crack of my knees as I hit the hard floor sends a flare of white-hot agony shooting through my body. There's a sharper crack as I pitch forward and my head hits the floor.

Then . . . nothing.

Until now. Here I am, hurting and with many more questions than answers. All I know for certain is that Libby and I are in the same place. And where's that? A world of trouble I didn't volunteer to visit. I force myself to try sitting up again. Every muscle braced and clenched, I push myself upright.

'Libby, what – and I sincerely mean this – the actual bollocks is going on?'

'We've been snatched off the street and brought here. Now you know as much as me,' Libby replies. 'Hang on. Let me try to get you free, then you can do the same for me.'

For the first time, I notice that Libby's wrists are bound with a cable tie in front of her. I try to stand, but my head immediately starts to swim again. All I can do for the next few moments is kneel as if in prayer and wait for the pounding in my head to lessen. She shuffles over to kneel behind me. Though her wrists are bound, I feel her hands moving over the ties around my wrists. I'm so glad to see her, hear her, feel her fingers against my skin. I'm not alone.

'Are you OK? Did you . . . did you faint or something in the van?' I ask, recalling how still she was in the van after we were abducted.

'No. A cloth smelling of something sweet was put over my mouth and nose,' says Libby. 'That's all I remember until I woke down here. Now the skin round my mouth and nostrils is burning.'

'They drugged you?'

'Must've done.'

'Why you and not me?' I ask.

'No idea. Ask me another,' says Libby.

'Ow! I don't know what you're doing back there, but you're making things worse,' I tell her as the cable ties tighten.

'Patience.'

I'm about to yell at her for trying to slice my hands clean off my arms when suddenly I'm free.

'My turn,' Libby says.

Vigorously rubbing my wrists, I turn towards her and start pulling at the tie around her wrists.

'Not like that, you idiot,' she says. 'You have to stick your fingernail in the recessed bit and push it down, then you can slide the tie out. Don't you know anything?'

Glad to hear her? I'm beginning to rethink that one. I frown, my fingers still on her wrists. Shaka on a unicycle! Even when I'm doing her a favour, she still manages to make it sound like the other way round.

'I'm doing my best.'

Libby sniffs. 'Do better. You're hurting me.'

Breathe, Troy . . .

If it wasn't for the fact that I might need her help to get out of this room, I would've happily left her wrists tied. Would it kill her to be a little more pleasant? After a lot of prodding, poking and pulling, I finally manage to loosen the cable tie enough for Libby to slip her hands out. The look she casts at me as she rubs her wrists tells me she is less than impressed with my efforts. What does she want? My fingers aren't as slender as hers and besides, when fastened, these bastard cable ties are designed to stay that way.

Now that Libby is free, I take a proper look around.

We're in a dark, dank, dingy room filled with crates and boxes. And it stinks of things dead or slowly dying. A single light bulb hangs from a frayed wire on one side of the room, close to a wooden staircase that's seen better days. The bulb's sickly yellow light barely makes it to the nearest walls, casting the rest of the room in lurking shadows and creeping darkness. A windowless, confined space. A walk-in coffin with a light bulb. Not good. I swallow hard.

'Where exactly are we?' I ask again, failing to disguise the tremor in my voice.

'I don't know,' says Libby. 'How long were we in the van?'

'About thirty minutes, maybe more, maybe less,' I reply.

'Well, as an answer, that's worse than useless.'

Thanks, Libby, but I already knew that. I didn't exactly have a chance to set the timer on my phone.

The pain in my head slowly begins to subside – thank God. I head up the rickety wooden stairs.

'I wouldn't bother,' Libby calls after me. 'Whoever kidnapped us locked and bolted the door when they left.'

I try the door anyway, turning then rattling the door handle. I push against the door, then shoulder it. It doesn't budge. I kick it a couple of times. It barely moves. It sure as hell isn't made of MDF or chipboard. The ache in my toes and my bruised shoulder informs me that it's solid wood, no messing about. I head back down the stairs.

'Feel better for that?' asks Libby.

Ignoring her snide comment, I concentrate on using another sense. There are no ambient sounds – no cars, no voices, no plane noises. Nothing.

'You still got your phone?' I ask Libby. 'They took mine.'

She shakes her head. 'They took mine too.'

'So we're locked down here with no phones and no means of escape?'

'That's about the size of it,' Libby confirms.

No phone? I'm never without my phone. I even sleep with it under my pillow. Damn it! Why didn't they just take one of my arms and have done with it?

'Did you see or hear anything useful when they brought us in here?' I ask. 'Anything at all?'

Again Libby shakes her head. 'I mean . . . I thought I heard . . . seagulls of all things. But I can't be sure.'

Seagulls? Surely we hadn't driven anywhere near long enough to have made it to the nearest coast? Thirty to forty minutes was, however, plenty of time to get us somewhere near the capital's river. And the fact that I couldn't hear any traffic or people noises must mean we've been brought to one of the many areas of the capital that are derelict and deserted, earmarked for renovation that's been a long time coming. If we're banged up in one of those districts, we'll be skeletal remains before we're ever found. My heart bounces, super-ball-style. I've been concentrating on anything and everything except the reality of our situation. That's not working any more. Our predicament begins to well and truly sink in. This isn't a prank. Or a dream. It's as real as my last breath, as true as my next one.

'This has to be the basement of a house.' Libby says what I'm thinking.

I nod. 'But whose house? Have you had the chance to check out down here yet? Maybe there's a window or another door—'

'Yeah, of course I did,' she exclaims. 'The moment they threw me down here, I sprang up with my hands still tied and sprinted around the room twice, whistling the national anthem. Give me a minute to catch my breath and then I'll punch right through a wall and fly us out of here.'

Sarky trout. 'For Shaka's sake! A simple no would've done, Liberty.'

'Don't ask stupid-ass questions then.'

We scowl at each other. I have to bite my lip – literally – to stop myself taking her head off. Then it hits me. She's as scared as I am. That's why she's being so vicious. But she's always vicious. She must be scared all the time.

Let it go, Troy. You've got more pressing things to worry about.

Time to put some space between me and the poison mushroom – as Libby is affectionately known at school by all those who've been lucky enough to meet her. Finding a way out of this place is the top priority.

I don't do well in confined spaces.

I head away from the stairs towards the darker recesses of this dank basement. Libby follows. More boxes. More debris. Where I can actually get to the walls, there's just icy-cold, rough brickwork scratching at my fingers – and nothing else. At one point, something skitters past my foot. I only just manage not to squeal. I can imagine how that'd play with Libby. She'd never let me hear the end of it. We edge around as best we can, feeling our way where the light doesn't quite reach and shadows like snatching fingers claw at us.

As I feel my way along walls that are shrouded in gloom, I ask, 'Libby, did you notice anything about the scumbags who grabbed us?'

Behind me, Libby sighs. 'I caught a glimpse of the driver when I was thrown over the shoulder of crapstick number one.'

She pushes past me to feel her way along the crates against the wall. Obviously I wasn't moving fast enough. I scowl at the back of her head, but she's oblivious. Naturally. When Libby looks at me, she sees a Cross and then she stops looking. She doesn't see anything else; she doesn't want to see anything else because, as far as Libby is concerned, there's nothing more to see. Remembering how she used to be when we initially met during our first year at Heathcroft High makes me shake my head. The difference between Libby then and Libby now is startling and wider than the Grand Canyon.

I resume my search, examining each crate we pass. Some have lids; most don't. Every single one is empty. As I feel along the walls, I'm checking for draughts that might indicate another door or painted-over window. Occasionally, I tap the walls, listening out for a hollow sound that could mean there's a forgotten room beyond. The solid cold of the rough brick is a constant beneath my fingers.

'Did you see the driver's face?' I ask.

In front of me, Libby nods. 'He was skinny and wearing a black leather jacket and a fox mask covering his whole head. The one who carried me in here was taller and broader and wearing enough aftershave to choke a horse.'

At once I remember the aftershave. It was so strong it caught in the back of my throat. But that doesn't move us any further forward.

'How can someone drive along the city streets wearing a fox mask and not get pulled over or at least noticed?' I frown.

Libby shrugs. 'Maybe he put it back on once the van had stopped?'

Which I have to admit sounds more reasonable. Time to stop skirting round the issue.

'Why are we here? D'you know?' I ask. 'What do they want with us?'

Libby turns to me, shaking her head. Even in this half-light, I can see her blue eyes shimmering with unshed tears. She turns away, embarrassed.

'None of them said anything?' I ask.

'A lot of cussing from the one who carried me down here. That's it.'

A couple of minutes later, we've explored the entire basement. No windows. No doors. No cupboards. No hidden alcoves. The boxes and crates are all empty, and the bucket and two rolls of toilet paper in one corner of the room shout that we're not about to be released any time soon.

We are in a world of trouble.

I regard Libby, refusing to believe that our situation is as hopeless as it appears. Tears are spiking her lower lashes now. Her lips are quivering. She's that close to breaking down completely. Oh hell, no!

'You're not going to start blubbing, are you? That'll make your cheeks wet, but how will it help our situation?'

Libby shakes her head, her expression dripping annoyance. OK, so that worked!

'I would get stuck with you, of all people. You're not exactly one of those guys, are you?'

I frown. 'What guys?'

'Those guys who can take a box, a paper clip and some chewing gum and build a tank to get us out of here.' Libby looks me up and down, unimpressed.

Oh my God! She's serious! I should be used to that expression when she looks at me by now, but I'm not. It pisses me off.

'I'm all out of chewing gum,' I inform her.

'Improvise.'

'I've got news for you, Libby. Guys like that don't exist outside of action films.'

'Well, what *can* you do?' Libby throws down the challenge.

'Plenty.'

'Nothing useful though, eh?'

I study her. 'I've just realized I've died and gone to hell.'

'I'm in your hell then?' she mocks.

'You *are* my hell, Libby. You always have been.'

Libby's eyes narrow. 'I'm not in any rush to have your babies either, Troy.'

I cough a couple of times, before wiping my mouth with the back of my hand. 'Don't even joke! God, I just threw up in my mouth at the prospect.'

'Screw you, Troy.'

'Only if I was comatose and floating in a vat of penicillin,' I shoot back.

We glare at each other, the loathing deep-seated and mutual.

Libby sighs, looking away first. 'How about we work

together to get out of here first and resume hating each other afterwards?'

I nod. My dislike of Libby is hardly the most important thing at the moment. 'Suits me. So what d'you suggest, as I'm so useless? Come on. I'm all ears.'

'We need to come up with some way of getting out of here.'

'Duh!'

'I just meant that, as the only way out is up those stairs and past our kidnappers, we need to be prepared the next time the door opens.'

I nod. 'That makes sense.'

'Glad you think so.'

'What we need is a way to arm ourselves with some kind of weapon.' But what?

The boxes are made of wilting, rotten cardboard so they're no use. I check out the nearest crate. It's solid wood, reinforced with thick metal strips along its sides. No way am I taking one of those apart with my bare hands. I push it to the closest wall, picking up speed as I approach. The thing smashes into the wall, then rebounds to crash into my legs. It hurts. A lot. Won't be doing that twice. I try picking it up to slam it back down again. Maybe it'll fall to pieces that way? Nope. All it does is scratch up my hands. So much for that then. I push the crate till it's under the light bulb, a metre away from the foot of the wooden steps. At least it makes a solid chair. I need to think. Not panic. Think.

'Budge up then.' To my surprise, Libby sits next to me, her body warm against mine.

I move over so that we're no longer touching. Glancing around, I wonder if it's worth taking a second look in all the boxes and crates. Maybe we missed something. But it's wishful thinking. Besides, no kidnapper with any brains would put us in a room with potential weapons or an escape route.

'I've been thinking about why they drugged me and not you,' says Libby.

'I'm listening.'

'I reckon they only meant to grab one of us. Before I passed out in the van, I heard one of them say that, as we were together, they had no choice but to take us both.'

I regard Libby. 'Which one of us did they mean to take then?'

Libby shrugs. Her words circle and land heavily on my shoulders. If what she said is true, then that means one of us is expendable. Libby and I study each other as the truth sinks its claws into us.

'Troy, I . . . I'm scared,' Libby admits.

We sit in silence, alone together. Another look around the basement, with its clutching shadows and its intermittent skittering noises. The walls are breathing – in out, in out. The ceiling is slowly but inexorably coming down to crush me. I close my eyes.

Mind over matter.

You can do this, Troy. Breathe in. Breathe out. Think it and blink it all away.

I open my eyes. The walls have stopped breathing, the ceiling has stopped descending, but I'm still locked in the basement – with Libby. It's only a matter of time before the walls start to heave again. If we're not rescued soon, losing it will be a matter of *when*, not *if*. Libby moves closer. We're almost touching. Almost but not quite. Silence reigns for too long. Despair, like icy hands, steals round my chest to hug me, squeezing and freezing by degrees, making it hard to catch my breath. It's a struggle to think clearly, what with the sheer dread bubbling up inside. I force it down, knowing it's in me now and won't depart until I'm out of this basement. In fact, the longer I'm in here, the harder it will become not to freak out. I can't do that, not in front of Libby of all people – but she's already told me she's frightened. Whether I like it or not, we're in this together.

'I'm scared too,' I say quietly.

What the hell has happened to bring both of us to this dank basement and this predicament? If I can figure that out, then maybe, just maybe, I can think of a way to get us out of here.

Daily Shouter Online

Kamal Hadley's love child, Yaro Hadley-Baloyi, reveals all about the father who disowned him

Yaro Hadley-Baloyi has broken his silence regarding his politician father, Kamal Hadley, who died last year. It has recently come to light that Kamal Hadley, who served as Home Secretary of the Liberal Traditionalist party from 1998 to 2008, had a dual-heritage son whom he kept hidden from public gaze. Kamal Hadley, who often spoke out against miscegenation at the start of his career, is now being called 'a raging hypocrite' in some political circles. He famously disinherited his daughter, Persephone Hadley, when she became pregnant by Callum McGregor, a Nought who was later hanged for terrorist activities.

THEN

Daily Shouter Online

The Democratic Alliance ahead in the polls for the first time

The Democratic Alliance party are ahead in the polls for the first time, with the general election only days away. Tobias Durbridge, Nought, 36, and Lydia Scruggs-Morsanya, Cross, 47, are currently neck and neck in the polls to become both leader of the DA and Prime Minister should the DA win the election.

Opinion

The *Daily Shouter* believes that our country is not yet ready for a Nought Prime Minister. It must surely happen one day, but Tobias Durbridge is not ready for the role. For one, he is far too unseasoned. Though popular with younger voters, the *Daily Shouter* questions whether his words and demeanour carry enough gravitas to be taken seriously. The Prime Minister should be a statesman, someone who will be respected by our country's friends and enemies alike. Though he has been a Member of Parliament for a number of years, as well as a former Mayor of Meadowview, that hardly qualifies him to run the country. His degree was completed part-time and his family is totally unsuitable. The *Daily Shouter* has learned that his sister, Jessica, used to have a drug problem. In only a few days, our country will have to make a decision on not just which party but which leader shall govern us. The *Daily Shouter* says that, if you must vote for the DA, then Lydia Scruggs-Morsanya is the only right and logical choice for leader.

'Libby, you can't just assume you'll get the votes of everyone who isn't a Cross,' says Raffy. 'That's not how it works.'

I scowl at Raffaella, or Raffy as she prefers to be known. She's a Nought, the shortest girl in our year and one of the smartest. And, unlike most people I've met, she doesn't just speak to hear herself. She only opens her mouth when she's got something to say – and it's usually worth listening to. Except for now. What's my friend talking about? The others running against me in the forthcoming school election are no competition at all – that's why I'd get most of the votes. Besides, 'Why on earth would the Noughts in this school vote for anyone else?'

Raffy shakes her head, her auburn cornrows working loose. By the end of the day, they'd be out completely – as per usual. 'Libby, it's not a foregone conclusion. You need to let everyone know what you stand for. If you want to be head girl, you've got to convince the majority of the school to vote for you and your policies, not just Noughts.'

'No one's going to vote for you if they don't know what they're voting for,' says Maisie, who looks enough like me for the two of us to be mistaken for sisters. But our looks are where the similarities end. Maisie is laidback to the point of tipping over. Me? Not so much.

'And, even if you get the vote of every Nought in the school, that's still not enough to win the head-girl election,' Raffy adds.

I frown. My friends are right. Looking around the sixth-form common room, I notice it's unusually full for the beginning of the lunch break. Usually, at this time of day, there's less than a dozen people in here, but there are at least three times that many scattered throughout the room. I'd say the room – like the school – is just over one-third FEN (Fenno-Skandian, Eastern and Nought) and just under two-thirds Cross, mostly of Zafrikan heritage. A couple of metres away sit Troy and his friends, Zane and Ayo. Troy Ealing – the fly in my ointment, the boil on my backside, the pain in my neck. Troy Ealing with his perfect mahogany skin and his perfect teeth and his perfect smile. God, but that guy loves himself, and he expects everyone to feel the same way. And to think that once . . . No! I'm not going there! I turn back to Raffy and Maisie.

'At least when people vote for me they know that what they see is what they get,' I tell them. 'I'm not about to start trying to bribe people by making promises I know I can't keep.'

I notice the volume of chatter has died down around me as those closest start to listen to what I'm saying. If Raffy reckons I should let people know what I stand for, then that's exactly what I'll do. I get to my feet. Time to turn up the volume.

'What this school needs, what we all need, is someone

who will take the role seriously. Someone who will be an advocate for us students against the teachers. Someone who isn't afraid to speak the truth, even when it's unpopular.'

A few heads turn my way.

'What this school needs is a head girl who isn't hidebound by so-called tradition.' A few more heads turn. 'The status quo? The same old, same old? That doesn't work for everyone. I want to be the voice of those who aren't afraid of change.'

I'm the centre of attention. Good. Even Troy is watching me. No harm in doing some campaigning here and now. Every little helps.

'If you vote for me to be head girl, I promise I will take it to the teachers and fight for the whole student body, unlike some of those I'm running against who are too gutless to stand up and be counted. It doesn't matter to me if you're Albion, Zafrikan, Western, Eastern or Fenno-Skandian, I'm here for you and you will always have my full support. Votes for Dina and Meshella are wasted votes. They only care about their own. And Zane's only running because he thinks it'll impress us girls.'

'Oi!' Zane calls out.

Eyebrows raised, I look at Zane pointedly, daring him to deny it. His face immediately flushes red. 'That's a lie. I want to be head boy because . . . because . . . er . . .'

I turn to Troy with a satisfied smile. 'I rest my case.'

'You arse!' Troy exclaims at the expression on his biracial friend's face. 'Is that seriously why you're running for head boy?'

'Course not!' Zane's face is now an interesting shade of beetroot.

'Once more with feeling.' Is the disdain in my voice noticeable? I hope so! 'Whereas I will represent everyone and I can be trusted to keep my word, unlike Meshella and Dina.'

'Why can't they be trusted, Libby?' Ayo calls out. 'Because they're Crosses?'

'You said that; I didn't,' I call back. 'But if the shoe fits—'

Murmurs ripple around the common room.

'Playing the race card, Libby?' Troy calls out, a scalpel-sharp edge to his voice. 'That's low, even for you.'

'Troy, I'm not going to let you put me off my stride.'

'What strides would they be?' asks Troy. 'You think you're going to get us Crosses to vote for you after you insult us by saying we only care about our own? Are you really that stupid?'

I look around. Some people are frowning at me; others are giving me serious side-eye. What did I say? I replay my words. I didn't say anything that wasn't true. Some of the Crosses have obviously taken it in a bad way. Time for some damage control.

'You misunderstood me—' I begin.

'No, I think we're all smart enough to understand exactly what you meant,' Troy interrupts. 'Channelling your mum there, Libby?'

I scowl at him. Why bring my mum into this?

'Liberty, why don't you sit down?' someone calls out from across the common room.

Troy applauds in agreement.

'I didn't mean Crosses couldn't be trusted as such,' I say hastily. 'I only meant that it's natural that you Crosses would look out for your own first. Meshella and Dina would say as much if they were here—'

'No, they wouldn't,' Troy argues. 'And it's funny how you wait for both of them to be out of the room to trash-talk them. What else would you be saying about Zane if he wasn't sitting next to me?'

Shut up, Troy. Shut up. Shut Up. SHUT UP!

'I just mean that, as head girl, I promise to work on behalf of each and every student in this school.' I force a smile.

'Well, I don't need a crystal ball to know that if you became head girl it'd be a disaster. You'd play one group against another against another until the whole school fractured and became just as toxic as you,' says Troy. 'That's not gonna happen. Not on my watch.'

'I don't know what you're talking about.' I hate the picture he's painting of me, like I'm some kind of self-centred bigot, playing divide and conquer. I'm not.

'You know what?' Troy stands up, addressing the whole common room. 'At the beginning of term, Mrs Paxton said I should run for head boy and I turned her down, but I've changed my mind. I'm going to run and run hard for head boy – and, unlike some, I won't be trash-talking the opposition to make myself look good. I'll be running a positive campaign, addressing the issues we all care about. I'd appreciate your support and votes.'

A spontaneous round of applause fills the common room. People clap and stamp and whistle their support. Troy turns back to me with a smirk on his face. The gauntlet has been thrown down. Hard. I now have some serious competition in the race to be head student. Troy will bring it. But let him do his worst. He won't win.

I don't care what it takes, but I will be head girl of Heathcroft High, and nothing and no one is going to get in my way. Or take it away from me. As a Nought with no money, making head girl of Heathcroft High plus my predicted final grades are my one shot at getting a scholarship to university. It's my only way up and my only path out. I won't let anyone get in the way of that. Especially not Troy Ealing.

four. Troy

Yeah, that wiped the smile off your face, Liberty Jackman!

Mrs Paxton has been hassling me since the beginning of term to run for head boy. During our last conversation on the subject, she said, 'Head boy would suit you and your temperament, Troy. You could really shake things up in a constructive way. We should all strive to make a positive difference.'

Do me a favour. 'No thanks, Mrs Paxton.'

The head wasn't going to give up. 'Just think about it. Promise me you'll consider it?'

I smiled politely and nodded while thinking, *I'd rather be kicked in the bollocks, thanks for asking!*

To be honest, I suspect she was expecting me to run because of my family background. What? Did she think that with my sister Callie and what happened to her dad, Callum McGregor, I'd want to stand up for truth, justice and the Heathcroft High way? If so, then disappointment was coming at her, top speed. In fact, if that's what she was expecting, then it's kinda insulting. Not a fan of people assuming they know all about me. My family's personal business is private and I've worked hard to keep it that way. Apart from Mrs Paxton, a couple of teachers who'd been at

Heathcroft High forever and one other person at school, my family's secrets are safe. I haven't even told my best mates. In all my years at Heathcroft, no one has ever confronted me about Mum and Callum McGregor, and that's the way I like it.

So, as far as I was concerned, the school election? Count me out. And it would've stayed that way if Libby had kept her mouth shut. She's glowering at me. Is that supposed to make me back down? Apologize? Tremble? Do me a favour! God, but she really is pathetic. And to think that during our first year at school we were actually friends. Best friends.

Libby walks over to stand before me. I rise to my feet. Tense. Waiting. What's she going to do?

'You won't win, Troy,' Libby leans forward to whisper. For my ears only.

'That's OK with me,' I reply, equally softly. 'Just as long as you lose.'

Daily Shouter Online

Nought footballer Dolph Lilac quits because of 'racism'

Nought footballer Dolph Lilac called a press conference earlier today to announce his retirement from professional football. 'I'm just sick and tired of it. Not the game but the so-called fans,' said Dolph. 'The verbal and physical abuse comes flooding at us Nought players in every game. Each time one of us Noughts gets the ball, the clicking noises and chants of "maggot" start and we have rotten meat flung at us by idiots in the crowd. Far from racism in football being eradicated, it seems to have actually got worse over the last few years and the AFC are doing nothing about it except spouting platitudes about how it's a bad thing.'

Dolph Lilac went on to say, 'Last week, after I scored the winning goal for my team, opposition fans invaded the pitch and I was actually in fear for my life. Enough is enough. After talking it over with my wife, I've decided to call it a day.' The Albion Football Commission has since issued a statement in response: 'Dolph Lilac is wrong to say we are doing nothing. We have called for an inquiry into last week's pitch invasion and will be seeking a ban of at least two games for any season-ticket holder found guilty of threatening behaviour.'

NOW

five. Troy

How long have we been down in this basement? Over an hour? It feels like it. The air down here is thick, heavy, unpleasantly warm. Libby and I have been sitting on this crate, contemplating our fate, and the inactivity is getting to me. It's taking everything I have and then some just to keep it together. I glance at Libby. Her expression might be carved from stone.

'You OK, Libby?' I ask softly.

'No. Are you?'

A moment's pause. 'You're right. It was a stupid-ass question.'

Libby smiles faintly.

We keep our voices low and quiet as we both watch the top of the stairs, straining to hear something. Anything.

Silence.

We exchange a look. I'm scared to shout and bang on the door and draw attention to us. I'm scared to stay still and quiet and hope they just forget about us. Basically, I'm scared shitless. Libby slips her hand into mine. I freeze. My first instinct is to pull away, but I don't. Giving her hand what I hope is a reassuring squeeze, only then do I let it go.

'I've been thinking,' says Libby. 'We haven't seen our

abductors' faces. That's good, right? A positive sign? That means they have no reason to . . . to kill us 'cause we can't give their descriptions to the police. Right?'

The desperate hope in Libby's voice . . . I can't stamp on that.

So I nod and say, 'Yes, but we should still try to figure out who took us and why.'

'I've been thinking about that,' Libby says softly.

'So have I,' I confess. 'In my case, the line forms on the left.'

'Why?'

Oh God! I really don't want to say, but what choice do I have? This is not the time for hiding or dressing up the truth.

'Because of my sister.' It feels strange, almost traitorous to state it out loud, but having the words out rather than within has an unexpected effect. They settle me. I'm calmer.

Libby studies me then shakes her head. 'You're wrong. I have a line forming on the right.'

I frown, my question evident from the tracks furrowing between my eyebrows.

Libby answers my unspoken question. 'I'm so sorry, Troy. It's hard to say it but . . . I think we're here because of my dad.'

THEN

six. Libby

As I walk along the corridor towards the library, I allow myself a slight smile. My campaign is going well. I've got my friends Raffy, Eden and Maisie lobbying on my behalf, talking me up and extolling my virtues. They're the only real friends I have at this school. We're four Nought girls who've come through school together. If it wasn't for them on and at my side, I don't know how I would've survived. Eden is already talking about all the things I can do when I'm head girl, like I've already won. According to her, I'm ahead in the straw poll they took last week when they went round all the upper-school classes asking everyone how they intended to vote. Since then Troy has joined the race. OK, so Troy is also gaining traction in the fight for votes, but I've made a point of going round to each classroom during the lunch hour and speaking for a few minutes about what I stand for and what I intend to do for each and every student. And I steer well clear of 'us and them' rhetoric. I've learned from my mistake in the common room. Luckily for me, memories are short. Well, not Troy's — but I don't want to think about that.

I'm within arm's length of getting what I want. It smells of fresh-cut grass. It's warm, furry and purrs beneath my fingertips. It tastes raspberry-sweet and sharp against my tongue. Its siren song stirs my blood. Ambition is working all my senses. This time next week I'll be head girl and it's going to look so good on my university application forms. As a Nought, I know I have to be twice as good to get half as far as a Cross. My mum has drummed that into me since before I could walk and talk. Being head girl of a school like Heathcroft High will guarantee that I get to study medicine at my first choice of university. I've got it all worked out. I'm going to be a surgeon. Maybe even a neurosurgeon. The best damned one in the country. My hands are going to make my fortune. And then no one, but no one, will look down on me or laugh at me behind my back because of my mum. I'll be my own boss. I'll be Liberty Jackman − renowned doctor. And, even if being head girl only gets me a partial scholarship, at least it'll be something. Some way, somehow, I'll find the rest of the money needed to get to uni. Even if I have to work two jobs while I'm studying. Every time I mention going to uni, Mum scoffs and tells me I'm wasting my time.

'You could be a hairdresser or work in a shop. There's nothing wrong with those professions.'

When it comes to what I should do once I leave school, it's the only song Mum sings and those are the only lyrics she knows.

'You're right, Mum. There's absolutely nothing wrong with those jobs, but I want to be a doctor,' I tell her.

'A doctor? A Nought doctor? That'll be the day.'

I only just manage to keep my expression neutral.

'There are Nought doctors,' I point out.

'Damned few and far between, and do you really think Crosses will want you looking after them? They'll insist on one of their own. And, even if you do qualify as a doctor, I guarantee you'll be questioned every day by some dagger moron about whether or not you're really qualified.'

I wince. Mum can never mention Crosses without calling them daggers or worse. After all these years of hearing it, I should've got used to it by now, but it still jars.

'I don't care. I'm going to be a doctor, Mum.'

'And who's going to pay for your training?' says Mum. 'Because it won't be me. I don't have that kind of money.'

'I'll find a way.' That was my motto. My mantra.

I have no idea how I'll do it, but I won't give up. I can't.

And the first step towards the realization of my dream is to be voted head girl. Since Troy announced that he's going to run for head boy two days ago, he and his friends have put up posters all around the school detailing his plans – what he grandiosely calls his manifesto. Plans like setting up a student council to meet with the staff once a fortnight. Or plans to stop whole-class detentions in the lower school for the actions of one or two disruptive students. I have to admit they're reasonable ideas and he's making sure everyone knows about them. That's what I should've done from the beginning – put up posters all over the school. The moment Troy got approval from Mr Pike, the teacher co-ordinating the head-student election, to run, he hasn't let up. I've been campaigning all term, but it never occurred to me to stick up posters until Troy did it.

Luckily, good ideas love company so I stole a leaf out of his book. I took a selfie, used the school library computer to enlarge the photo and then turned it into a set of posters, printing a metric ton of them. My smiling face had the straight-up slogan – VOTE FOR LIBERTY JACKMAN – above it and the words VOTE FOR STUDENTS' RIGHTS below it. My friends and I put them up all over the school. I only have a few more days to make my message count. And I intend—

Wait . . . What the—?

Fists clenched, my face burns as I stand outside the school library. On the poster of me taped to the noticeboard by the door, someone has drawn horns sprouting out of my forehead and the word FAKE has been writ large across my face.

I don't need to be a genius to know who's responsible.

OK, Troy. You know what? You want a war? You got it.

Speak of the devil. There he is, rucksack over his shoulder, laughing at something his equally moronic mate Ayo has said. Troy, Ayo and Zane are heading my way. Then Troy notices me and his smile vanishes. I step into his path.

'You really are pathetic. You know that, right?'

'Hello to you too, Princess Petunia. What's biting you now?' Troy says with an exaggerated sigh.

I point to my poster on the wall. 'That! Is that really the best you've got? So much for not trashing the opposition. That's so pitiful. And stop calling me Princess Petunia.'

'Whatever you say, Ms Dibby.'

Bastard! He knew that name wound me up. 'Stop calling me that too.'

Ayo and Zane stand on either side of Troy, grinning at me, revelling in my humiliation.

'Libby, I've got ninety-nine things I'd rather do than talk to you, including having my toenails extracted,' says Troy. 'What d'you want?'

I point at my poster again. 'You did that, didn't you?'

Troy contemplates the poster like he's never seen it before. Who does he think he's fooling?

'I don't need to resort to stuff like that to see you lose. That poster is pretty accurate though.'

'Drop dead, Troy.'

'You know what, *Liberty*? Contrary to what you obviously believe, I don't spend my hours thinking up ways to annoy you,' Troy snaps. 'Actually, I don't think of you at all, so could you miss me with your bullshit, please?'

I scowl at Troy, my heart slamming against my ribs. Flashes of light and white appear before my eyes. Why can't I catch my breath? Then I realize what's happening. I tear the poster off the wall, turn and stride away from Troy, heading for the girls' toilets.

Don't melt in public.

Don't melt . . .

I have to get away before I embarrass myself. A couple of girls I recognize from the year below mine are already in there. Ignoring them, I head for a cubicle, slamming the door behind me before leaning against it. *Breathe in. Breathe out.* I want to slide down the cubicle door and keep falling right through the floor, but force myself to stay upright.

Breathe in.

Breathe out.

I grab for my pencil case from my rucksack, which is

now resting on the mucky cubicle floor. Digging into it, I look for the sharpest thing in there. My safety pin. My pin of safety. I pop it into my mouth to rest on my tongue before rolling up my left sleeve. Retrieving the pin, I open it, running my thumb over its point. Caressing it. One deep breath later and I scrape the pin along my skin. Slowly. Deliberately. From inner wrist towards my elbow. One direction only. Scrape. Scrape. Little beads of red appear along each line.

Breathe in . . .

Breathe out . . .

Concentrate on each and every bead of red. Watch them swell. Grow. Then still.

At last my heart rate begins to slow down. I close the safety pin and push it back down to the bottom of my pencil case. My life-saver. My forearm is stinging. I focus on the burning prickle of my skin. The one thing in my life I truly control. There's only one person in the entire school who knows what I do to keep from . . . exploding. One person who shares my secret – Troy.

And he only knows because he once caught me with my pin of safety, as I secretly call it, in our first year at school. I begged him not to tell anyone. I made him promise. Well, no one else at school has ever spoken to me about it so I guess he's kept his word. That's the only thing Troy has going for him: he always keeps his word. But he's the cause of this fresh set of scars on my forearm.

I may be adept at direct confrontation, but that doesn't mean I enjoy it. I get flustered, start sweating and my heart races like an Olympic sprinter.

All these years of living on a knife edge with my mum, I guess. When I was younger and more fearless, I tried standing up to her. After one particularly vicious argument, she hit me so hard . . . well, I ended up swallowing a tooth. She was all tears and apologies afterwards, but the damage was done.

My motto now – at least at home?

Anything for a quiet life.

When Mum comes at me in one of her moods, I know enough to keep my mouth shut. I look down and try not to catch her eye. Nine times out of ten, looking her in the eye makes things worse. So I always back down, beta to her alpha wolf. But every daydream is filled with getting up, getting out, getting away.

At least here at school I can be closer to my true self. Not closest but closer. Less hiding, less lying. More vocal. But arguments still make me sweat. Particularly arguments with Troy.

And I don't need to wonder why.

What the actual hell?

Furious, I watch Libby stride away from me. How dare she? I don't appreciate the way she automatically assumes I'm the one defacing her stupid posters. Dina, Meshella and Zane are also running for head student. Not just me and her. It could quite easily have been one of those three or their friends. Why assume I have nothing better to do?

Typical of Liberty and her way of thinking. She can't stand me, so I must be guilty. No proof required.

She's an every-day-of-the-week-and-twice-on-Sunday member of the church of the vicious minds. You'd think, after all these years, she'd know stabbing people in the back isn't my style. I don't need to resort to writing facile remarks over her posters. The head-student debate will be in assembly in front of the whole upper school next Wednesday, with the vote taking place later the same morning. Two teachers are then responsible for collecting and counting the votes, and the winner of the election is announced in a special assembly that same afternoon at the end of the school day. I can't wait for next Wednesday. Truth to tell, I'm surprised by how much I'm looking forward to it. During our debate, I intend to take Libby down so hard and fast that she'll never get up again.

I know just how to do it too.

And it won't be behind her back.

Daily Shouter Online

Revealed: in the run-up to the election, Tobias Durbridge speaks out against confirmed residential status

Tobey Durbridge, Shadow Home Secretary for the opposition Democratic Alliance party and Prime Ministerial candidate, has spoken out against confirmed residential status, the government ruling that requires all those of Fenno-Skandian heritage who were not born in Britain to apply for confirmed residential status.

'It is outrageous that Fenno-Skandians who came to this country as babies or young children and who might now be in their seventies and eighties are being told to apply to stay in their own country,' said Tobey Durbridge at today's opposition news briefing. 'A number of my constituents have recently asked me if the current government is deliberately doubling down on deporting as many Noughts as possible in the hope of skewing the voting in the forthcoming general election.'

eight. Libby

I'm sitting at the back of the library, staring out of the grimy windows across the staff car park. The grey clouds drip their insipid colour into the very air. Everything about today is grey. School is over, but I'm in no hurry to get home. It's been a bitch of a day. Sly smiles and snide asides about my defaced campaign posters have followed me round the school. And Meshella Musenga has made a point of 'accidentally' bumping into me whenever we're within a couple of metres of each other. What is her problem? Is it what I said a couple of days ago about her only looking out for her own? How was that wrong? Isn't it only natural? It's not like saying that made me a paid-up member of Nought Forever. It's just that Mum says Crosses look after their own first, last and always, and that we Noughts need to do the same.

Mum says . . .

Mum says a lot of things, too much of which bypasses her brain before it comes out of her mouth. So I should've known better. Why didn't I think harder before I said anything?

My damned eyes are beginning to leak.

'Goodness me, Libby. You're here again?'

I dash a hand across my cheeks before dredging up a smile for Mrs Robe, the school librarian and one of only two Nought members of staff in the school — apart from the dinner ladies and the cleaners. 'I can't keep away, Mrs Robe.'

Mrs Robe casts a speculative look in my direction. Did she see me tearful? God, I hope not. After smoothing down her light brown hair, cut into a neat bob, Mrs Robe glances at her watch. 'The library is closing in five minutes, OK? It's just you, me and the cleaners left in the building at this point.'

I close my books and pull them into my bag. When I look up, the librarian is watching me.

'Everything all right, Libby?'

'Yes, miss. Of course.' I force a smile.

'I haven't seen your mum at the last few parents' evenings.'

Warmth floods my face. 'She's been busy.'

'Oh. OK.' Mrs Robe nods but doesn't look convinced.

Silence sits like a voyeur with popcorn, watching both of us.

'Libby, are you sure you're OK?' says Mrs Robe.

'I'm fine.' Please stop asking.

'If there's anything worrying you, I'm here,' she says. 'You can talk to me. You know that, right?'

A flush of unwelcome red climbs up my neck to perch on my cheeks. 'Nothing's wrong, Mrs Robe. Honest. I was just doing my homework and lost track of the time, that's all.'

I stand up. This conversation is over.

'Goodnight, miss.'

''Night, Liberty.'

Heading out of the door, I don't need eyes in the back of my head to know that Mrs Robe is still watching me. I let my guard down. Mistake. I need to be more careful. But I'll say one thing about my mistakes – I tend to only make them once.

nine. Troy

The late September afternoon is too warm. The sky is grey but it's still cloyingly humid. My jacket is tied around my waist and my shirt is sticking to me like one huge plaster. It's been a bitch of a day. Ayo and I are walking home after football practice, which has left me sweaty, tired and strangely irritable. It's the long walk home from school that's really got to me. I stupidly forgot that my car is out for repairs after I backed over a sneaky bollard that was lower than the boot so wasn't immediately visible.

'For Shaka's sake, Troy! Your car has a parking camera at the back,' Mum ranted when I told her what had happened. 'You just weren't paying attention and that's going to cost you. Don't even think about asking me to help pay the repair bill.'

Which was exactly what I'd been about to ask her. That bill is going to put a severe dent in my savings. Plus that morning, when I'd asked Mum for a lift to school, she shook her head and said, 'Can't help you, honey.'

'What about Nana Meggie? Can't she drive me?'

'Your nana has given up driving. Besides, I have no intention of waking her up just to suit you,' said Mum. 'Start walking, child. You wouldn't want to be late, would you?'

At first I thought Mum was winding me up, but she waved her hand in front of her face and said, 'Does it look like I'm joking? I've got an early meeting with a particularly obnoxious turd that I don't want to be late for, so off you go.'

'Who's your meeting with then?' I couldn't help asking.

Mum sighed. 'A guy I used to know back in the day. He was a piece of work then and he's an even bigger piece of work now. He's got something I need and it's going to cost me to get it back.'

'What's he got? And cost you what?'

'Never you mind. Hurry up and get to school.'

Mum's gaze fell away from mine like she regretted saying as much as she had. I knew from experience I wasn't going to get any more out of her so I chucked my rucksack over one shoulder and headed out of the door, making my way to the bus stop – just in time to see the bus drive off without me.

Like I said, a bitch of a day.

'What's going on between you and Libby?' asks Ayo, walking beside me.

I frown. 'Nothing. What makes you think otherwise?'

Ayo contemplates me like I'm under a microscope. My eyes narrow. 'What?'

'There's not getting on with someone. There's detesting someone. And then there's what you two do,' says Ayo. 'Whenever you're together, I have to break out my woolly hat and gloves 'cause the temperature drops by twenty degrees – at least.'

I shrug. 'Pfft! Can't get on with everyone.'

Ayo eyes me speculatively.

'What?' Oh my God! Ayo is beginning to work on my nerves.

'Nothing,' he says, when it's obviously something. 'It's just that you and Libby – well, that's a whole new level.'

'Does it really show that much?'

'Are you kidding me?' Ayo scoffs, eyebrows raised.

Damn it! That's why for the most part I try to stay away from Libby. She and I invariably rub each other up the wrong way. Antagonism crackles between us like static electricity, but I certainly don't want to be responsible for driving Libby towards a pair of scissors or anything else with a sharp point.

'I'm just not a fan of her and her bullshit,' I say. 'She can't ever be honest, even with herself.'

That piques Ayo's interest. 'What d'you mean?'

'Doesn't matter.' I shake my head. 'So d'you wanna go and see the new *Black Panther* film this weekend?'

Ayo and I discuss the last two *Black Panther* movies and the forthcoming one until we reach the security gate that leads to my house. Ayo lives in the gated estate about a mile further along the same road. My house and its grounds are almost the same size as three houses where Ayo lives. Stupid, I know, but I always feel just a slight tinge of embarrassment when I reach our security gate. I love that we live in a large house and I have my own bedroom and my own activity room, but Mum has always brought me up to value and be grateful for every single thing I have.

'Don't get too caught up in *things*, Troy,' she warned me, and more than once. 'Things can be taken away just as easily as given to you; things can be lost as well as found, sold as well as bought, stolen as well as recovered. Measure yourself by the things you have and, if you lose it all some day, you won't know who you are. D'you understand?'

I shook my head every time Mum asked that. I mean, why would we lose anything, or have it taken away? It makes no sense.

Ayo waves bye and peels off to continue down the road to his house. Entering the code to open the gate, I head along the driveway. Nope, tired doesn't even begin to cover how I'm feeling. Knackered, more like! The moment I open the front door, the welcome smell of roast lamb hits me. I take a deep, appreciative breath.

'Hey, Troy,' Mum calls out. 'How was your day?'

I pass the dining room on the way to the kitchen. The tablecloth has been changed and the table is laid.

'Can I have a snack before dinner? I'm starving.' I dump my rucksack by the door and follow Mum's voice into the kitchen where I head straight for the fridge.

'"Hello, Mum. How are you today? That's a lovely dress you're wearing,"' Mum mocks.

I straighten up and grin at her. Actually, the dress she's wearing does look like it was bought this century, her braided hair is loose around her shoulders and she's wearing lipstick and stuff! She does look kinda nice. 'Hello, Mum. How're you today? Lovely dress you're wearing!'

'Don't strain yourself, Troy,' says Mum, unimpressed. 'And don't go packing your face. Dinner will be ready in an hour.'

'Actually, you're looking relatively reasonable,' I say. 'What happened? Cosmic ray?'

'Child, you're not too old for a spanking.'

I burst out laughing. Likely! I'm over six foot tall and Mum is five foot and a small something. 'Mum, you've never spanked me in my life and you're so anti–violence, it's actually embarrassing.'

'That can be rectified,' Mum warns, though the twinkle in her eyes gives her away.

'Yeah, right,' I say.

I'd seen Mum get upset after inadvertently stepping on a beetle on the pavement. Any and every march for peace, love and understanding in the capital and she's there.

I'm a PACIFIST, honey. Deal with it.

How many times had I heard that when I was growing up? Mum says she's seen too much violence in her life to be anything else.

'Troy, I mean it,' Mum says with a frown. 'Don't go spoiling your appetite.'

'Just have a sarnie then.' My nose is back in the fridge.

'No sandwich. Have some fruit, Troy, and save the textspeak for your phone. Don't they teach pronouns at your school any more?' Mum sighs. 'Pronouns are friends. Don't drop them – use and cherish them.'

I roll my eyes. Not this again! How many times have I heard this particular nag?

'How's the election going?' she asks. 'Are you winning hearts and minds? Are you setting the world to rights? Are you championing the fight for liberty and justice? Are you? Are you?'

'Mum, d'you have to be so extra?' My eyes roll. 'It's not that big a deal.'

'Oh yes it is,' Mum immediately contradicts. 'It takes no work at all to sit and grumble. It takes courage to stand up and be counted. Good for you.'

Which is precisely why I didn't want to tell Mum I was entering the school election in the first place.

'You want my advice?'

It's a rhetorical question, so I emerge from the fridge with an apple in hand and wait to hear the answer.

'Be true to yourself, Troy. Don't turn into someone you don't like or even recognize simply because you think it will win you this contest,' says Mum, suddenly very serious.

'It's not a contest, it's an election.' I bite into the apple, which has more of my attention than my mum.

'Oh, honey, elections are the most cut-throat contests there are,' she says. 'My second piece of advice? Watch your back.'

Her tone of voice has me straightening up. 'Wow, Mum. It's a school vote to choose our head student, not a general election.'

'Ah, Troy, you're so young!' she says. 'Whether it's a general election or an election to decide who's the best at picking up litter – when it's a position you really want, there's no difference. When it comes to politics, people will lie, cheat and steal to get what they want. And don't talk with your mouth full.'

I sigh inwardly. Typical Mum! Always blowing simple things out of proportion. Being head student really isn't all that. It looks good on university applications and it means sitting in on a few staff meetings throughout the school year, but that's about it. I must admit though, if I'm voted head boy, I have plans to make the role bigger, like attending school-policy meetings, not just boring staff meetings. But the role is hardly vital to world peace. Mum is taking this – along with everything else – too seriously.

'I wish your dad was here to see this. He'd be so proud of the way you're stepping up to fight for what you believe in.' Mum gives me a hug. I put up with it for a good three seconds before trying to shrug her off.

'OK, let go now, Mum.'

She hugs me tighter.

'Mum! Get off!'

She hugs me tighter still. 'This hug is from your dad as well as from me so it's got to be twice as long.'

I sigh. 'Mum, you're talking shite again.'

'Language, child. I'm your mother!'

But at least she lets me go. She smiles, but not enough to lighten the trace of sadness dimming her eyes.

'I miss him too, Mum,' I say quietly.

She opens her arms to give me another hug. Hell, no! I leap back. 'Had today's quota of hugs, thanks.'

Mum laughs, her hands dropping to her sides. I love to see her laugh. After Dad died, it was as if her smile died with him.

It was the spring term of Year Ten. March 8th to be exact. The voice of Miss Juniper, the school secretary, played out over the school public-announcement system.

'Could Troy Ealing report to the head's office? Troy Ealing to the head's office, please.'

'Ooooh!' the rest of the class called out spontaneously.

The automatic assumption was that I'd done something heinous and was now in deep manure.

'Er, do you mind?' said Mr Marshall, annoyed. The class quietened down. 'Off you go, Troy. Don't keep the head waiting.'

I closed my history books and scraped them off my desk into my backpack. What was going on? I racked my brains for something I might've done that would warrant a visit to Mrs Paxton. When I reached the school office, I was stunned to see who was waiting for me.

'Mum? What're you doing here?'

'Troy, it's your dad. He's been in an accident,' she said, hugging me to her.

'What kind of accident?' I tried to pull away but Mum wouldn't let me.

'A bad one. He's in hospital. Come on, love. Let's go.'

A bad one . . .

Those words and no others kept echoing in my head. I don't remember much of what happened after that. Time moved in a series of snapshots, fast and sharp like finger snaps. Getting in the car. Getting out of the car. Outside the hospital. Inside the hospital. The click of Mum's heels as we walked along a corridor. The smell of bleach and vomit. Beeps and whirrs and flickering lights overhead. The sour taste of fear in my mouth.

Is Dad OK?

Please let Dad be OK.

Mum and I sat in a waiting room with faded green plastic chairs.

A Cross female doctor with neat, close-cropped hair and

wearing a white coat entered the room. She was tall, willowy, holding herself straight, proud to make the most of every centimetre of her height.

Mum stood up. Her hand on my shoulder stopped me from doing the same. She stepped forward to speak to the doctor. How many seconds passed? Five? Ten at the most. Mum's whispered 'No . . .' echoed in the room. She swayed to her knees.

I jumped to my feet.

Mum buried her face in her hands. Tears dripped between her fingers. Her body shook, racked with silent sobs. She didn't make another sound. I ran to her. Hugged her. Held her. My own tears fell like winter rain. In the course of a day, hours, minutes, both our lives changed.

To this day, I've never heard these words spoken to me – 'Troy, your dad is dead.'

Still can't remember when or how I learned exactly *how* he'd died. It must've been later that same day. Dad was a hit-and-run victim. The car that killed my dad was a dark blue Whitman Scorpius. A vintage car. Very expensive, very rare. The driver didn't stop but accelerated away as my dad lay dying on the road.

The police never found the car, let alone who was driving it. The person who killed my dad got away with it. No repercussions, no comeback, no clapback, nothing. The driver and the car were long gone. That was the day I learned the truth – the bitter truth – about the real world: sometimes the guilty get away with it.

The very worst thing is knowing Dad's killer is out there somewhere, enjoying life, while my dad isn't. I had to watch Mum fall to pieces. If it weren't for Nana Meggie and Callie, I don't know what we'd have done.

'Earth to Troy. Come in, Troy.' Mum's voice drags me out of unhappy memories.

'Seriously, Mum, being head student isn't all that,' I say, covering the tracks of where my thoughts had taken me.

'That depends on your point of view, Troy. Just because you think a certain way about something doesn't mean everyone else feels the same,' she says. 'Believing that is not just narrow but dangerous.'

For Shaka's sake! 'Mum, I only wanted a snack, not a lecture.'

'Sorry.' She smiles ruefully. She walks over to me, studying, scrutinizing my face. I frown. What's she doing? 'I love you, Troy.'

My frown deepens. 'Are you dying?'

Mum bursts out laughing. 'No. Hopefully I have a few decades left before that happens. Can't I say I love you now?'

'Fine, but don't say that in front of my friends though, yeah?'

Mum smiles and kisses my forehead. 'Wouldn't dream of it. Now go and change for dinner.'

Hang on . . . Mum is looking fresh, roast lamb for dinner on a weekday and the table in the dining room is laid. Damn, but I'm slow.

'Mum, is it just you and me for dinner tonight?' I already know the answer.

Mum's gaze falls away from mine. 'Er, I invited Sonny to join us.'

Again? I open my mouth to protest, only to snap it shut again. Over the last couple of years since Dad died, I've watched Sonny worm his way back into Mum's life. When Mum first introduced him to me, about two months after Dad's death, she said he was an old friend. Wasn't quite sure I believed that. Too many times I've watched him watching her and that look on his face . . . Like he's already nuts about her and is trying — and failing miserably — to hide it. No . . . actually, it's more than that. Sonny is seriously hung up on Mum but, judging by his demeanour when he's around her, it isn't exactly making him happy.

'That OK, love?' says Mum. 'About Sonny joining us?'

I shrug. 'It's your house too.'

She bursts out laughing. 'Why, thank you!' Her smile fades. 'Troy, why don't you like Sonny?'

'Never said I didn't,' I reply.

'You never said you did either.'

'Don't think about him one way or the other,' I lie.

'Troy, can't you—?'

'What?'

Mum sighs. 'Never mind. Go change and do your home-work before dinner.'

For once, I don't argue. Appetite gone, I throw the barely touched apple in the bin before I leave the kitchen. After the crap day I've had at school, I really don't need it to continue at home. The last thing I want is a row with Mum.

Sonny . . .

Dad was barely cold in his grave before Sonny came sniffing around, presenting himself as a friend who had not just one but two shoulders for Mum to cry on. Recently, during the last couple of months, Mum and Sonny have started having dinners out alone, just the two of them. I know Dad died over two years ago, but it's too soon for Mum to be dating again. And if Sonny thinks he's going to replace my dad . . .

Listen to me. Damn it! I feel like a selfish dickhead with a huge dollop of arsehole on the side. Shouldn't I give Sonny more of a chance for Mum's sake? Sonny obviously loves Mum and is waiting patiently for her to see him as something more than a friend. And Mum deserves to be loved. But who am I trying to kid? I've tried – tried hard – over the last few months, yet I still haven't warmed to Sonny. Would I feel the same about anyone trying to fill the gap left by my dad? Probably. But in this case it's Sonny.

And I don't know what to do about it.

ten. Libby

My heart thumps as I put the key in the front door. Home is where the heart is, but my heart isn't here. I never relax when I open the door, never feel at peace. In fact it's just the opposite. School, homework, being head girl, going to a good university, becoming a doctor, they're all rungs on the ladder of escape to get me out of this house. Up or out, I don't particularly care which, as long as it's away from here. Away from *her*. I can't afford to fail, yet sometimes my fear of failure cripples me. I'm scared of starting to get away, testing and tasting what it's like on the other side, only to take a false step and be dragged back down into the mire Mum calls her life. Our life. No! Once I'm out of here, I won't let her get hold of me. If I do, she won't just drag me down, she'll push me under and drown me.

I'm afraid of drowning.

Always have been. I love the sea – when I'm standing on a beach. I can put up with swimming if I'm in the shallow end of the pool and within an arm's length of the side at all times, but I hate being in water. The thought of having my head submerged makes me break out in an icy sweat.

I don't need a head doctor to tell me why either.

Mum's little game when I was a toddler.

She used to hold me by my feet when I was in the bath and pull. She never pulled me all the way under the water, just till my chin was wet usually. Sometimes my bottom lip. Once or twice my top lip. Just enough for me to scream and panic and cry. Then just enough so I couldn't scream. And afterwards the coughing and tears were always dismissed by Mum. After all, it was just a joke. Just for a laugh. Ha ha.

Where's your sense of humour, Libby?

It drowned a long time ago.

I have showers now. Only showers. Always showers.

Mum has resigned herself to who and what she is. She hasn't changed in all the years I've known her and she's proud of the fact that she'll never change. Her mind, her views, her attitudes, her few loves and many hatreds, they'll be with her till the day she dies. And top of her hatred list is my dad. He found out she was pregnant and did a runner apparently. Mum hasn't seen him since. And me? I know nothing about him and that's fine by me. If he doesn't want me, I don't want him either. Most of Mum's modelling and acting work dried up years ago, but we do OK, I guess. We have a roof over our heads and food in the fridge. And the bills get paid. I'm not sure how, when Mum only gets maybe one paid acting or modelling job a year as far as I can see, but somehow we get by. It's probably thanks to the parade of boyfriends Mum has brought to the house over the years. So yeah, we manage.

But it's not enough.

I push open the front door yet make no attempt to enter. Not yet. The smell of stale rubbish, even staler perfume and red wine hits me like a wrecking ball. The house stinks like a seedy wine bar.

'Mum?' I whisper.

No reply.

A deep breath. Louder this time. 'Mum?'

No reply.

A sigh of relief. Huge and heartfelt. I shouldn't feel this way, elated at being alone, reassured by the house being empty.

But an empty house is the only time this place feels even remotely like home.

Home means my music and my choice of food to eat without constant criticism.

Home means serenity and calm.

Home means the absence of fear.

A home without Mum means peace.

I glance down. A single envelope sits on the doormat. A letter addressed to me. Unusual. I never get letters. Frowning, I bend to pick it up. A white envelope, no address on the back. As I head upstairs to my bedroom, I tear open the letter and begin to read.

What I read stops me in my tracks midway up the stairs.

What I read sends shock waves cresting through my body.

Time stands still as my mind races. So many pieces of the puzzle of my life with Mum begin to fall into place. My expression set, I continue up, making for her bedroom.

I need to start digging. Mum has buried the truth and I need to find it. All of it.

eleven. Troy

It's almost midnight. A single knock, then the door swings open. My sister, Callie, stands in the doorway, framed and posing. The only thing missing is a trumpet fanfare. God, she's so extra! Callie swans into the room, barely glancing in my direction. Suppose I'd been doing something or watching something that required more than one knock's notice? I close the lid of my laptop.

'Hey, squirt,' says my sister. 'I was hoping you'd still be awake.'

'If I wasn't, I would be after that entrance. And my name is Troy. It's one syllable for God's sake. T–R–O–Y. Troy.' Unbidden, Libby pops into my head, scowling at me as I call her Princess Petunia. The dog of hypocrisy starts nipping at my heels. I ignore it.

My sister's eyebrows quirk. She looks just like Mum when she does that. 'Someone's in a good mood!'

For Shaka's sake! How hard is it to call me by my proper name? That dog is now taking chunks out of my ankles. My sister thinks I'm overreacting, and maybe I am, but – damn it! – it would be great if just one thing could go right today.

Dinner with Sonny had been a disaster, to say the

least. I'd been on my best behaviour, making an effort to get on with him for Mum's sake, but then the topic of conversation had moved on to politics. Like most self-made rich people I've come across, he was of the view that, if he could make something of himself, so could and should everyone else.

It was after he made a pointed comment about how, when he was my age, he was already out working full-time that the gloves came off.

'Showing your true colours?' I asked Sonny. 'I never took you to be an "I'm all right, Jack, go ahead and pull the ladder up" kinda guy.'

'I am not,' Sonny said with indignation. 'But too many people these days are looking for handouts. If I want something, I go after it and nothing gets in my way.'

'Well, bully for you,' I said with disdain. 'Some people work just as hard if not harder than you, but simply aren't as lucky.'

'Troy . . .' warned Mum.

'Lucky? I make my own luck,' Sonny told me. 'Always have done. You wanna know some other names for *luck*? Bloody hard work! Dedication. Persistence.'

'Bullshit.'

'Troy!' said Mum.

Sonny's lip curls in disdain. 'You're here in this huge six-bedroom house surrounded by a couple of acres of manicured lawns and you're going to lecture *me* about working hard for what I have? Seriously?'

'Sonny!' Mum admonished.

'Mum, he's talking out of his —'

'TROY! SONNY! That's enough. Troy – apologize at once!' said Mum.

'Pfft! For what?'

At which point, Mum did her nut, yelling at both of us. She insisted that we change the subject, but the damage was done. Dinner after that had been uncomfortable to say the least. I said no to dessert and escaped to my room, and for once Mum was happy to let me leave the table early.

'So why're you in such a bad mood, squirt?' asks Callie. 'Did someone at school steal your crayons?'

Ha bloody ha! OK, so my sister is ages older than me – well, eighteen years older to be precise – but I'm taller than her, better-looking, just as smart and not her *baby* brother any more. So hardly a *squirt*.

'For all you knew, I might've been fast asleep,' I point out.

'Not likely.' Callie indicates my laptop. 'Which government institution were you hacking into?'

'Was doing my Chemistry homework actually.'

'Yeah, right,' says Callie. 'And it says something that I think you're hacking into somewhere you shouldn't rather than trying to find footage of men or women displaying all they have and haven't got.'

'If I were trying to find films like that, it'd be of women, not men,' I tell her.

'Whatever,' Callie says dismissively. 'I couldn't care less which way your pendulum swings.'

I shake my head. 'Is there something in particular you wanted or are you just here to be generally annoying?'

'OK, spill, Troy. What's biting you? We usually have to be together for a least five minutes before you try to pick a fight.' Callie sits on the chair by my desk, only to immediately leap up again. A frown, a quick glance down and then she lets rip.

'What the actual hell? Troy, I swear every time I come into your room, I feel like I need a tetanus shot.' Callie removes a less than fresh pair of underpants from the chair. Holding them gingerly by the waistband between her index finger and thumb, and as far away from her nose as she can get them, she drops my underpants on the floor like they're toxic. They aren't that bad!

'Troy, you are disgusting,' Callie says with some force. 'How are we related?'

'Like this, sis.'

'I'd shift your underwear into the laundry basket before Mum sees it if I were you,' my sister warns.

'Don't nag. Damn, I get enough of that from Mum.'

'Don't be such a slob then. I was never like that,' says my sister.

'No, you were perfect in every way.' Is that a hint of sour in my voice? Hell, yes. Though Callie's immediate snort of self-derision makes me smile and the sour fades.

'*Perfect?*' Callie's eyebrows shoot way up. 'Boy, you have no idea what I was like when I was your age, but I was about as far removed from perfect as it's possible to get.'

'Mum's always going on about how you knuckled down and got on with your schoolwork when you were in your late teens,' I say, before adopting Mum's voice and tone. ' "Callie very rarely went out at your age. Callie focused on her studies. Your sister was determined to make something of herself. What're you doing with your life, Troy?" And on and on ad nauseam.'

'Get Mum to tell you about me and Uncle Jude some time,' says Callie quietly.

'Your dad's brother?'

Callie nods. My sister very rarely talks about her childhood and, every time she does, there's a palpable sense of sadness that flows from her before she changes the subject. But now she's actually inviting me to speak to Mum about her past? That's a first. I open my mouth to ask more, but then I notice her expression. Whoa! From the look on my sister's face, her thoughts have plunged her into some dark waters. Any lingering traces of resentment are banished in an instant. Callie isn't sitting with me in my room any more. No, she's long ago and far away. Lips pursed, eyes glistening, body absolutely still and hunched; my sister's reminiscences aren't exactly accompanied by joy. Was she thinking about her dad again and how she never got to meet him?

'Penny for them?' I say, wondering what she's thinking.

'My thoughts aren't worth that much,' she replies, still focused on the past.

Time to drag my sister back to the present.

'Callie, what d'you think of Sonny?' I say the first thing that comes into my head.

My sister's eyes snap back to mine, immediately alert. Like a butterfly emerging from a cocoon, Callie my sister has retreated and Callie the lawyer is out and beating her wings.

'Why d'you ask?'

'Callie, don't go all barrister on me.' I grimace. 'Just give me a straight answer. What d'you think of him? D'you trust him?'

'Is there any reason why I shouldn't?'

For Shaka's sake! Getting a straight answer is like trying to get blood from a piece of flint.

'Sonny loves Mum. He has done ever since I can remember,' Callie says carefully. 'He'll make her happy. Don't you think Mum deserves to be happy?'

I nod. 'Yeah, she does.'

'Troy, what's going on in that head of yours?' She comes over to sit next to me.

I shrug. 'Just worrying about nothing.'

'Any worries you'd care to share?'

'Nah. I'm just being silly.'

'That I can believe,' says Callie. 'You needn't stress about Sonny. He'd cut off all his limbs before he'd do anything to make Mum unhappy. And he's been like the dad I never had. He's the one who taught me the sign language that I taught you.'

'Yeah, I know.' I fake a smile. 'Don't worry. Sonny is having no effect on my stress levels.'

'Well, I'm afraid I've got plenty to raise your blood pressure,' says Callie, suddenly serious. 'I hope you're sitting comfortably.'

Oh hell!

Now what?

Already, Callie is eyeing me apologetically.

'I'm not going to like this, am I?' I state.

She shakes her head. 'Just don't hate me, OK?'

And what gets to me is that Callie believes whatever it is she has to tell me might make me do that.

twelve. Libby

I hear her before I see her. The sound of a key scratching at the front-door lock. Mum's obviously having trouble fitting one inside the other. At least a minute passes before the door finally opens. Not good. That's how I judge just how wasted Mum is – by how long it takes her to open the front door. Reluctantly, I make my way downstairs. One look is enough to make my heart tumble. Mum stands at the door, swaying slightly. Her pupils are barely visible, mere pinpricks at the centre of her grey-blue irises. Her yellow blouse is dishevelled and buttoned up wrong. I'm pretty sure she didn't leave the house that way. Mum is very careful about how she looks before she goes out anywhere. Coming back home? Not so much.

Pete the creep, Mum's boyfriend, slinks into view, the usual hateful, knowing smirk already on his face. He wears denim jeans, a black T-shirt decorated with the profile of a silver wolf howling and a leather jacket that's too well worn to be fashionable. His long black hair is tied back in a ponytail. He has one hand on the front-door lintel above his head, like he's posing for a photo shoot. No doubt he thinks he looks too cool, but he comes across as exactly what he is – a total loser. He's over forty and trying to convince everyone he's half that age. Pathetic. My lips press together in a bloodless line as I glare at him, unblinking.

Creep! Loathsome, scumbag, son-of-a-bitch, low-class, bastard blanker. I don't even feel guilty about applying that word to him. In his case, the word fits.

'Hey, baby girl . . .' he says.

The expression on his face makes my stomach churn. His words make me sick, like one second away from actually heaving. I'm not a baby and I'm certainly not his girl. I bite back the curse that has sprung fully formed into my mouth.

Ignore him, Libby. He's not worth it.

'Mum, are you OK? I need to talk to you.'

Pete enters the house, not bothering to shut the door. He stands to one side as if inviting me to walk past and close it. I have no intention of going anywhere near him. When he sees his ploy isn't working, he kicks the door closed. The glass panes rattle in the door. Mum doesn't say a word.

'Tonight, your mum told me all about your dad,' Pete informs me. 'It was a very interesting discussion.'

That's more than she's ever done with me. Clenching my teeth so hard it's a wonder my molars don't crumble, I pin Mum with a contemptuous glare. She visibly squirms, then looks away – anywhere but at me. It doesn't stop me scowling at her.

'Mum, where've you been?' I ask. 'I was worried sick.'

'Shame your mum didn't tell me before, because then you and I would've had so much more to talk about,' Pete interjects with a grin so oily I'm surprised it doesn't just slide right off his foul face.

Owl-like, Mum blinks at me like she's trying to remember who I am. After so many times of this, it shouldn't hurt, but it does. As always. Her lipstick is slightly smudged and the mascara on her left eye has run.

A good time was had by all.

'I was going out with Pete. I told you,' Mum slurs.

'No you didn't.'

Pete again. Always encouraging Mum to drink this and snort that. And she's weak enough to give in to him. Mum has been going out with Pete for over six months now and the more I get to know him, the more shivers of revulsion slither over me whenever he's nearby. The last time I found myself alone with him, he stroked one finger slowly up and down my bare arm, his finger running over the scars on my forearm. Just remembering it makes me shudder.

'How did you get these scratches?' he asked.

'Next door's cat – if it's any of your business. And get your hand off me.'

But he just carried on stroking up and down my arm. When I threatened to tell Mum, he laughed in my face.

'Go ahead. Tell her. And I'll tell her what a tease you've been, flashing me and trying to get me to dump her for you. Let's see who she'll believe.'

No contest. I already knew the answer to that question.

'I dist— distinc— totally remember telling you that Pete and I were out tonight. We're celebrating our seven-month anniversary,' says Mum, swaying like a sapling in a high wind.

Why bother to even argue? Mum won't remember a word of this conversation in the morning. Hell, ten minutes from now it'll be out of her head.

'I bet your dad dotes on you, Liberty,' says Pete softly. 'You being his only child and all.'

What the hell is he talking about? Didn't Mum tell him that I've never even met my dad? My nails bite into my palms as I scowl at him, wishing he'd just drop down a deep hole and die.

'Pete, stop it,' Mum admonishes. 'I need a drink.' She weaves her way to the kitchen. 'You want one, darling?'

'No thanks. I've got plans,' says Pete. 'Be seeing you, Libby.'

Not if I see you first, I think sourly.

He blows me a kiss, chuckling at the look of utter loathing darkening my narrowed eyes. Only when he's closed the front door firmly behind him do my fists slowly unclench. Mum brought that toad to our house again, despite the fact that I've told her more than once that he makes me feel uncomfortable. Tomorrow morning she'll tell me she forgot, or she couldn't make it home alone. Always some excuse. Much as I want to question Mum about the letter I received earlier, I know there's no point. Not when she's in this state. It'll just have to wait till tomorrow. Better yet, I should gather all the information I can so Mum can't easily lie to me any more.

'Goodnight, Mum,' I say through gritted teeth, heading back upstairs.

'Don't I get a hug?' Mum staggers to the foot of the stairs, her arms open wide. Funny how she only wants to hug me when she's drunk.

'Mum, you've got food down your front,' I point out.

She pulls her half-unbuttoned yellow shirt out of her

black skirt to peer down at it. Vomit, food remnants or booze, it doesn't matter. It's nasty. 'How did that get there?' she says, frowning and still swaying with the effort of staying upright.

I run downstairs to reach her before she topples over, but she manages to right herself. At the disgusted expression on my face, Mum's lips thin. Mistake. From the moment I heard the front door open, I should've broken out my poker face. Shaking my head, I turn and carry on back up the stairs. For once, I'm not close to tears. I'm too angry for that. The words in the letter have seared their way into my skull. Besides, if I confront Mum now, she'll turn on me for making her feel guilty and we'll only end up quarrelling again. And then worse. Mum is a mean drunk and meaner when she's high. Time for me to retreat to my room, but this time I won't forget to lock the door.

NOW

thirteen. Libby

Before either of us can speak, the bolts are drawn back and a key turns in the door above us. Troy is already on his feet. I move to stand beside him but he reaches out without looking and pushes me back, partially shielding me with his body. Stunned, I stare at him but he's looking up at the door, waiting for it to open. His whole body is tense, coiled like a snake about to strike. He's not even blinking. In spite of where we are and the neck-deep shit we're in, Troy's actions unexpectedly make my eyes prickle.

The door opens. The man wearing the rabbit mask appears at the top of the stairs, a phone in his hand. A moment, then he raises it, centring on Troy and me, and takes a couple of pictures. The flash of his phone dazzles. I blink rapidly. Rabbit Man stands watching us without saying a word. Is it my imagination or does he seem to be studying me in particular?

Troy sidesteps to stand directly in front of me. So it wasn't my imagination. I reach out to hold onto Troy's arm. His muscles are bunched and rock solid but it's his stillness that's most unnerving — like he's poised and waiting for hell to erupt. Peering over Troy's shoulder, I watch as Rabbit Man turns his attention to Troy, glaring at him with hostile contempt. Even in the half-light of the basement I can see – and feel – the cold in our kidnapper's eyes. And still no one speaks. Rabbit Man turns and leaves the way he came, bolting the door behind him.

Moments pass.

'You OK, Libby?' asks Troy, his eyes still on the door.

The choking lump of fear in my throat makes any answer impossible. At my silence, Troy turns to face me, a frown pulling his eyebrows close together.

'Libby, it's all right. He's gone,' he says.

I am glass. One inappropriate word, one wrong gesture and I will shatter into a million pieces. I want – no, I *need* to scratch at my skin, plant my nails into my forearm and dig deep. Troy moves closer to stand in front of me and takes my hands in his.

'Libby, he's gone. We're still standing.' Troy forces a smile.

I look up at him.

'Libby, breathe,' he orders.

He makes a show of inhaling and exhaling like he's demonstrating how it should be done to someone who's never tried it before. But it works. My heart rate begins to slow. The need to claw at my arms doesn't disappear but it begins to recede. And all I can do is thank whoever, wherever, that I'm not alone. After what happened to Troy at my house all those years ago, I'm lucky he doesn't spit in my eye.

Troy smiles. 'OK?'

I nod.

I'm not – neither of us is – but for the moment it'll do. In this moment, it's all we've got.

THEN

fourteen. Troy

Callie looks around my room, at the posters she's seen a thousand times before, at my duvet cover – anywhere but at me.

'Come on, Callie. Spit it out,' I tell my sister.

'Just remember that I'm your older, more intelligent, prettier, awesome sister and I love you very much.'

Warning bells begin to peal in my head. Callie is on the verge of being maudlin, and my hard-nosed, hard-headed sister is never soppy.

'Callie, we both know that of the two of us I got all the best genes in this family,' I state, wishing she'd get to the point.

Her smile fades.

Crap! Hadn't meant it that way. I take hold of her hand and smile to show it was just a joke. The clouds over Callie's expression clear and she smiles faintly.

'You certainly got more than your fair share of modesty,' she says. 'I'll give you that.'

The twinkle in her eye is back, thank goodness. My sister already has to put up with enough crap and condescension about her dad being a Nought. She isn't about to get more of the same from me. My dad, Nathan Ealing, was Mum's second husband. Well, I say second husband, but technically

Mum wasn't actually married to Callie's dad. He died before they could get married or even live together. My dad owned a restaurant called Specimens before he died. That's where he and my mum, Sephy, met. Mum doesn't like to talk about her past. She says the past is to learn from, not live in. Hell, I only learned when I was nine, almost ten, that Callie's dad's full name was Callum Ryan McGregor and exactly who – and what – he was. Before that, I only knew he was called Callum and that Callie was named after him. How messed up is that?

Callie purses her lips. I know what that means. 'I need a favour from my favourite brother.'

'I'm your only brother, Callie, so that doesn't count.'

'Pfft! Details!'

'I thought you were all about the details—'

'Unless I want a favour from you.'

'Like what?'

Unusually for my sister, she hesitates.

'Get on with it,' I say, exasperated. The suspense is killing me.

'I took on a case recently, a high-profile case. It hasn't even been formally announced yet. I'm working to ensure it stays out of the news, but I can't guarantee that.' My sister traces the pattern on my duvet cover before taking a breath and looking me in the eye. 'And I just want to warn you that there may be some fallout in your direction so I need you to be on your guard.'

I stare. This is a full one hundred and eighty degrees away from what I'd been expecting. 'On guard? Why? Your cases are nothing to do with me. What kind of high-profile case?'

Callie sighs. 'I can't say until it's officially announced.'

'Who am I going to tell? Don't you think I should know, especially if your case is going to have some kind of impact on me?'

'It won't. I'll make sure of that.' Callie's expression hardens by degrees. Her eyes take on a steely look that is rarely displayed outside court. 'Anyone wants to take on my family? They'll have to go through me first.'

'Callie, what's going on?'

Silence.

In that moment, I realize something. Whatever happens now will define our future relationship. Either Callie trusts me or she doesn't.

Maybe Callie feels that too because she says, 'I'm defending Tobey Durbridge on a charge of murder.'

Staring so hard was putting serious strain on my eyeballs. 'You *what*? The politician? *That* Tobey Durbridge?'

Callie shrugs. 'The one and only.'

I can't believe what I'm hearing. 'Who did he kill?'

She frowns. 'It's alleged that he killed Daniel Jeavons.'

'The mobster?' My mouth falls open. Wow! The shocks just keep on coming.

Callie's expression is grim. 'The one and only.'

'Wait. What? Tobey Durbridge killed Daniel Jeavons and you're going to defend him? Dan Jeavons' lowlife friends aren't going to be happy about that and they won't be afraid to show it. Are you nuts?'

'Troy, you have heard of innocent until proven guilty, haven't you?' Callie frowns. 'Tobey didn't kill Dan.'

'What makes you so sure?'

'Because Tobey told me so,' she says, as if I'd asked a stupid question.

'And if I told you I was the king of the whole of Zafrika, would you believe that too?' Was my sister serious?

'Tobey and I grew up together. We were close, OK? He wouldn't lie to me,' she insists.

'He might if—'

'He wouldn't.'

'But he would if—'

'Troy, I'm telling you, Tobey wouldn't lie to me. He just wouldn't do that.'

My sister is adamant that Tobey is innocent. He would never lie to her, so how could he possibly be a killer? Usually, my sister keeps all emotion out of her court cases.

'It's the only way to do my job effectively,' she's told me more than once.

But anyone with half an eye could see that Callie's emotions are involved. Her past friendship is affecting her current judgement. Her lack of logic when it comes to this guy is troubling.

'If you two are so close, how come you haven't mentioned him recently?' I can't help asking. 'How many times have you seen him to talk to in the last few years?'

'That's not the point. Tobey and I were never friends for a reason or a season, but for life. If you must know, we were more than friends, until something happened which exploded our friendship.'

More than friends? It's hitting home just how little I know about my own sister. It wasn't for want of asking either.

'What happened?' I ask.

At first I think Callie isn't going to answer. Either that or she's going to tell me to mind my own. Instead, she sighs. 'Beware of jealousy, Troy. It makes you do stupid things. Unforgivable things.'

'Like what?'

'Like something that burns through you like acid every time you remember it, so you try not to think about it.' Callie lowers her gaze. 'Except, as time goes by, you find yourself thinking about it more, not less. When I was your age, Troy, I made a huge mistake. Colossal. Now it's time to atone.'

'What mistake did you make?'

'Something I have no intention of sharing with you, so don't even ask,' Callie replies.

Worth a try!

'Is that why you're defending Tobey? As an apology?'

Callie doesn't speak. She doesn't have to. Neither of us have to say it, but her need to atone might just end up rebounding on me and Mum. If what they say about Dan Jeavons and his friends is true, then Callie's need might end up with someone getting hurt. Or even killed.

fifteen. Libby

I lie on my bed, curled into a ball, facing the wall. The cotton pillowcase beneath my cheek smells of the lavender perfume Mum bought me over two years ago for my fifteenth birthday. I'm not a fan of lavender, never have been – but it's one of the few presents Mum has ever given me. My birthday tends to be something Mum remembers after the event. I gave up reminding her round about my ninth or tenth. I read somewhere that moths don't like lavender and the smell helps you to sleep so I always squirt a little on my pillow whenever I change the pillowcase. The thing is, now I have trouble sleeping without it.

'Liberty? Liberty darling, let me in.'

'Mum, it's late and I'm tired. Go to bed. We can talk in the morning.' I clench my fists to stop my hands shaking. I don't need this. Not tonight.

Mum, please go away.

Mum rattles the door handle. 'Liberty, open the door, please. This is important. I have something to say to you.'

That was stupid. I shouldn't have answered. I should've just pretended to be already asleep. Now she won't stop.

'No, Mum. Go back to bed. We'll talk tomorrow.'

'Liberty Jackman, you open this door. NOW!'

I sit up in bed, pulling down the oversized T-shirt that serves as my nightie. I know from past experience that, if I don't open the door, Mum will get louder and more belligerent until the neighbours either come knocking or phone the police, who inevitably knock louder. I stand up, my heart thumping.

'Mum, please. I just want to go to sleep. I'm very tired.'

'This won't take long, Libby. Open the door. Don't make me repeat myself,' says Mum.

Libby, don't be a damned fool. Don't open that door.

The voice of reason lives rent free in my head, but, like an unwanted squatter, I resent and resist it and once again choose to ignore it.

Libby, don't—

My fingers creep towards the lock beneath the door handle.

'Liberty love, please.' Mum's voice is soft, caressing, barely above a whisper.

I turn the lock slowly. The door opens.

I don't see it coming. There's just a sudden impact to the middle of my face, a flash of hot and red, a crash of head-splitting agony. My legs give way beneath me and I crumple into darkness.

I can't believe what my sister is telling me. Tobey Durbridge has been charged with killing the most notorious gangster in the country. I may not have been a great follower of current events, but shouldn't that fact have hit every online news bulletin on the Internet? A story like that would surely have flashed up on my laptop, yet there'd been nothing about Tobey's arrest.

'Why isn't this all over the news?' I ask.

Callie lifts her chin defiantly. 'I took out a super-injunction. Until it's lifted, the press aren't allowed to mention anything about Tobey being arrested or the charges he's facing. They can't even refer to the fact that they can't mention it.'

'What happens if they do?'

'Go directly to jail. No mitigating circumstances, no appeals, no second chances.'

'So what can they report on?'

'Dan Jeavons is dead. That's about it. They have to stick to the victim and the crime, not the potential suspects.'

Wow! Eyebrows raised, I contemplate my sister with a new appreciation. She could do that? Suppress the biggest story in years? I guess she could and she did. So all the hype about her is right. I'll have to start paying more attention.

'But what about Tobey? Shouldn't he at least resign from the government or something?' I ask.

'He'll announce he's standing down within the next forty-eight hours, claiming it's temporary, for personal reasons. As soon as I get the case dismissed, he can pick up where he left off.'

I feel like I've been given a front-row seat from which to watch the wheels of power and privilege work. And my sister is one of the key cogs in the whole mechanism. Justice for all – as long as you have pockets deep enough to pay for it.

'What has Tobey got to do with Daniel Jeavons?' I ask. 'How do the two of them even know each other?'

I would've thought their paths were very unlikely to cross.

'They grew up together,' Callie informs me.

My eyebrows shoot up. 'Tobey told you this?'

'No, I have first-hand knowledge,' she says. 'I grew up with both of them.'

By now I'm bug-eyed. 'What? You know . . . knew Dan Jeavons?' The words squeak out of me. 'What the hell? You never said. How come I'm only finding out about this now?' Hearing that Callie knew Dan Jeavons is like hearing that my sister was friends with Jack the Ripper.

'Troy, it was no biggie. I grew up with Dan. He got into some things he shouldn't've, went on the run, gave himself up, served his time and came out of prison. And after that he made sure never to get caught again.'

Well, that says a lot.

I look at my sister like I'm seeing her for the first time. Never before have I felt our age gap as keenly as I do at this moment. Eighteen years means a lifetime of experiences for her that were way before my time. Eighteen years of doing and being, living and loving that I know nothing about – unless Callie or Mum chooses to tell me.

Callie says, 'I'm surprised you've even heard of Dan Jeavons, to be honest. Since when have you taken an interest in criminal lowlifes?'

Is she kidding? 'There isn't a person in the country who hasn't heard of Daniel Jeavons,' I reply. 'You should've told me before that you knew him personally.'

Callie is unrepentant. 'Like I said, we were sort of friends a long time ago.'

'Sort of?' Funny sort of friend who my sister labelled a criminal lowlife.

'To tell the truth, Dan gave me the creeps,' she admits. 'He was always looking at me like he didn't need X-ray glasses to see what was beneath my clothes. Take a tip from me, Troy: don't stare at girls like that. It gets old real fast.'

As if! Besides, if I stared at anyone in my class like that, I'd get a mouthful of scorching verbal – at the very least.

'If you're worried about the fallout from this case, can't you palm it off on someone else?' I ask.

Callie scowls like I've just insulted her. 'Tobey is my true friend and I'm not going to turn my back on him. I guarantee a lot of his so-called friends will be doing that in the weeks ahead. I won't be joining them.'

Why did Callie have to be so noble all of a sudden? But

then I realize something – it wasn't all of a sudden. Media reports and throwaway gossip about my sister always talk about her integrity, taking on cases that no one else would touch so that justice could be properly served. She's gained a lot of admirers that way, but has also made some powerful, outspoken enemies.

'Let me guess, you've already started receiving threats about taking on Tobey as a client?'

Callie nods. 'The trolls have begun to crawl out of their slimy holes. Threats have started coming into chambers, and Sol, my boss, is livid that I took on the case without discussing it with him first.'

'What kind of threats?'

Callie's eyes roll. She's trying to make out that it's no big deal, but her actions speak far louder than her words. 'Warnings to back down. Step up. Drop it. Don't drop it. Take the case. Don't take the case. Or else.'

'How does anyone even know about it when it hasn't been in the news?'

'I told you I took out a super-injunction to suppress the story so the press aren't allowed to report on it, but the officers who arrested and charged Tobey are bound to tell their families who blab to their friends.'

'Hmmm . . . You've had threats before—'

'Not like these. There's a new tone to some of them . . .' Callie's voice trails off.

'Threatening me and Mum as well as you.'

'Exactly,' she admits. 'I'm big enough and ugly enough to take care of myself, but I'm not going to risk anyone trying to harm you and Mum. If by some miracle the prosecution manage to get the super-injunction over-turned, I'll assign a close-protection officer to look after you and Mum. Until then, just be vigilant. OK?'

'Callie, you're probably worrying about nothing. I'm not gonna start looking over my shoulder everywhere I go.' Bugger that for a game of soldiers.

'Look, Troy, this isn't a joke or a game. I'm taking these threats seriously. So are the police – and so should you.' Callie's tone is sombre. 'There are people out there who wouldn't hesitate to hurt you and Mum to get to me.'

Her razor-wire words slowly but surely sink in.

'How is Gabriel taking all this?'

Gabriel Moreland is Callie's knob of a boyfriend. I've only met him twice, but each time he spoke to me like my shoe size and IQ were a matching pair. With his power suits and his power fade and his power-toned muscles and his power-plucked eyebrows, he was all about money and the status that synchro-swam with his job title. The last time we'd met was at the Mafanikio Ball, a big, glossy annual dinner-dance for lawyers, which also included a charity auction of donated gifts. Callie had unexpectedly invited me to go with her and I'd bitten her hand off. It wasn't often I got to attend formal functions. My sister and I sat at a table of ten, including Gabriel. Our meal was over and the auction due to begin. My first auction. I couldn't wait to see how it worked. Some of the submitted gifts included a spa weekend, a flying lesson, driving a Formula One car for an afternoon, a few paintings, rare books and a trip in a hot-air balloon. I could've gone for any of those – except the spa weekend. Hard pass on that one. Not that I could afford any of the auction items if the guide prices were anything to go by.

While waiting for the auction to start, for the first time that evening Gabriel spoke to me. 'So, Troy, what do you plan to do once you've left school?'

'I don't know,' I replied honestly. 'I wouldn't mind teaching chemistry or maths, but I haven't decided yet.'

'Teaching?' Gabriel looked me up and down with disdain. 'You know what they say – those who can, do; those who can't, teach.'

I glanced at Callie. Had that been a frown on her face? It had come and gone so quickly it was hard to tell.

'I mean really – don't you have any ambition?' Gabriel said with contempt.

I replied, 'You wanna know the difference between a mosquito and a lawyer? One is a blood-sucking parasite and the other is an insect.'

Gabriel's eyebrows shot up at my retort.

'Troy, you're sitting at a table of lawyers,' Callie reminded me pointedly. 'And we're not all like that.'

My face flushed hot as I looked around. My joke had gone down like a cup of sick. A perfect example of not reading the room. Damage limitation was required. 'Callie, I know that's not you. It's just a joke I heard,' I tried feebly. 'Besides, I know you wouldn't work or go out with other lawyers who are like that either.'

A few hard glares, a couple of forced smiles.

The other lawyers might've been OK, but Gabriel sure wasn't. I knew a dickhead when I saw one. He wasn't just conforming to every negative stereotype, he was basking in them. After my comment, the gloves came off. Gabriel spent the rest of the evening ripping into me. Ass hat! He was so patronizing, he was lucky I didn't knee him in the nuts. God knows I wanted to. But what burned me more than anything – and still burns, if I'm honest – is that Callie sat next to him and didn't say a word as he verbally crucified me.

'Well?' I prompt. 'Don't tell me, let me guess. Gabriel isn't happy and is telling you to drop the case.'

'I have no idea how Gabriel feels about it. Nor do I care. He and I aren't together any more,' Callie retorts.

'Oh? When did that happen?'

'The day after the Mafanikio Ball.'

'Really? Why?'

'I didn't appreciate the way he spoke to you,' Callie says with a shrug.

'No, why did you really break up with him?'

Callie quirks an eyebrow, tilting her head to one side as she looks at me. It hits me like an express train that she's deadly serious.

'You dumped him because of *me*?'

'No, I dumped him because of him,' she says firmly. 'He went out of his way to be a dick to you and I'm not having that, not from him, not from anyone.'

'Why was he so unpleasant?'

'Maybe he thought that making you look small would make him look bigger,' Callie says, unimpressed. 'He was wrong.'

'But you didn't say anything at the time,' I can't help pointing out. 'You sat next to him and didn't say a word.'

'I wasn't about to make a scene in front of my colleagues

and the whole lawyer fraternity,' Callie replies. 'I've told you before, Troy, learn to pick your moments.'

She had told me that – and more than once. If it'd been me, I would've told Gabriel something about himself right there and then, but Callie always views things from every angle before she makes a move. That's probably why she always thrashes me at chess and is formidable in court. A satisfied smile creeps across my lips. Gabriel got dumped. Ha!

'Troy, don't get puffed up,' she says. 'I would've dumped him if he'd spoken to anyone the way he spoke to you. When people show you their true selves, you need to believe them. I always do.'

One shiny moment for my ego and then my sister has to go and stick a pin in it. Typical!

'So you'll be careful? And report anything suspicious straight back to me?'

'Course.'

Callie's eyes narrow. 'Troy, promise.'

For Shaka's sake! 'I promise.' It's only a takeaway, disposable promise, barely acknowledged by me. I'm sure Callie is overreacting and worrying about nothing.

Callie nods, then leaves the room, taking my promise with her.

seventeen. Libby

I try to open my eyes, but the pain is blinding. My left eye feels like it's been sewn shut with a rusty needle and my whole face is throbbing. A sound comes rumbling towards me like a rainstorm approaching. The voice is muffled at first, but grows more distinct by the second.

'Libby darling, I'm sorry. Wake up. I'm so sorry. See what you made me do.'

Mum.

I lie crumpled on the floor. Forcing my right eye open, I see Mum standing over me, swaying slightly, still drunk. Or high. Immediately I scramble away from her until my back hits the wall. Mum looks at me, a strange expression on her face. She reaches out with one hand. I notice the back of her hand is bleeding where she's been scratching it.

'Libby—'

I shrink away from her. Mum's hand falls to her side, her expression freezing by degrees.

'You are your father's child,' she tells me, her voice dripping with contempt.

It's not the first time I've heard that, but now I understand the comment for what it truly means.

'And that's why you hate me,' I reply quietly. 'That's why you've always hated me.'

I voice what I should've figured out years ago. Mum straightens up, very still. We regard each other, the truth naked and ugly between us.

I struggle to my feet. Mum takes a step back as if she thinks I'm about to launch myself at her. I take a step forward. She takes another step back. For the first time, *I'm* in control, not Mum. The heady rush of realization is intoxicating.

'Mum, I will never allow you to hit me again,' I tell her quietly. 'And tell your boyfriend that, if he ever lays a hand on me, I'll chop it off and then go straight to the police and have him arrested.'

A moment's consternation on Mum's part, then she turns and staggers out of my room, slamming the door shut behind her. Her final word. I rush to lock the door, then lean on it, my forehead against the cool wood.

Stupid to open it in the first place.

Stupid for putting up with a mum who drifts through life with nothing but hatred for company.

Well, no more.

Swallowing hard, I reach out for the door handle, only to snatch back my hand. No! She isn't going to do this to me. I open the door before my courage can dance away again. The landing is empty. I head for Mum's bedroom. No more living with lies. No more living in fear.

I open her door without knocking. Mum is sitting on the edge of the bed, her head in her hands. The moment I enter the room, she looks up. Not allowing her a moment's thinking time, I launch straight in. 'Mum, where's my trust money?'

Mum's expression is instantly incredulous. Wary. 'What trust money? What're you talking about?'

'The money my dad pays you each month to look after me, for my future college fees and other expenses,' I reply. 'The dad you took great pleasure in saying didn't give a damn about me.'

Mum's face began to redden. 'I don't know what you're talking about.'

OK, so that was the way she was going to play it, was it?

I tell her, 'The bank sent me a statement today and I phoned them to find out if they'd sent the letter to the right person.'

Mum's cheeks are almost puce by now.

'How dare you!' She is actually beginning to shake with rage. 'How dare you open my letters!'

But I'm calm. Cool. Confident. 'It was addressed to me, Mum. They've been addressing letters to me about the trust since I was sixteen, apparently – so if there's any inappropriate letter-opening going on, it's not from my direction.'

'I'm your mother. You can't talk to me like this!'

I shake my head, recognizing this current argument for what it is. 'Mum, pick one thing to get mad about and stick to that. You're firing in all directions at the moment.'

'I . . . I . . . don't . . .' Mum splutters.

'So I'll ask again: where's my trust money, Mum?'

Her mouth opens and closes like a goldfish. She blinks rapidly, trying to summon up a suitable answer. None is forthcoming. The hunted, haunted look on her face confirms my worst suspicions. My heart is flip-flopping, though I'm careful to keep my expression neutral. My poker face is recharged and back in action. It wouldn't do to let Mum see the disappointment on my face – again. Mum's expression hardens as she finally settles on the way she's going to play this. She's about to kick off, but not in an alcohol- or drug-induced rage this time. No, this one is provoked by something less tangible, more unadulterated. Guilt.

'The letter had a bank statement attached to it stating that my trust fund is now down to double digits,' I get in before she can. 'I didn't even know I had a trust fund so when I phoned the bank I asked for more details.'

Mum blanches. 'You had no right to do that.'

'It's my trust fund, Mum, and the bank statement is in my name. That gives me every right. You said my dad was a nobody who walked away when you were pregnant. Yet he cared enough to set up a trust fund for me. A trust fund that used to have a lot of digits before the decimal point.'

But not any more.

'I'm not having this conversation.' Mum's voice hardens to match her expression. 'And don't you ever open my post again.'

'It was *my* letter, Mum, addressed to *me*. I just told you that. You're the one who's been opening my post all these years, not the other way round.' It's like she just doesn't get it. 'I'm eighteen in a few weeks, and d'you want to know what my present to myself will be? I'm going to find a lawyer to go through my trust-fund account with a fine-tooth comb. And if . . . *when* I have proof that you've been taking money meant for me, I'll make sure you pay – one way or another.'

'Are you threatening me?' Mum gives me a hard stare.

I don't answer. How can I? I'm not sure if it's a threat or a promise or just hot air created in the heat of the moment, but Mum isn't the only one who's pissed. All this time she's made out that my dad did a runner and didn't give a toss about me. Liar.

'I've spent years wondering why you didn't just farm me off to a relative or put me in a children's home,' I muse. 'And now I know the reason: because without me you would've had to work for a living. No me, no trust fund. All this time, you've been living off my money.'

'I don't have to listen to this. Get out of my room.'

'Mum, I mean it. The moment I turn eighteen, the first thing I'm going to do is check out my so-called trust fund. If you've stolen my money, I'm going to the police. I'll do whatever it takes to get it back and be free of you. In fact, I'm going to write to my dad care of the bank and ask if I can live with him.'

'Yeah, that'll happen,' she scoffs.

'Even if he says a flat-out no, I still won't stay here with you. Either way I'm outta here.'

'You do what you have to do,' says Mum. 'And so will I.'

She glares at me, her gaze scornful. For the first time, it doesn't hurt. It doesn't even sting. I'm beyond that now. I head back to my room, locking the door behind me. Lying on my bed, the words of the letter from the bank keep dancing before me. Trust fund . . . account balance . . . Lots of technical banking jargon that all boils down to one thing – no more money. When I phoned the bank earlier, giving the account number and sort code provided in their statement to me, the first thing I asked was how much had been paid in each month and how much the account had at its peak. They wouldn't tell me until I answered their security questions, like my mum's maiden name and my mum's date of birth. I was thankful Mum had picked security questions that all revolved around her. Once through security, I got shocking answers to my questions.

Mum said my dad walked out on us and never looked back. He looked back enough to pay for my upkeep each month. He looked back enough to never skip a month. Not one. Apart from the regular monthly deposits, every year on my birthday and at Crossmas, more money was added to my account, only to be withdrawn within a couple of weeks. My dad had remembered my birthdays. It was all academic though because my account had been bled dry.

They say you can't miss what you've never had, but I was already missing the financial security that had been snatched away from me – stolen away and spent by my mother.

And, more than that, I missed my dad. A dad I'd never met, never known. I missed the idea of him, as well as the reality. A dad who was supposedly so worthless that, under the father's name on my birth certificate, Mum had put UNKNOWN. Why had she done that? A way of spiting, spitting at and splitting both of us? Fed up with me plying her with questions about my dad, Mum had thrown the birth certificate at me when I was six or seven. I hadn't understood what UNKNOWN meant, so Mum had explained it meant unwelcome, unwanted. I'd believed her.

The bank wouldn't or couldn't tell me my dad's name either. The source of the money on the statement was listed as TD Holdings – whatever that meant. I googled the name, but all that came up with was some insurance company. My dad is out there somewhere, and if Mum lied about him not caring, maybe she'd lied about everything else. Maybe he does want to get to know me. Maybe I'm not as unlovable as I've been made to believe all my life.

I now have a new mission – to find out more about my dad and make contact with him.

And neither Mum nor the devil himself will stop me now.

Daily Shouter Online

Prime Minister Mansa Julliard speaks out against latest confirmed residency riots

Liberal Traditionalist Prime Minister Mansa Julliard has condemned yesterday's riots in the capital. 'Those arrested have no interest in debate or political discourse,' she said last night. 'They merely seek to destabilize this government and our great country, encouraged in their lawlessness by dissident voices such as that of Tobias Durbridge in the main opposition party.'

What started as a peaceful march to the Houses of Parliament quickly descended into a brawl between anti-government activists and the police. One protester told the *Daily Shouter*, 'It's a shame that a peaceful protest against an unjust law can get hijacked in this way.' Another stated, 'I don't understand what's going on in this country. I'm a sixty-year-old Nought woman, born and bred here. I really thought that we, as a nation, were coming together and making progress. The fact that the Confirmed Residency Bill could become law just shows that racism wasn't on the way out, it had just gone underground. And now it's back and roaring. This is my home. I'm not going anywhere.'

eighteen. Troy

Well, this chews bag! I really have better things to do with my Sunday, but, after our last train-wreck dinner together, Mum has arranged for us to spend the day with Sonny at his home. We've been invited for Sunday dinner. According to Mum, Sonny is even going to cook it himself. Big whoop!

I sit in the passenger seat of Mum's car, staring out of the window. We've been on the road for over an hour now, having left the city behind a while ago. The farmhouses around here are few and far between. I'd heard of the back of beyond, but I'd never driven through it before.

'Troy, I want you on your best behaviour,' Mum warns.

'Yeah, well, I hope you told Sonny the same thing,' I say. 'He's the one who started it.'

'Troy, I'm not playing.' Mum's eyes narrow into slivers of ice. 'You are to behave yourself or you and I are going to fall out – big time.'

'Yes, Mum.' It really isn't worth arguing about. I resolve to just keep my mouth shut for once and try to get through the day without Mum shouting at me.

Damn it, but Sonny lives in the middle of nowhere. Typical! Kilometres and kilometres of nothing to do but look at the greenery. How does he stand it? And Mum wouldn't even let me bring my tablet so I could at least play games or watch films while at his house.

'I want you two to sit and talk to each other. Really talk,' Mum declared. 'I'm sure you'll find you have a lot in common if you give each other a chance.'

Yeah, right.

At last we turn into a wide driveway, flanked on both sides by trees. That's when I catch my first glimpse of Sonny's house and, OK, I admit, it's impressive. I thought our driveway was long and strong, but Sonny's is like the grown-up version. Poplar trees, tall and skinny sentinels, line the way up to his manor. I get out of the car, my mouth hanging open. Mum smiles wryly at me.

'Catching flies, hon,' she says.

My mouth snaps shut.

'Sonny lives *here*?'

'Most weekends he does,' says Mum.

'Him and what army?'

'Just him.' She chuckles. 'Well, he has staff of course, but it's his house. During the week, he stays in his flat in town.'

'I thought he wrote songs,' I say, puzzled.

'He does. At least one fifth of the songs currently in the Top One Hundred were written or produced by him,' Mum explains. 'He uses different names for the different genres of songs he writes.'

Ah! That explained why my Internet search had been lacking in information.

I look around. 'And he owns all this land too?'

'Yep. All fifteen acres,' says Mum. 'There's a quarry to

the north and woodlands to the south and east, and the lake over there to the west is also his.'

'OK, so Sonny's not dating you for your money then!'

Mum stares at me, then bursts out laughing. 'Is that why you've been so hostile towards him? You thought he was after my money? Aw, Troy – bless!'

Mum only says 'bless' like that when I've said or done something particularly moronic. She's still chortling as we make our way up to the front door. We don't even have to knock before the door is opened by Sonny himself.

'Welcome. Hey, Troy. How're you doing?'

'Fine, thanks,' I mumble.

Sonny looks from Mum to me and back again. Mum is grinning. It wasn't *that* funny! 'What have I missed?' he asks.

'Troy thought—'

'Mum! Don't you dare!' I warn.

She takes one look at the scowl on my face and shakes her head apologetically at Sonny. 'Just some mother–son humour.'

'Fair enough,' he says. 'Come in.'

Thankfully, he doesn't push it, though I have no doubt that Mum will tell him when the two of them are alone. Sonny steps aside so that Mum and I can enter his house.

'Make yourself at home, Troy,' he tells me.

I take him at his word, and off comes my jacket, then my jumper, and I fling both over the stair banister. After all, we're going to be here for quite some time.

'How's Callie Rose?' Sonny asks Mum.

'She's great. Going from strength to strength,' she says

proudly. 'One day that girl of mine is going to be Attorney General for the whole country.'

'I don't doubt it for a second.'

'She has a big court case to prepare for or she would've come too,' Mum explains.

'No worries. Tell her I said hi,' says Sonny. 'Troy, would you like me to show you my recording studio?'

'You've got a recording studio here in your house?'

'I do. Wanna see it?'

'Yes, please.'

'I'll head to the kitchen and help with dinner,' says Mum.

'Sephy, I didn't invite you to dinner so you could cook for me,' Sonny protests.

'You know you burn water,' she teases. And she heads straight for the closed door on the left-hand side of the grand polished-wood staircase that sweeps down to the middle of the vast hall. She opens the door on to a huge kitchen decorated with white cupboards and black marble worktops. It takes a moment to click, but click it does.

'You've been here before, Mum?' I call after her.

She turns, and the tips of her ears are red and she can't quite look me in the eye. Sonny's cheeks are a fiery tomato-red too. I turn back to Mum. She'd been to Sonny's house before, and more than once, and I bet it was for more than coffee. Ewww.

'I . . . er . . . well . . .'

'Is that a yes then?'

'A couple of times,' Mum admits.

So it's like that, is it?

She hurries into the kitchen, ignoring the knowing look

I give her. Sonny shows me his indoor swimming pool and gym, the attic which has been converted into a cinema room, the lot. And each room is like something out of a high-tech magazine. His house really is amazing.

'How long have you lived here?' I ask.

'Just over ten years,' Sonny replies. 'Some of my neighbours weren't thrilled when I bought the place, but I'm still here and they're not.'

'Why weren't they thrilled?'

'A blanker moving into a predominantly Cross area?' Sonny shrugs. 'Some of them were worried I'd drive down the house prices around here. When I made it clear I was staying put, some of them moved elsewhere – and good riddance.'

He says it likes it's a joke, but we both know he's serious. I shake my head. For Shaka's sake! We're now at the recording studio in a soundproofed annexe to the side of his house.

'Troy, you into music?' Sonny asks as he shows me around.

'Only to listen to,' I reply.

'You don't play an instrument or sing or spit bars?'

'Me? Nah.'

'Shame.' Sonny smiles. 'You sure you don't want to record a little something for your mum?'

'Er, that's a hard pass! I love my mum. I wouldn't do that to her,' I protest, at which Sonny laughs.

We actually end up having the first proper conversation we've ever had as Sonny shows me round his home. And he is all smiles and questions, and he listens to my answers.

By the time the tour is over, I am beginning to wonder if I've made a huge mistake about him.

Once we reach his kitchen, which is even bigger than ours at home, Sonny says, 'Dinner will be at least an hour so, Troy, why don't you grab one of the quad bikes from the garage and go and explore?'

My eyes widen. This sounds great. 'Really? Can I?'

'Er, a quad bike. I don't think—' Mum begins.

'Sephy, let the boy go and have some fun. He'll be fine and it's perfectly safe as long as he sticks to the tracks,' Sonny interjects. 'Troy, feel free to go anywhere you like except north to the quarry, OK? It's not safe up there and, if you fall into one of the many caves or pits up there, it could be weeks before we find your corpse.'

I start to laugh. Sonny doesn't. Instead, he raises an eyebrow at me. Oh my God, he's serious.

'Fair enough,' I reply, the smile dying on my face. 'I'll head round the lake and through the woods.'

'Just stick to the established tracks and you won't get lost or in any trouble, OK?'

I nod vigorously. Mum still doesn't look happy, but she doesn't tell me no.

'Troy, make sure you wear your jumper and jacket,' she says.

'But, Mum—'

'Jumper and jacket or forget it,' says Mum firmly.

I exchange a long-suffering look with Sonny, who smiles in sympathy.

'Sonny, tell her!' I plead.

'Are you having a laugh?' He splutters. 'Me? Get between the two of you? I don't think so.'

No help there then.

Reluctantly, I put on my jumper and jacket. Beads of sweat are already breaking out on my forehead and my armpits are prickling.

'Let's go, Troy. I'll show you how the quad bikes work,' says Sonny.

'Sonny—' Mum still isn't happy.

'Don't worry, Seph,' he soothes. 'My quad bikes are so easy to manage, a four-year-old could ride them.'

We head to Sonny's garage, which is like the showroom of an upmarket car dealership. It is huge, almost as big as the downstairs of his house. Luxury cars I've only seen on TV line one wall. Motorcycles requiring serious muscles to control line the opposite one.

'This is something else.' I'm wide-eyed like a child at Crossmas. 'These are all yours?'

'Every one of them,' Sonny says. He's not boasting, just stating a fact.

After I pick his brains about a couple of his vintage cars, he leads the way to his three quad bikes.

'They're for me and my two nieces,' he explains.

Sonny shows me how they work, and what he told Mum about how easy they are to manage isn't a lie. Right foot pedal to go. Left foot pedal to stop. Steering wheel to steer. Emergency stop cord around my wrist to immediately cut power to the engine should I fall out. Push button to start. And that was it. Five minutes later, I'm heading for the lake, whooping with glee as Sonny chortles behind me. I've never been on a quad bike before and it is the boss!

'One hour, Troy. No longer.' Mum appears at the back door to call after me.

'Yes, Mum!' I call back without even looking round.

I have one hour and I intend to make the most of every single second.

Sticking to the tracks, I drive round the lake several times. During my second lap, I pull off my jacket and jumper, dumping them in the seat beside me, and I feel better for it. The lake water glistens blue and gold in the sunlight, like liquid diamonds. The air smells so . . . clean. No diesel, no petrol fumes, no pissy aromas. I could get used to this! I head for the woods, lifting my foot off the accelerator so I don't go crashing into anything. After all, it's not my quad bike. Driving through the trees is a revelation. I don't have to race to still enjoy myself. At first I think the only sounds are from birdsong and the quad bike, but, as I listen, I realize my mistake. There's an underlying rhythm to the stillness, almost like the woods are breathing. The crackle of twigs, the sound of lapping water, a hoot, a dog barking far away. I can well understand now why Sonny bought this place. If I had serious money, I'd do the same.

Weather-wise, the temperature is just how I like it – cool but sunny. Even the slight chill in the air can't dampen my excitement. After exploring the woods for ages, I glance at my watch. Fifteen minutes left – and the only place I haven't yet checked out is the quarry.

If I take it slowly and carefully, what harm can it do? What's the point of having all this land if some of it is out of bounds? I leave the woods by the track furthest away from the house, and, once I'm sure I can't be spotted from any of the windows, I head north. The dirt track is worn, but that's the worst of it as far as I can see. No potholes, no troughs, no cave-ins, no caves. Am I missing something? I head further north at a slowish speed.

What was Sonny talking about?

This route is no more dangerous than any of the others on his estate. I round a bend in the track skirting a fringe of trees, and then I see it about twenty metres ahead. Like some titan has taken a huge scoop out of the earth and left a massive hole instead. The quarry. I slow right down as I approach, my foot barely on the accelerator pedal. Ten metres from the edge I stop the quad bike and get off. I edge forward like I'm a hundred and ninety, not wanting the ground to suddenly give way beneath me. Maybe this was what Sonny meant about caves and cave-ins. If the ground is going to collapse anywhere, it'd be here.

One step.

Another.

I peer over the lip of the quarry. Far below I can see the smashed remains of two cars and the burnt-out remnants of one other. How long have they been down there? And why would Sonny allow anyone to use the quarry on his land as a dumping ground for vehicles? I can't tell the make of the burnt-out car, but, of the smashed-up ones, isn't the one closest to the lip of the quarry a Whitman Scorpius? A navy blue one, by the look of it. I frown. What a waste of a classic car. Why would anyone—?

A dark blue Whitman Scorpius.

I fall to my knees. Minutes pass as I stare down at the mangled yet still identifiable car. There must be some mistake. I keep searching for proof that I'm wrong – but I'm not.

I don't know how much time passes. The cold of the ground seeps into my bones. Or am I the one freezing the earth beneath me? Numb, I finally get to my feet.

That car . . .

The same make and model that killed my dad in the hit-and-run incident.

It has to be a coincidence. It just *has* to be. Eyes down, I head back to the quad bike. Thoughts sting like angry wasps as I gingerly turn it round, only to find I'm no longer alone. Up ahead on the only track away from the quarry sits Sonny on another quad bike, watching me.

nineteen. Libby

'Who's my dad, Mum?'

Mum scowls at me. 'How long are you going to keep this up, Libby?'

How long have you got? 'Who's my dad, Mum?'

Late Sunday afternoon and my attention isn't on my homework or even on the forthcoming school election. It's on my dad. I have so many questions there's no room in my head for anything else.

'You and I have no more to say to each other until you tell me who my dad is,' I tell Mum again. If she thinks I'm joking, she's going to find out otherwise.

'Maybe I don't know,' says Mum.

'Really? You've been taking money from this man for almost eighteen years, but you don't know who he is? I'm supposed to believe that?'

Mum's lips tighten until they're just a slash across her face. 'I'm the one who had you and took care of you. Your dad wasn't interested. He told me to have an abortion and, when I refused, he promised he'd have nothing to do with either of us and he kept that promise. Paying into a trust fund all these years was his way of turning his back on us and not being saddled with a guilty conscience to go along with it.'

'Who's my dad, Mum?'

'Stop asking that question,' she snaps, exasperated. 'Believe me, you're better off not knowing.'

'Who's my dad, Mum?'

'You want to know? I mean, d'you *really* want to know?' The change in the tone of Mum's voice should've set off warning bells, but it doesn't.

'Yes, I do,' I reply. 'I wouldn't have been asking for the last two days if I didn't.'

'OK. You want to know the crappy truth – I'll give it to you. And don't say I didn't warn you.'

And then Mum lets me have it.

Straight between the eyes.

twenty. Troy

All the way back to the house, Sonny doesn't say a single word to me. His quad bike is always just behind mine. He isn't taking any more chances of me going places and seeing things I shouldn't. His eyes bore into my back. I press the pedal to the metal, desperate to get back to the house and Mum. My anxiety ratchets up every moment Sonny is behind me. By the time his house comes into view, I feel physically sick with relief.

'Just park at the front,' Sonny calls out.

I turn. He is wearing a smile like a first-year school uniform on a sixth-former. It's a bad fit. I skid to a halt and dart for the house. The door is shut but not locked.

Pushing it open, I yell out, 'Mum!'

She emerges from the kitchen, a carrot in one hand, a knife in the other. One look at me and her smile fades, a question mark drawing her brows closer together. 'You OK, Troy?'

My relief at seeing Mum is short-lived. Sonny is right behind me.

'Sephy, I've already told you, I didn't invite you here so you could do all the work,' he says.

'I'm only doing the veggies,' Mum says, smiling. 'Besides, you know I love to cook. It relaxes me.'

'I'll help, love.' Sonny heads over to Mum, the two of them sharing a smile.

Love? Is that where their relationship is at now? My heart dive-bombs.

What to do? Follow them into the kitchen and tell Mum what I saw? But then what will Sonny do? We're alone in his house, kilometres from anywhere. After dithering in the hall for several moments, I follow the sound of Mum's laughter into the kitchen. She and Sonny stand side by side, preparing veggies, their bodies dangerously close to one another. Mum is topping and tailing carrots, her focus on them, though she's smiling at something Sonny just said, but Sonny's eyes are on Mum and the look on his face . . . He's got it bad and he's not even trying to hide it. The lack of space between the two of them makes up my mind. Following my sister's advice for once, I realize I need to pick the right moment – and this isn't it. I go into the sitting room to watch TV, but no matter how hard I try to concentrate, my mind is elsewhere, my thoughts racing. I need to tell Mum what I saw before Sonny can get rid of the evidence, but how do I even begin to do that? How do I start?

Dinner is excruciating. I push my food around with my fork, east, west, north, east again. Bits of beef, mashed potato and carrots circumnavigate my plate. Again and again my gaze is drawn to Sonny. I can't get the dark blue Whitman Scorpius in the quarry out of my mind, its metal mangled, twisted, broken. A reflection of my dad's state once that car had hit him.

What should I do?

Tell Mum. That's what I should do. Now. Do it now.

Troy, just open your mouth and tell her.

What words should I use?

By the way, Mum, I just thought I'd mention that your new boyfriend might've killed my dad. Pass the gravy.

Yeah, right.

And what if it is all just a coincidence? Stranger things have happened. I glance up at Sonny again, only to find him watching me, his eyes narrowed and speculative. The exact same way he looked at me when he caught me at the quarry.

He did it.

In that moment, I know he did it.

He killed my dad.

And he knows that I know.

'Don't you like your food, Troy?' asks Sonny.

I look down at the mess on my plate. 'I'm not hungry.'

'That's not what you said in the car on our way here,' Mum reminds me. 'In fact, you wanted to stop off for a snack before we got here.'

'I've lost my appetite,' I mumble.

'Troy, what on earth is wrong with you?' Mum frowns. 'You've barely said a word since you got back from your quad-bike ride.'

Sonny sighs. 'Troy, should I just tell her? Get it over with?'

My head jerks up in surprise. My mouth falls open. He's going to confess? Just like that?

'Sephy, don't get mad because no harm was done,' says

Sonny, his eyes still on me, 'but I caught Troy over by the quarry.'

A moment's stunned silence, then Mum scowls at me. 'You went to the quarry after Sonny warned you not to?'

'Mum, I've got something to tell you—'

'Sephy, calm down. Troy's fine. The ground is uneven and liable to cave-ins over there, plus the quarry is filled with wrecked and burnt-out cars, but Troy's back here in one piece so it's all good,' interrupts Sonny with a smile. 'It's a shame the previous owner used the quarry as a dumping ground for old cars and bits of machinery. There's even a Whitman Scorpius and a vintage Wells Phoenix in the pit. Imagine dumping a Wells Phoenix! Those cars were works of art. The cars in the quarry are too wrecked and burnt-out to salvage though, which is a damned shame. But you know what? First thing tomorrow morning, I'm going to get someone to clear out the place and make it safe. Troy has convinced me that I've put it off long enough.'

I stare. The fluency and ease of his lies are masterful. At any other time, I'd applaud. Instead my heart flips. By getting in first, Sonny has very effectively spiked my guns.

'Mum, there's a Whitman Scorpius in the quarry,' I tell her.

'Yeah, Sonny just said that,' she says.

'A *dark blue* Whitman Scorpius,' I repeat. 'The same car that killed Dad.'

'Oh my God! Was that the make of car that killed Nathan?' Sonny turns to Mum, his eyes wide with shock. 'I'm so sorry. I didn't know.'

I glare at him, not buying his surprised act for a second.

'Mum, don't you think it's one hell of a coincidence that Sonny has the same make and model of car as the one that killed Dad?' I ask. 'Even the colour is the same.'

She blinks at me in disbelief. 'Troy! Are you saying what I think you're saying?'

'Mum, you didn't see Sonny's face when he caught me there,' I blurt out. 'He was furious. He knew I'd put two and two together.'

'And made thirty-three and three-quarters,' she says. 'Troy, have you lost your mind?'

'Troy, are you serious?' Sonny says with dismay. 'You really think—?'

'Mum, it's the same car.'

'And how many Whitman Scorpiuses do you think there are in the country? The police told me over one hundred thousand,' says Mum.

'But Sonny has one in his quarry. Dad's gone and he's here and—'

'Troy, that's enough.'

'But I saw—'

'I said – ENOUGH.' The look on Mum's face . . . I've never seen her so fuming angry.

'Troy, I'm disappointed.' Sonny shakes his head, morose. 'I had no idea you resented me quite so much that you'd automatically assume the worst.'

'Mum, he's hiding something. I know it.'

'That car was in the quarry when I bought this place. Sephy, if you want to call the police and have the car forensically tested, then feel free,' says Sonny.

'Don't be ridiculous,' Mum snaps in his direction, though

it's aimed at me. 'I wouldn't dream of doing any such thing. As if you'd own the car that killed Nathan. Troy, you and I are going to have a serious talk when we get home.'

Sonny reaches over to place his hand on Mum's. He shakes his head. 'It's OK, Sephy. Let's just drop it and move on.'

'I don't think so,' says Mum, glaring at me.

'Please, love,' says Sonny. 'For me?'

There it was again. That word. *Love.* I scowl at Sonny, my stomach roiling. He's too busy gazing into Mum's eyes to even notice. Mum, however, notices enough for both of them. She regards me, her eyes shooting fiery jets like flame-throwers. I immediately look down at my meal. Too late.

'Sonny, let me just have a word with my son.' She stands up and leaves the dining room, fully expecting me to follow her — which I do. With each step, my heart sinks lower. The moment we're out in the hall, Mum carefully shuts the door behind us.

'How dare you?' she bursts out, her voice low, but her tone no less intense for it. 'How dare you embarrass me like that? Accusing Sonny of all sorts.'

'Mum, the car that killed Dad is in Sonny's quarry — or don't you even care how Dad died any more?'

A stillness descends over Mum. Silent moments pass. I want to reach out with both hands and snatch back the words, but it's too late.

'Troy, if anyone else had said that to me, my hand would now be decorating their face — and that's in spite of being a pacifist,' Mum says stonily. 'I am seriously disappointed in you. Now get back in there and apologize to Sonny. Then I don't want to hear another negative comment from you for the rest of the time we're here. Is that understood?'

'Yes, Mum.'

Mum glares at me, unblinking, her face a mask. I've messed up. I should've kept my suspicions to myself – at least until I have proof. And what I just said to Mum . . . Damn it. Mum still grieves for Dad and I was grossly unfair to say otherwise. An apology sits and withers in my mouth, the moment lost. I've messed up big time. We head back into the dining room and sit down. Mum looks at me expectantly.

'Sorry, Sonny,' I say grudgingly. 'I shouldn't have said what I did. I guess my imagination is doing too much homework.'

'Damned right it is.' Mum's lips are pursed, her eyes hard. I'm not used to her looking at me like that.

'Apology accepted,' Sonny says, with a smile as warm and cosy as a pair of slippers.

And I hate him all the more for it.

For the rest of the evening, I keep my head down, my mouth shut and my eyes open, watching Sonny every chance I get. He, on the other hand, is Mr Friendly.

'Troy, can I get you a drink?'

'Troy, have you had enough to eat?'

'Troy, would you like . . . ? Do you have . . . ? Can I get you . . . ?'

He's really working it, the butter-wouldn't-melt act. He's also working my nerves – as my sister, Callie, would say.

Sonny offers me the chance to play the latest virtual-reality zombie apocalypse game, and I only say yes 'cause Mum is watching me. It goes some way to placating her and I need all the good will I can get. I win the first two games, but Sonny easily wins the next two, leading me to suspect he was humouring me when we first started playing. At last it's time to leave. We are at his front door when Mum says, 'Damn it! I'll be right back. I left my phone in the kitchen.'

Muttering to herself, she heads back inside to get it, leaving Sonny and me alone in the hall. We both regard each other, but I look away first, unable to hold his gaze.

'You really do believe that I had something to do with Nathan's death, don't you?' Sonny sounds bemused at the idea. More acting.

I take a quick look around. Mum is still in the kitchen.

'I know you did,' I say quietly, deciding to be honest.

'I don't suppose there's anything I could say to change your mind?'

I shake my head.

Silent moments pass as Sonny studies me. He shrugs, stating steely-soft for my ears alone, 'Then I guess it's up to you to prove it.'

Daily Shouter Online

Tobias Durbridge is the new Prime Minister as the Democratic Alliance sweep to power

This morning the country woke up to a new governing party – the Democratic Alliance – and its first ever Nought Prime Minister, Tobias Durbridge, as voted for by an overwhelming majority of the public. Speaking to the *Daily Shouter* after his historic win, Tobey Durbridge proclaimed, 'This is a great day for our country. No longer will politics be for the benefit of the few and work against the interests of the many. We in the Democratic Alliance will seek to ensure that the rights and freedoms of all in society are protected.'

Click below for a full analysis of the way the country voted.

twenty-one. Libby

My chin rests on my upturned palm as I gaze out of the window into the web of lies my mum has spun around me. A web of lies that surrounds my Monday afternoon like a net. I'm still trying to digest the information she fed me the night before.

My dad . . .

My dad is . . .

'Libby, where is your head today?' my biology teacher asks, exasperated.

Blushing, I turn to face her. 'Sorry, Mrs Baxter.'

'Tell me what I just said?'

I was afraid she'd ask me that. I haven't a clue what she's been chatting on about and my expression says as much. 'Something about the forthcoming school election?'

'I was saying that as one of the election adjudicators, and one of the teachers who'll be acting as scrutineer and counting the votes, I want everyone to take this election seriously. This may be just a school election, but it's important,' sniffs Mrs Baxter. 'Politics is important. You're never too young to understand that. Politics is power. Politics is *life*.'

Politics is life? Is she for real? I school my features and say, 'Yes, Mrs Baxter.'

Behind me, Meshella snickers. I frown as I contemplate Mrs Baxter, the other Nought staff member. As a Nought, maybe politics means more to her than the average Cross teacher. Maybe it means more to her than it does to most Crosses. Is that what she's trying to tell me? That, as a Nought, politics matters more to me?

'Mrs Baxter, why has this school never had a Nought head girl or boy?' I ask.

Mrs Baxter's neck and cheeks bloom red. A sudden tension fills the room, so tangible I feel I could reach out my hand and touch it. All eyes are now on our teacher.

'Just because something hasn't happened in the past doesn't mean it can't happen now or in the future,' says Mrs Baxter, picking her way through the words like she's in a minefield. 'There are more Noughts attending Heath-croft High than ever before—'

Behind me Meshella mutters something to Dina seated next to her.

'And for Noughts in general, throughout the country, there are more opportunities open to them than ever before,' Mrs Baxter continues. 'Look at our general election. Tobias Durbridge, a Nought, is now Prime Minister of this great country.'

More mumblings from behind me about the new prime minister. Now I take them personally. I turn my head to frost Meshella, waiting for her to make another comment. I long for her to say something so I can punch her lights out.

'Face forward, Libby. Our best hope is that the politics of

the past, the rhetoric of division and exclusion, stays where it belongs – in the past,' says Mrs Baxter.

'Are you saying that all Cross politicians were bigots?' asks Meshella.

'I'm not saying that at all,' Mrs Baxter replies, frowning. 'That is the very definition of a straw-man argument, Meshella. I say one thing, you tell me I'm saying another so you can shoot down that straw man. Don't put words in my mouth. I'm sick of people putting words in my mouth.'

We sit in stunned silence. Mrs Baxter's voice doesn't normally rise above mousy diffidence.

'Has having a Nought prime minister gone to your head, Mrs Baxter?' sneers Meshella.

Mrs Baxter draws herself up, her shoulders back, two sharp points of red on her cheeks. 'Meshella, that piece of rudeness will cost you five demerits. Go and report to the head. NOW!'

With a huff, Meshella stands up, grabs her rucksack off the floor and heads out of the door, slamming it behind her. Mrs Baxter glares after her. She turns to the rest of us, blood in her eye.

'If anyone else has anything rude and inappropriate to say, go for it. I'd be more than happy to send you to the head as well.'

No one says a word. I turn in my chair to face forward. Seems I've had Mrs Baxter wrong all this time. I'm beginning to realize that I've done that a lot – got people wrong. It feels like I've spent so much time, too much time, seeking answers to the wrong questions. I raise my hand.

'Yes, Libby?'

'Why d'you think Tobey Durbridge and his party won the election, Mrs Baxter?'

She looks around the room. 'Because he got the most votes.'

Some titters. Mrs Baxter smiles, adding, 'Because I think people are ready for something new, someone different. A change. Sometimes change is scary, but that's the only way we grow and move forward. Remember, class, if you always do what you've always done, you'll always get what you've always got.'

Mrs Baxter's words shoot straight through me like arrows.

You'll always get what you've always got . . .

That described Mum and me exactly. Round and round in our *danse macabre*. And it would stay that way until one of us broke free – or died. Whichever came first.

twenty-two. Troy

'Mum, what was Callie's dad like?'

'Pardon?' Mum starts in surprise. 'Where has that come from all of a sudden?'

'I've been wondering,' I say. 'Callum McGregor, what was he like?'

I'm stirring the cheese sauce for our dinner of macaroni cheese and lamb chops. I continue to stir, even though I can feel Mum's eyes drilling into my nape. Outside, the sky is almost sepia, a brown-grey haze filling the air. Rain pelts against the kitchen windows, rapping to be let in.

'Callum was . . . well, he was a warrior. He was fiercely loyal and he fought for what he believed,' says Mum carefully. 'I didn't always agree with his methods, but I understood his need to stand up and be counted. Your dad was the same. When a street rat named Jordy Carson tried to extort money from him, Nathan told him to get lost.'

'What happened to Dad?' I ask.

'He got beaten up,' says Mum. 'But he never backed down. I was so proud of him for that. Even Dan Jeavons tried extorting protection money from your dad and, although he threatened him, he got the same answer. Scumbag! Why the questions?'

'Hang on. Dan Jeavons threatened Dad? I didn't know that.'

'Is there any reason why you should?' asks Mum.

'Did Dan ever threaten you?'

Mum shrugs.

That's not an answer.

'Mum?'

Mum's gaze slides away from mine.

'He did, didn't he?' Every muscle in my body tenses.

'Troy, calm down. The man is dead now. He can't harm anyone any more,' Mum soothes.

I force myself to take a deep breath, to calm down. If Jeavons was in front of me now . . .

'Is that what Sonny is too? A warrior?' I ask when I can trust myself to speak again.

'Troy, what's going on? Talk to me,' says Mum. 'I'm trying to figure out what's going on in that head of yours, but I'm failing.'

I shake my head. I hate lying to Mum. I hate lying full stop. I'm no good at it. 'Mum, you worry too much.'

'I'm worrying about nothing then?'

'Yep, as always. I'm guess I'm just trying to find out if you're serious about Sonny. Does he make you happy?'

A moment's silence. 'Yes, he does. In fact, I've got some news. Sonny has asked me to marry him.'

The wooden spoon in my hand clatters to the floor. Moments pass and there's no sound in the world but my heart thumping a stricken tattoo in my chest. Eventually my world stops spinning.

'Did you say yes?'

'I said I needed to talk to you first,' says Mum. 'This affects both of us.'

'I see.'

'So what d'you think?' she asks.

The look on her face . . . So hopeful. So expectant. As far as Mum is concerned, another word for happiness is Sonny. And, beyond a shadow of a doubt, Sonny loves her. I bend to pick up the spoon. It falls out of my sweaty hand. I grip it tighter then toss it into the sink. Grabbing some kitchen towel, I wipe up the sauce on the floor, before heading over to the sink. I don't look at Mum.

'Troy?' she prompts.

'Do you love him?' I scrub at the wooden spoon with the scourer.

'We wouldn't be having this conversation if I didn't,' says Mum.

That's what I thought. Rinsing the spoon under the hot tap scalds my hands. I don't make a sound.

'Troy, look at me,' Mum pleads. 'D'you really hate the idea that much?'

'It's just . . . Dad . . .' My voice is weak.

'I know.' Mum walks up behind me and hugs me round my waist, resting her head on my back. 'I miss your dad too, love. Every day. When your dad died . . . well, I swore I'd never even contemplate being with anyone else again. What with Callum and then Nathan, your dad, I figured I was bad luck. Jinxed. I warned Sonny I should come with a health warning, but he finally persuaded me that that was nonsense.'

'Of course it's nonsense, Mum. You can't honestly believe you're jinxed.'

'I was beginning to wonder.' She lets me go and turns me round to face her. 'So? D'you think you, me and Sonny could live together as a family?'

'If I say yes?'

'Then I tell Sonny that maybe some day.'

'And if I say no?'

'Then Sonny and I stay as we are. This far, no further.'

Mum smiles and I realize she means it. She'd actually do that for me. I swallow hard, trying to shift the lump in my throat. Oh, Mum . . .

'Mum, I want you to be happy. You deserve it.' And I mean that.

Mum's smile turns into a grin of relief. 'I love you, Troy.'

'Love you too, Mum.'

I head back to the hob to stir the cheese sauce. It's too late. The sauce is boiling and burnt. I stir it anyway, my mind a hornets' nest.

Proof . . . Sonny challenged me to prove his involvement with my dad's death. What I should've done was go directly to the police to get them to investigate. But, if I'd done that, Mum would've been so angry with me. And, more than that, she'd have been so hurt.

'Oh, and Sonny has had the quarry cleared and he's having it made safe,' says Mum. 'That's a relief, right? He told me to let you know.'

I just bet he did. My heart drops and stays dropped. Any evidence relating to Dad's death is now well and truly gone. I've left it too late. What the hell do I do now?

twenty-three. Libby

I lie on my bed, staring up at the ceiling. Mum is with Pete in her bedroom. The two of them have been as thick as thieves since I made Mum tell me the truth about my dad. They've barely spent an hour apart. And Pete keeps looking at me with that sneering, knowing smile of his, like he knows something I don't. God, but he makes my skin crawl.

Knowing the truth about my dad is seriously doing my head in. For the first time in what feels like forever, I'm starting to hope. Maybe he'll want to get to know me. Maybe he misses me as much as I miss him, even though we've never met. Maybe I could actually go and live with him. Maybe — that's another word for hope. Hope is dangerous. I should know. For years, I hoped Mum might come to love me. Just a little. But it never happened. Hope lost is worse than no hope at all. When I thought I had none, what I did have were my plans for the future and the lines on my arm. They were mine and mine alone. Now there's a chance for something more and my mind is racing with . . . possibilities.

Tomorrow is head-student election day, but I don't even care. Not any more. I've already sent an email to Dad's office. I couldn't wait. I needed to make contact. I just have to hope that whoever deals with his emails will pass it on to him. After school tomorrow, I'm going to visit Dad and demand to see him. And I won't move until I get to meet him. If he tells me to my face that he doesn't want to have anything to do with me, then at least I'll know for certain where I stand. I keep telling myself I'll be no worse off than I am now. How many times have I told myself that I don't need anyone? Often enough for me to actually start believing it. But I've been kidding myself. I'm desperate for Dad to like me, to want to be part of my life just as I need to be part of his. I'm desperate to belong somewhere. Be a part of something. Matter to someone. Otherwise, what's the point?

Dad *will* want to see me. I'm hanging on to that hope with everything I am. He'll love me, and finally I'll have someone in my life who likes me for who I am. Wouldn't that be something? I'm scared though, I admit it. And the thing that scares me the most as I lie here and dream about the perfect reunion in the perfect setting with the perfect outcome? What if I dreamed the whole conversation with Mum where she finally told me the truth about my dad? What if I'm still asleep and dreaming? If I am, then maybe, if there really is a God, I won't wake up.

twenty-four. Troy

Debate day has finally arrived and, quite frankly, I'm struggling to care. I have other things on my mind – like Sonny. While I'm racking my brains trying to figure out what to do, life is pulling me along regardless. Here we are, the final three head-student candidates, standing on the stage in front of the whole upper school. Me, Dina and Libby. All the others, including my mate Zane, have dropped out or have been removed from the running – like Meshella. Apparently, she said something she shouldn't've to Mrs Baxter, one of the biology teachers. Removing her from this election was the head's punishment. When I asked Zane why he'd bailed, he replied, 'I'm making a political statement.' It took me too long to realize he'd dropped out to increase my chances of getting elected head boy. It was only the thought of a severe punch to the arm that stopped me from hugging him. Man-style of course!

The kicker is, my original motive for entering this election has been swallowed up. At first I wanted to win just to stick it to Libby. That soon morphed into me wanting to win because I thought . . . no, I *knew* I could stand up for the rights of us students – and not in the divisive way Libby has been wittering on about. I'd been looking forward to this day for ages. A chance to show the whole upper school not just who Libby really is, but who I am. But now all my plans on that front seem insignificant. Sonny keeps creeping to the front of my thoughts. Since Sunday dinner at his house, he hasn't budged out of my head. And, like a gutless wonder, I've said and done nothing since. Except worry. And now he wants to marry my mum.

Over my dead body.

Looking around the school hall, I see most of our audience look like they could quite easily give it a miss too. People are fidgeting, chatting, looking down at their watches. They can't leave any more than I can. It's only the thought of Libby becoming head girl that has got me up on this stage in front of the entire upper school in the first place. The voting takes place later today and I don't care if I lose, as long as Libby doesn't win. This election isn't on my list of priorities, not any more. I glance across at Libby. For once, she's not working the room, no false smiles at anyone and everyone whose eye she manages to catch. That's so plastic. And what's up with Dina? She looks like she's about to have all her front teeth extracted. God, this is all so . . . pointless. I shouldn't be here. I should be at the nearest cop shop, demanding they check out Sonny's alibi for the day my dad died.

Sonny . . .

Hell! I can't stop thinking about him.

Since our dinner at Sonny's, I've had sleepless nights and can't concentrate. Finally, I realized I needed to talk to someone, confide my fears, before my head exploded, or I did something really stupid. So yesterday I phoned my sister, asking to meet up.

'I can't tonight,' Callie said. 'I've got meetings and a report to prepare. How about tomorrow evening? Isn't it the head–student election tomorrow? If you win, I'll buy you dinner.'

'And if I lose?'

'I'll buy you dinner.'

'I was hoping to see you today, not tomorrow, but OK,' I agreed reluctantly.

'Troy, is everything all right?'

'I need your advice.'

The stunned silence from my sister spoke volumes. I had never, ever asked for her advice before. She'd given it freely on countless occasions, but this was the first time I'd specifically requested it.

'Is something wrong? Is Mum OK?'

'Mum's fine. I just need to talk to you about something.'

'And you don't want to tell me over the phone.'

I shook my head as if Callie could see me. 'No. I need to speak to you in person.'

'Look, I could try to come round tonight, though it'd be after midnight—'

I couldn't do that to her. She already sounded dog-tired. 'No, tomorrow will do.'

'OK. Tomorrow evening it is then,' said Callie. 'Let's make it early. Around six?'

'That's fine. How's your case going by the way? Proved him innocent yet?'

'I'm working on it,' Callie replied. 'Look, why don't I just see you at home?'

'No! I want to talk to you outside the house.'

'Hmm. OK. I'll book a table somewhere and send you details,' said my sister.

Over twenty-four hours to wait before I can speak to her about Sonny, but it'll have to do. She'll put me straight, one way or another. Everything inside me shouts out that I can't let Mum marry that man. He might be a murderer . . .

What if he isn't?

But what if he is?

The not-knowing-for-absolute-certain is doing my head in. The headache I woke up with is definitely getting worse, not better.

Troy, focus on the here and now.

The debate is about to start.

The noise in the assembly hall is a low rumble as the entire upper school, including all the teachers, are now seated, waiting for the debate to begin. Mrs Paxton raises her hands for quiet. Immediate silence. I swear that woman could quell a horse stampede with one look. The head's impressive locks are piled high on her head in a grey-white bun that in itself commands respect. Callie says that Mrs Paxton used to frighten the hell out of everyone even when she attended this school. I guess time moves on, but some things never change.

Without warning, Dina lurches towards Mrs Paxton and they begin an urgent conversation in hushed tones. Dina has her back to everyone else seated in the assembly hall, but, from where I'm standing on the stage, I can see that she is adamant about something. She keeps shaking her head, though Mrs Paxton is trying to tell her something.

Finally, the head sighs and nods reluctantly. Dina immediately rushes down the stairs and leaves the hall. Frowning, I watch her speedy exit. What's that all about? Is she ill?

'Good morning to you all,' Mrs Paxton begins. 'The role of head boy or head girl has been established at our school for decades. It is a time-honoured position where one head student is elected by the whole upper school to represent them and their interests. Teachers do not get a vote. After all the weeks of campaigning, our final two candidates are Libby Jackman and Troy Ealing. Unfortunately Dina Myan is feeling unwell and has asked to be withdrawn from consideration. Libby and Troy will take part in a debate where they will answer questions that you, the students, have previously submitted. If we have time, we'll take more questions from the floor. Each candidate will have up to sixty seconds to answer each question. At the end of that time, a buzzer will sound, and the candidate will be allowed to finish their sentence. This debate will last for one hour and I want you all to pay close attention. Listen to the arguments put forward by both aspirants and, when it is time to vote, I urge you to select the best person for the role. These elections, like all elections, should be taken seriously. The winner will speak for you and represent you, so choose well.'

Thanks, Mrs Paxton. Like I'm not nervous enough already. Why has Dina pulled out? Is illness the real reason? I see Zane seated down in the hall, and catch his eye. He shrugs at me, obviously having no clue either.

'Now all the question boxes from around the school have been emptied into this one, and I will be drawing the questions out at random.' Mrs Paxton opens a large black cardboard box and draws out the first folded piece of paper. She reads it and smiles. 'An excellent question to start us off. "Why should we vote for you?" Which one of you two would like to take that one first?'

Mrs Paxton looks expectantly at me, then at Libby. Libby steps forward, her microphone in her hand, that false smile already on her lips.

'To answer that excellent question, I urge you all to vote for me because I *care*.'

Oh. My. God! Pass a sick bag.

I shake my head at the performance. Libby casts me a look. 'Troy, my opponent, is already shaking his head. He thinks caring is weak. A dirty word. I disagree. I care about what kind of food is served in our food hall. I care about increasing our school counsellor's hours so that she works full time, not just three days a week. I care about making sure we all get proper, timely feedback as far as our classwork and our homework are concerned. I care about after-school clubs and music lessons for all those who want them, not just those who can afford them. I care about having not just one but two school librarians to help out in our library. I *care*. Can you say the same, Troy?'

Libby smiles triumphantly and lowers her mic. She's that confident, I'm surprised she didn't just drop it.

Bitch, please!

Casting Libby a withering look, I raise my mic. 'Take a look at Liberty, everyone. Take a long, hard look. I readily admit that she's a better politician than I will ever be. Check the way she started her speech – with an immediate attack on me. She made one statement about herself, then proceeded to trash-talk me, implying – based on absolutely no evidence whatsoever – that I don't care about what happens at this school. Sit comfortably and watch Liberty go totally toxic on me. I'll tell you exactly what she'll say. Liberty is going to promise to listen to each and every one of you. She's gonna be there for you, fight on your behalf. She's on your side. But don't believe a word of it. Like most politicians, she'll make promises she has no intention of keeping. Like most politicians, she'll say and do anything to become head girl, including promising each of you her firstborn if that's what it takes. Don't fall for it. I'm Troy Ealing and, for those who don't know me personally, I'll tell you who – and what – I am. A straight talker. With me, what you see is what you get. I want to be head boy not because it looks great on a university application form or for a chance to get back at all those I've got a grudge against, but because I believe I can make our great school an even better place.'

A ding. My allotted time is up.

I'm just getting started.

Libby scowls at me. It's on!

twenty-five. Libby

How dare you, Troy Ealing? What right d'you have to say that? I'm not running for head girl just to get back at all those who might've pissed me off in the past. I'm not that petty.

How dare you?

'Our next question is . . .' Mrs Paxton frowns slightly as she reads on without speaking. 'OK . . . our next question is, "Name two good things and one bad thing about your opponent." Troy, would you like to go first?'

This should be good. Eyes narrowed, I wait to hear just what he's going to say.

Crap! *Two* good things? About Libby? That's a tall order. Like Mount Everest tall.

'Er . . . I hear Libby is loyal to her friends and that she's good at history. The bad thing would be her ambition to become head girl for all the wrong reasons. Not for your benefit, but for her own. Libby has about as much political insight as a stale cheese sandwich. And she couldn't care less about any student issues. She sees being head girl as a stepping stone, nothing more.'

OK, not my best effort, but all I could think of on the spur of the moment. Libby's expression hardens like quick-drying cement. She's going to let me have it – both barrels.

'It's hard to come up with one good thing to say about Troy Ealing, never mind two,' says Libby. 'But I can think of a bad thing. Back in the day, Troy's mum got knocked up by a Nought extremist called Callum McGregor who was hanged for being a terrorist. Is that really the sort of person we want as head student repre-senting our school?'

The shocked gasp that ripples through the hall is nothing compared to the crippling gut punch I feel at Libby's words. Gut punch? Hell! It was more like being kicked in the nuts by a horse, then run over by a tank. My mouth falls open as I stare at Libby, unable to believe that she went there. She actually went there. She's the one person I told in confidence when we used to be friends. Even when our friendship died, I still believed she'd keep my secret, just like I kept hers. Quid pro quo. I glance out across the assembly hall. The volume of the murmurs is steadily rising. I raise my mic.

'My mum's past has nothing to do with me. That's her business, not mine. My mum was married to Nathan Ealing and he's my dad. So at least I know who my dad is. Can you say the same, Libby? From what I hear, your dad could be any one of twenty different guys.'

More gasps from around the hall.

'Right. That is quite enough of that from both of you,' Mrs Paxton intervenes, her dark brown eyes flashing. 'This is a serious debate about your proposed student policies and what each of you can bring to the role. This is not a race to the bottom where each of you shows just how low you can go. I won't have it. Not in this school. Ever.'

'Sorry, Mrs Paxton,' mumbles Libby.

I was the one who should've received that apology, not the head.

Mrs Paxton turns to me, waiting to hear similar fall from my mouth.

'My apologies, Mrs Paxton,' I say clearly. 'You're right, I shouldn't have descended to Liberty's level.' I look at my opponent with scorn. 'When she went low, I should've gone high because *both* my parents taught me better. And I apologize to all of you in the audience. Just because most real politicians behave like Libby doesn't mean any of us have to follow their example. I mean, I certainly don't.'

'I'm glad to hear it,' says Mrs Paxton, still vexed. She dips into the box again. 'I expect all of us to continue this debate in a civilized manner. The next question is . . .'

I look across the hall as Mrs Paxton asks the next question. Every student is now facing forward in rapt attention. The only thing missing is the popcorn. I turn to Libby. She's looking at me with total loathing. I return her look with interest.

If we weren't standing in front of hundreds of witnesses, I'd show her exactly what I think of her swipe at my mum. If it's the last thing I ever do, I'll make her pay for that.

twenty-seven. Libby

Total bastard!

twenty-eight. Troy

Toxic bitch!

twenty-nine. Libby

Well, that went to hell in a handcart real fast. Only the second question and Troy's retort had me rattled. Maisie, Raffy and I spent a couple of lunchtimes in one of the music rooms, practising my responses in the debate. They asked me all kinds of awkward questions to make sure I wouldn't get flustered or angry and I'd sailed through all that. But the moment Troy opened his mouth—

Damn it!

I didn't mean to reveal stuff about his mum like that. Truly I didn't. During our first year at the school, when Troy and I had actually been friends, he'd confided in me about his mum. He knew my greatest secret. I knew his. But one jibe during the debate from Troy and all that stuff about his mum came flooding out of my mouth. Why hadn't he retaliated and told everyone about my arms? In his shoes, I would've – an admission that made me feel like an even bigger bitch. I hadn't set out to do it. I'd just wanted to wipe that smug-git look off his face. But it was more than that.

Be honest, Liberty. You wanted to hurt him like he hurt you when he dropped you as his friend. Plus you wanted to win this so you could impress your dad.

The end result was I messed up – big time. The gasp that went round the hall when I said what I did . . . And Mrs Paxton looked at me with such disapproval and, worse still, disappointment. Even Maisie, who's always had my back, shook her head at me from her chair in the assembly hall. I've let everyone down, most of all myself. I'm better than that, but now no one in school thinks so. I can't understand it. I didn't appreciate just how deep my hurt ran until I heard myself slagging off Troy's family.

For the rest of the debate, I tried to stick to the issues, but the damage was done. Afterwards, I retreated to the girls' toilets to be by myself for a while. On my way to the first empty cubicle, I caught sight of myself in the mirror, only to look away. Fast. I couldn't bear to see myself, to see what I'd become. Sitting on the toilet seat, I tried to figure out just when I'd turned into the woman I despised most in the world.

During our first year at school together, Troy and I had been so close. He got me. I got him. I'd even begun to . . . well, never mind. Back then, Eden started calling us 'the twins', which made us both laugh, Troy being a Cross and me being a Nought. But that stuff was superficial – then. Troy promised me we'd be friends forever. I believed it – no reason to doubt him. But then he met my mum and found out she was a 12/NF supporter. A 12-words/Nought Forever paid-up member. I'd invited Troy round to my house for tea and Mum had been fine with that – until she'd seen that Troy was a Cross.

Just thinking about that evening still makes me cringe. Mum was polite to Troy, but only just. And, when we were alone in the kitchen together, she told me fiercely, 'We don't invite bastard daggers into this house, d'you hear? Don't ever bring him here again. What? D'you think I spout the twelve-words slogan at you just to hear myself?'

Behind Mum, Troy's silhouette was visible through the frosted glass of the ajar kitchen door. He'd heard every word. My face burned with embarrassment. Troy was my best friend in the whole world. To hear my mum say that . . . It was a slap in the face aimed at Troy that I felt down to the depths of my soul. I had to force myself to go back to the living room, my face still burning red. Troy was sitting on the sofa, playing my PlayBox game like he had stayed in the room the entire time. But he looked at me and I looked at him and we both knew. The look he gave me . . . I'll never forget that look as long as I live.

That was the first time I thought about the 12-words mantra Mum was talking about. Really thought about it. The Nought supremacist ideology summed up in just twelve words.

We must secure and preserve the rights and future of all Noughts.

So outwardly harmless. So inwardly monstrous. The motto of white supremacist Nought Forever supporters, including my mum and her friends. Nought Forever was supposed to be the more acceptable modern face of the extremist group – the Liberation Militia. From what I'd seen and heard, the NF's views were just as extreme, just as filled with vitriol against Crosses, and in fact anyone who wasn't a Nought. After that disastrous evening at my house, the friendship between Troy and me had kicked the bucket. It's like he thought that because my mum was a bigot I had to be one too. That hurt.

Well, if he didn't want to be around me, I didn't want to be around him. Mum was right about Crosses. They only cared about themselves and couldn't be trusted. That's what I told myself. Except hadn't my actions throughout the campaign and in the debate proved that I was different but no better than my mum?

I'm still blushing at what I said. I've blown this stupid head-student election out of all proportion, telling myself it was what I needed to make my life better. If I won, Dad would be more likely to want to get to know me. But what's the point of winning if I can't even look at myself in the mirror? It just isn't worth it. So I'm going to remake myself from the head down. I'm going to bow out of this election. Concede defeat. If Troy wants to be head boy, then all power to him. I have other things to concentrate on, like meeting my dad. I want to build a relationship with him.

That's why, come lunchtime, I'm standing outside Mr Pike's office, trying to pluck up the courage to knock on his slightly open door. He's the Head of Languages and speaks Kiswahili, Xhosa, Latin, Russian and Greek fluently. He's the teacher in charge of the head-student poll – one of the two teacher scrutineers – and he's probably right in the middle of counting the votes. I'm not going to be popular with him if I bow out now, but that can't be helped. There are raised voices coming from inside the room, getting ever louder.

'We should be thankful for what Liberty did,' says Mr Pike.

I'm being talked about. I lean in closer to eavesdrop.

'Now that it's common knowledge, there's no way the son of a Nought terrorist sympathizer can be our head boy. No way,' Mr Pike continues.

My eyes widen with shock.

'Come on, Leeto, even if that's true, it was a long time ago.' That sounds like Mrs Baxter, my biology teacher.

'Of course it's true. After what Libby said, I checked on the Internet.'

'Oh well then! My apologies for doubting your sources,' says Mrs Baxter, her voice dripping with sarcasm.

'The point is,' Mr Pike goes on, 'if it comes out that our head boy's mother is Persephone Hadley, whose first child is the daughter of a hanged Nought terrorist, how soon before every right-minded parent takes their child out of this school? You'd be able to shoot a cannon down our school corridors and not hit a student. And the national press? Jesus! They'd have a field day.'

Every right-minded parent—?

'Every right-minded parent?' says Mrs Baxter, echoing my thought. 'What the hell does that mean? There hasn't been a hanging in this country for over three decades. These are different times. For Shaka's sake, Persephone Hadley's daughter, Callie Rose, is a renowned lawyer. If any Cross is going to judge a student on the past actions of their parents, then good riddance if they walk. That's not how things work any more.'

'Don't delude yourself. That's exactly how things work,' Mr Pike argues.

'It shouldn't be about your family or your past—' Mrs Baxter says.

'And in some far-off utopia that's probably the case. Meanwhile, back here in the real world, it makes one hell of a difference.'

'Not if we ignore all that poisonous stuff. We can at least try to rise above it—'

'Oh, for God's sake! Get real, Monifa,' Mr Pike scoffs. 'Politics gets nastier and more vicious with each passing year. It's not a parade of ideals or ethics any more. It's about celebrity, false promises and image. And, if we allow Troy Ealing to become head boy, the image of this school will take a severe beating.'

Mrs Baxter sighs. 'Well, as it's the students who vote, not us teachers, there's not an awful lot we can do about it.'

'The students may be the only ones to vote, but it's the two of us who count those votes . . .'

A long pause.

'Are you really proposing that we . . . that we *cheat*?' asks Mrs Baxter, appalled.

'We're saving the school,' Mr Pike insists.

'Mrs Paxton—'

'Mrs Paxton is retiring next year,' Mr Pike interrupts. 'Let's make sure the school is still up and running after she's gone.'

'Is this really what we're going to resort to? *Cheating?*'

'I don't like it any more than you do,' says Mr Pike. 'For Shaka's sake, that's some choice – the son of a Nought terrorist sympathizer or a Nought.'

'I beg your pardon!'

'Wind your neck in. All I mean is, it's not exactly upholding the proud traditions of this school, is it? To have a Nought as head girl. I think Dina Myan should receive the most votes, don't you?'

'She pulled out of the election.'

'I suggest we put her back in,' says Mr Pike. 'If we declare that she received the most votes, who's going to contradict us – as long as we back each other up?'

'Now you listen to me, Leeto Pike—'

'No, you listen, Monifa. We have to act for the good of the school. That means Dina has to win—'

I don't wait around to hear any more. I have to find Troy. *Fast*.

After five minutes of fruitlessly searching the food hall, I spot Troy's friend Ayo. Marching over to him, I ask, 'Where's Troy?'

Ayo looks me up and down, eyebrows raised at my brusque tone. I don't have time for this.

'Please, Ayo, it's important. Where's Troy?'

'He popped out the back of school to get some fish and chips from Stratees.' Ayo frowns. 'Why?'

'That's my business.' As I turn to head out of the food hall, my phone rings. I wouldn't bother answering it but it's Mum. She hardly ever phones me so, in spite of myself, I take the call.

'You're welcome!' Ayo calls after me.

'Hello?'

'Libby, I need you to do something for me.'

'What?' I ask.

'There's a journalist who wants to do a story on me and my career, but he asked to interview you too. His story has to be filed this afternoon if it's going to make this month's edition of the magazine. He's waiting at the school's back gate to interview you. Could you do this for me, please? It'll only take a couple of minutes.'

Are you kidding? 'No way. Mum, I'm at school.'

'Yes, I know. I told him that. He was happy to go to you so I gave him the school's address. He really needs to see you now or the story won't happen, and I need the money and the publicity. Please just do this for me and I'll never ask you to do anything like this again.'

An interview with a journalist who'll probably want to know all kinds of family details? Stuff I'd rather keep private? No thanks. 'I'm sorry, Mum, but he'll have to write his article without me.'

'Libby, please. Do this and I'll help you get in touch with your dad. In fact, I'll personally take you to see him. Deal?'

I sigh inwardly, calling myself all kinds of a fool, but Mum is holding out a carrot too tantalizing to ignore. 'Two minutes, Mum. That's all. I mean it.'

'Honestly, that's all he'll need. He's at the gate now. Thanks, Libby,' she says, and she hangs up.

I shake my head. How stupid am I? I should just tell Mum and this journalist where to go, but I'm heading that way anyway. Lips pursed, I promise myself that this journalist is going to get the equivalent of name, rank and serial number – and not much else. Then Troy and I are going to have a conversation, no matter how painful.

thirty. Troy

We aren't supposed to leave the school grounds at lunch-time, but I really need to get away from the looks and whispered comments that have followed me since the debate. Libby is just lucky I didn't come across her on my way out of school. She and I have unfinished business. I decided some haddock and chips from Stratees, the fish-and-chip shop at the bottom of the road, would improve my mood. Anything was better than the cold five-bean pasta mess that was the only thing left in the food hall by the time I got there. That five-bean pasta looked like it'd be great for filling potholes and not much else.

I still can't believe Libby used my private family business to further her campaign. What am I talking about? Of course I believe it. Knowing her, I should've expected it. Total bitch!

I head for the school side gate over by the tennis courts. The weather is distinctly chilly with grey-white clouds lining and redefining the sky. Five minutes to the end of the residential, tree-lined road, two minutes in the fish-and-chip shop, five minutes back to school and none of the teachers will be any the wiser. What I'm doing is against school rules, but at this moment in time I don't particularly care. Ayo offered to come with me, but I'm not in the mood for company.

I enter the shop, buy my meal, head back to school. Callie's warning plays in my head as I walk. On the opposite side of the road, a Cross woman walks her dog. She doesn't even glance in my direction as we pass each other. I sigh. I can't let my sister make me paranoid. Callie is definitely overreacting to a few stupid threats. And, besides, threatening me serves no purpose. Anyone who knows my sister is well aware of that. If anything, threats will make Callie dig her heels in that much harder.

I'd intended to save my food until I got back to school, but the smell is too enticing. Walking back, I open up the food box and retrieve a couple of chips to shove into my mouth. Crisp on the outside, fluffy on the inside, just the right amount of salt and vinegar bursting over my tongue. My eyes close momentarily as I slowly chew. Delicious. So worth waiting for – and better than the school muck. Definitely the best thing that has happened to me today. I break off a piece of fish and stuff that in my mouth. I'm not a great lover of fish unless it's swimming in vinegar and comes with big, chunky chips – and this is perfect. Having skipped breakfast, I seriously doubt if my meal will make it as far as the school gate.

'Troy, wait up!'

I look round, surprised not so much by hearing my name but by who is calling it. Libby. She trots up to me, her heels click-clacking on the pavement.

'Didn't you hear me calling you?' Libby huffs with attitude.

Seriously? After the stunt she pulled, she's acting like she and I are friends or something. This girl has got some nerve. I move to walk past her. She sidesteps in front of me. I swivel to walk past her again. She repeats her previous move. This is getting old real fast.

'Libby. Move.'

'You and I need to talk.'

'You don't have a damn thing to say that I want to hear.' I stuff another chip into my mouth, never taking my eyes off her.

Libby eyes my box of haddock and chips. 'D'you mind if I have some? I missed lunch.'

My mouth falls open, my half-chewed chips on full display. Libby wrinkles her nose at the sight. My lips snap shut. Since when did Libby eat anything or ask for anything from me? I'd've thought she'd rather bin-dive than take food from me, or any Cross for that matter. What's she up to? Suspicious, I hold out my fish-and-chips box towards her. If she's going to knock the box out of my hand or spit in it, then I swear to God it'll be on. Libby glances up at me, then helps herself to a handful of chips. I mean, a whole handful.

'Thanks, I'm starving,' she says with a forced smile.

My eyes narrow. Bitch, please!

What's she up to?

If Libby imagines I'm buying this sudden camaraderie act, then she has another think coming. Does she really believe I'm that stupid? She's not getting any more of my lunch either. I pop another couple of chips into my mouth and start back towards school. Libby falls into step next to me.

'Libby, what're you doing here?'

'I was supposed to meet someone at the school gate but they didn't turn up.'

'Maybe they're there now. Don't let me keep you,' I suggest.

Libby's mouth tightens slightly, but she carries on walking next to me. 'Actually, you're the one I want to talk to. It's about the election.'

A dusty grey van pulls up ahead of us, its hazard lights blinking. There's no other traffic on the road, which is only ever busy during the school run. I frown at Libby, who pops a chip in her mouth. A chip – singular. Even the way she eats is grating.

'How did you know where I was?'

'Ayo told me, but I had to wait to sneak out because Mr Lamont was telling someone off by the tennis courts.'

We walk in silence.

'You still haven't told me what you want, Libby.' I stuff another couple of chips in my mouth. 'Have you come to stick the knife in harder or just twist it some more?'

'Neither,' Libby replies, stepping in front of me again to make sure I have her full attention. 'Troy, we're being set up by the teachers. We're both being played, and I don't know about you, but I'm ready to fight back.'

thirty-one. Libby

Troy arches an eyebrow in that way of his. 'What're you on about?'

'Troy, this head-student election is being rigged and I need you to help me prove it,' I explain.

Troy's mouth falls open, once again revealing its half-chewed, mushy contents.

'Dude! Seriously?' I frown, pointing at his mouth.

Troy's mouth snaps shut. He chews quickly and swallows.

'Rigged? By who?'

'Mr Pike for one. He wants to rig the vote so that Dina wins, even though she pulled out,' I say.

'Mr Pike! Are you high?'

'No, and I'm not deluded either. He doesn't want the son of a terrorist sympathizer or a Nought to be voted the head student of Heathcroft – his words, not—'

'LIBBY!'

I register the shock on Troy's face a moment before his box of fish and chips hits the ground. Without warning, my arms are yanked behind me – hard – and what feels like a plastic tag is pulled tight round my wrists.

'GET OFF ME—' Troy yells.

A man wearing a rabbit mask has darted past Troy to put

an arm round his throat. Troy's eyes are bulging. I open my mouth to scream, only to feel an arm round my own throat, and then a piece of cloth is clapped over my nose and mouth. The cloth smells strangely sweet. A syrupy, chemical smell. I slam my head back into the man behind me and kick back as hard as I can. The back of my head smashes into something hard and plastic. A guy behind is wearing another mask as well, I realize. The man grunts so I've done some damage, but if anything the cloth is pushed harder into my face. The skin around my mouth begins to tingle. My head starts to swim. Black spots dance before my eyes, growing ever bigger. I watch as Troy struggles against being gagged, but he's losing.

Don't pass out, Libby—

The sweet smell of the cloth over my face is now sickly sweet, filling my nose, my mouth, my lungs. The hand over my nose moves away, only to return and push another cloth into my mouth. I'm lifted off my feet. I try to inhale to scream past the cloth in my mouth, but my breath is locked somewhere south of my shoulders, and my head is swimming so much by now that I don't know which way is up. My body flops as if all the muscles have melted. Almost immediately, I'm dumped down onto the raised, hard surface inside a van, which knocks all the air out of me. I fall sideways like a felled tree. I glimpse a guy in a tiger mask, his eyes the only part of his face that's visible. Inside I'm screaming, but the sound is too terrified to rise above my lungs. I can't move. My whole body has turned to lead.

'For fuck's sake! There's only supposed to be one.'

'So there's two. So we improvise.'

The men's faint, distorted voices are coming at me through cotton wool.

Get up, Libby. Come on. Get up. Get out.

I concentrate on moving my legs, but they no longer belong to me. My world is closing down. That sweet, chemical smell now shrouds my entire body.

The van door slams shut. It's different to a car door, louder and more resonant. Troy lies beside me, a cloth bag over his head. He's writhing and kicking out. Moments later, the van's engine starts and I can feel the vehicle vibrating beneath and around me. We shoot off at speed. So much so that there's another severe jolt as my body leaves the floor of the van for a moment before slamming back down. My head hits the floor first. A white, searing explosion of pain. And that sweet, chemical smell fills my whole world. I realize too late that I've been drugged. I'm going to black out. There are no more sights, no more sounds.

Only silence.

thirty-two. Troy

Owff! I'm bouncing around in the back of this van like a pinball. WTF—? I'd barely had a chance to register the two men jumping out of the back of the grey van that pulled up in front of us before all hell was let loose. I have no idea if the men who grabbed us are Nought, Cross or Martian. They were wearing hoodies and it was only when they raised their heads and I saw their animal masks that I realized we were in trouble. One in a tiger mask grabbed Libby. The one who grabbed me wore a rabbit mask. I had no chance to seize Libby and run. No chance to do anything but cry out her name before we were manhandled into the back of this van.

It all happened so fast.

'*Ihhheeeeh!*' I try to call out Libby's name, but I've been gagged with a grimy rag knotted at the back of my head. My hands are bound behind me with what feels like plastic cable ties. I can't see a damned thing past the filthy canvas bag they pulled over my head. I try to call out to her again. No reply. The van's engine, the honk of a horn and the rumble of traffic noises are all I can hear.

Is Liberty all right?

Who are those two men who grabbed us?

Where are they taking us?

What are they going to do with us?

All kinds of horror movies are playing in my head.

Is this about Callie defending Tobey Durbridge? If so, were they after me, and Libby just got in the way? Or maybe this has nothing to do with my sister and the forthcoming court case at all. Maybe they're perverts or traffickers, in which case we're really up shit creek.

Oh God . . .

Questions tumble over each other in my head. And regret. And remorse. I should never have ducked out of school. Strange — and terrifying — that I should hope and pray that we've been snatched to ensure that my sister will drop Tobey Durbridge's case. Because at least then Libby and I might stand some chance of emerging from all this . . . relatively unscathed.

But damn! What will they do to us if Callie won't drop the case?

What will they do to us if she *does*?

And, if Libby is collateral damage, what will they do to her? Surely they'll see her as expendable and get rid of her?

Guilt gnaws at me as I consider Libby. I had to watch as the tiger-mask man chucked her in the back of this van before my face was covered and the same was done to me. If something happens to Libby because of my sister . . .

NO!

That's not going to happen. Not if I have anything to do with it. God knows, Libby isn't my favourite person, but she doesn't deserve this. No one does.

We're turning right. Are we on the main road now? I should've tried to memorize the route we're taking. My phone! My phone's in my pocket. I lie flat and move my head up and down, trying to work off this hood. I catch a glimpse of daylight through the glass panels in the doors at the back of the van. It's working. I'm rubbing my cheek raw, trying to get this thing off, but I have to do something. Tilting my head back, I peer beneath the hood. Turning, I can just see Libby's feet to my left. She's not moving. At all. I inch forward but soon have to stop. There's not enough room to turn round and check her properly.

I turn onto my left side so that my right trouser pocket isn't pressed against the floor of the van. Now, if I can only get my phone out of that pocket . . . I bend my wrists in every position known to humans, and some that aren't, and I still can't get my hands anywhere close to my pockets. All I get for the effort are strained wrists, the plastic of the bindings cutting deeper into my skin and a burning ball of frustration in the pit of my stomach.

I have to get it together. *Think.*

It's too late to try and figure out our route and I have no idea where we're going, but I can at least try and work out where we are now. Car engines, the rev of a motorbike. Nothing significant there. Muffled laughter outside, gone just as quickly as it came.

Twenty minutes later and I'm just as clueless. I can hardly see, can barely move, and I still have no idea where we are or where we're going. My heart is beating so fast. Too fast.

Take a deep breath, Troy. Calm down. You can't think straight if you're panicking.

That's when it hits me, really hits me.

Libby and I are in a crap ton of trouble and it's all my fault.

Not for one single second did I take Callie's warnings seriously.

Big mistake.

HUGE mistake.

All I'd wanted was some chips and an escape from school. I'd thought Callie was being overcautious at best and had to be exaggerating at worst. If anyone thought they could get to Callie through me, they were seriously deluding themselves. At least, that's what I told myself. But apparently that's exactly what someone *has* decided. We won't even be missed until we're due home. No . . . hang on . . . The results of the school election are going to be announced at the end of the school day and Libby and I will be expected in the hall for that, along with the rest of the upper school. If we're both missing, surely the alarm will be raised then? Too late to help us, but at least the police will be notified and they'll start looking for us. The thought brings some comfort. Not much but some.

By the time the police start searching, we could be hundreds of kilometres away. Or worse.

Libby and I need to find a way out of this, but how?

How?

thirty-three. Libby

My heart is thrashing about like a landed fish. I groan, the sound smothered by the filthy rag in my mouth, which tastes of old sweat and petrol. Something slimy sits against my tongue, as if someone blew their nose on the rag first before stuffing it in my mouth. I try to force the disgusting thing out, but my tongue keeps rebelling. Steeling myself, I poke at it again. When enough of it has been pushed past my lips, I catch it under my cheek and then pull my head away until the disgusting thing is completely out of my mouth. I spit repeatedly into the hankie or whatever it is, trying to get its last remnants off my tongue. My hands are still tied behind my back. I'm not sure which is making my stomach churn more: abject terror or the lingering taste of the gag.

For Shaka's sake, don't puke.

It smells bad enough down here without me adding to it.

The hard floor scrapes against my back and legs. I take a deep breath and try to force myself to get it together and think rationally. My eyes are slowly growing accustomed to the dim, sickly yellow light, which barely reaches the far wall of this place. Nearby lies Troy. When they flung him down the stairs, he fell badly. He took quite a crack to his head, which I think knocked him out. God, I hope it's nothing more serious, though being knocked unconscious is bad enough.

'Troy? Troy, wake up. Are you OK? Wake up.'

He doesn't stir. He's just out for the count – I refuse to contemplate anything worse than that. What is this place? Where are we? It looks and smells like some kind of storage unit or maybe a basement? There are no windows, at least none that I can see.

Why am I here?

Barbed-wire thoughts slash their way through my mind. From a distance, a rumbling sound gets nearer and vibrates beneath me with a regular, thumping undertone to it. Are we near an underground station? Do Tube trains run beneath this building or close by? Heathcroft High is about seven kilometres away from the nearest Tube station so we must've been driven at least that distance and probably a whole lot further. I only came to when one of them carried me into this building over his shoulder. And even then I was as groggy as hell.

'Troy? Troy, wake up. Please wake up.'

But Troy is still unconscious. I twist, coiling my body round like a snake to lie on my back. My bound hands dig into my lower spine. Taking a deep breath, I jerk upwards. It takes a couple of tries, but at last I'm sitting, my hands still tied behind me. I rock back and forth, forcing my bound hands beneath my bum and hips, then under my knees and feet, curling to make it easier to bring my hands to the front of my body. At last it's done.

'Troy! Wake up, damn it. Troy—'

Troy's eyes flutter open. He looks bewildered. I don't doubt for a second that I'm his mirror image. The mere fact that I'm not alone is strangely comforting – even if it's Troy who's my companion.

Grunting, he struggles to sit up. He looks around, then at me, even more perplexed.

'Libby, what – and I sincerely mean this – the actual bollocks is going on?' he groans.

'We've been snatched off the street and brought here. Now you know as much as me,' I reply. 'Hang on. Let me try to get you free, then you can do the same for me.'

NOW

thirty-four. Troy

So here Libby and I sit, waiting to wake up from our shared nightmare. I'm hurting, especially my head, and the longer I'm down here, the worse it gets. I *need* to get out of here before I . . . Libby said our predicament might be because of her dad. Last I heard she didn't even know who that was. If she now knows, what could he possibly have done to have led to our current situation? No. My sister's job is the reason I'm down here. I'm sure of it. But it's messed up that I'm hoping one or other of us is right. The alternatives don't bear thinking about.

Or maybe this is Sonny's doing? A ploy on his part to get me out of the way? But what would that achieve? He's already got rid of the cars in his quarry. I have no proof of my suspicions so I'm no real threat to him. Going to all this trouble doesn't make any sense, unless he's afraid that Mum might start listening to and believing me.

'Why d'you think that man in the mask took our photo?' Libby's question is a welcome intrusion.

I sigh. 'To send to someone as proof that they have us? I hope.'

Libby nods. In agreement with my assessment or sharing my hope? It's hard to tell.

'Look, I don't mean to make this sound like some kind of competition Libby, but this situation . . . I think it's on me.'

'What d'you mean?' She frowns.

'My sister Callie is a lawyer – remember? Well, she's currently involved in a high-profile case and I suspect our being abducted has something to do with that.'

I force myself to look at Libby, expecting to see censure in her eyes. Instead, she holds my gaze, though even in the dim light I can see her cheeks reddening.

'What?' I ask. Am I missing something?

'What's the high-profile case your sister is involved in?' asks Libby.

'I can't say. I've been sworn to secrecy.'

'You can tell me,' she says. 'Who am I going to tell?'

I tilt my head. 'Libby, you of all people should know that, unlike most, I can keep a secret.'

Yes, that's a dig!

Libby nods, her cheeks reddening further. 'Maybe it's not you they're after. Maybe it's me.'

'Why would anyone want you?' That really wasn't meant to be a bitch-slap. It's just the way the words fell out of my mouth, but I can see from the look on Libby's face that that's how she takes it.

'You really are a total crapstick,' she retorts. 'If I have to be stuck down here in this hellhole, I can't think of anyone else I'd rather share it with.'

Not a compliment. I choose to ignore her snit and ask again, 'Why would they be after you?'

Libby takes a deep breath. 'Because of the new Prime Minister.'

'Tobias Durbridge?' I say, my voice unintentionally sharp. 'What about him?'

Libby looks me in the eye and states simply, 'He's my dad.'

Daily Shouter Online

Exposed: slain underworld kingpin Daniel Jeavons spun a web that ensnared judges, business CEOs and other pillars of society

Today the *Daily Shouter* can reveal that the ruthless underworld kingpin, Daniel Jeavons, whose body was found on 7 September, was aided during his reign of terror by pillars of society and prominent members of the establishment. Due to an active injunction against this publication regarding any discussion of Daniel Jeavons' business empire, we cannot reveal names, but we have proof that at least one circuit judge, a number of MPs and captains of industry were on the payroll of Dan Jeavons.

THEN

Way Back When

thirty-five. Tobey

Friday afternoon and it was the day of Callie's birthday party. I'd offered to help her set up after school. She'd kept saying no but I insisted. The rain was coming down in a fighting mood. Droplets the size of coins smacked at everything in their path and the blustery wind blew the rain every which way, making my hood and Callie's umbrella pointless as we made our way to her house. We both went in, laughing and shaking ourselves off like wet dogs.

'This weather is something else,' I said.

Callie's smile came and went.

'Where's your mum and Meggie?' I asked.

'Nana Meggie is spending some time with her sister, and Mum and Nathan are having a weekend break together by the sea,' said Callie.

'Your mum's trusting you with the house for the whole weekend?' I asked, surprised.

'Yep. So I'd better not mess up or it'll never happen again.' Callie pulled off her jacket and threw it over the banister.

I pulled off my hoodie and flung it over Callie's jacket. Dumping my rucksack at the foot of the stairs, I followed her into the kitchen.

'Most of the tables on the patio have already been set up

so hopefully the weather will improve soon. It's supposed to. The caterers are coming in an hour with the food, so until then could you help me with the decorations and getting the drinks chilled and in buckets?' said Callie.

Pause.

'Anything you want.'

Callie looked at me then, a charged silence descending between us. I stood still, drinking her in – the way she looked at me sometimes like I was a puzzle to solve, the sound of her voice when she was humming to herself, the way she laughed with her head tilted back, the way she dipped her chin when she smiled as if she didn't want anyone to see. I would grow tired of being with her about the time I grew tired of breathing.

This girl was my other half, and because of me she'd been shot and nearly died. She'd been in a coma for days – thanks to me. I still couldn't let that go. If I'd lost her, I would've carried on walking and talking and existing, but a major part of me, the *real* part of me, would've died with her. Looking at her now, it scared me just how much I lo— cared for her. After one brief moment of weakness many months ago, when I'd cried in front of her, I promised myself that Callie would never see me weak again. I'd prove to her – and myself – just how solid I was. I made myself stay away from her, pretending an indifference that was 180 degrees away from how I really felt. And I'll admit that part of it was to punish myself. It was my fault Callie had got shot in the first place, so I told myself she'd be better off if I stayed away from her. That was my penance, my self-inflicted stopover in purgatory. No, not purgatory. Hell.

During our time apart I'd missed her like crazy. My self-imposed punishment didn't last long. A few weeks at most before Callie's friend Sammi had taken me to one side and threatened to kick my arse if I didn't pull my head out of it.

'I don't know what you're playing at, Tobey, but Callie is miserable and you're the cause and I'm not having it,' she told me straight. 'If you don't want to be with her any more, then have the balls to come right out and tell her so. That way you'll both know where you stand. Don't just ignore her and duck out of rooms when she enters them.'

'I'm trying to do what's right for Callie,' I admitted.

'By deliberately hurting her?' Sammi said incredulously.

'That's not my intention.'

'Intention or not, that's what you're doing,' she said. 'Look, do you want to be with her or not?'

I nodded, unable to lie.

'Then stop acting like a dick.' And with that Sammi flounced off.

It had the desired effect though. After Crossmas I'd got back with Callie, and now here we were. Callie had never asked me why I'd backed away from her and she didn't recriminate – not once. Maybe she was waiting for me to volunteer the information. But what we have isn't the same. Since the new year she's been . . . cautious. Wary. I've caught her watching me when she doesn't think I'm looking. Yet when we're together, she has a hard time meeting my eyes. Is she afraid of what she might see, or what she might reveal?

'Callie, how's your mum– I haven't seen her in a while?' I asked to break the tension between us.

'Fine. You know she's Persephone Ealing now, right?'

My mouth fell open. 'She married Nathan? Last I heard they were going to wait till summer.'

'They both changed their minds and got married at Crossmas. She's full of the joys of spring at the moment. I wanted to invite you to their wedding as my date, but—' Callie shrugged.

No more words were required. I'd been too busy doing my running-man act to slow down enough to receive the invitation. Callie proceeded to tell me all about the wedding and some of the more amusing moments from the wedding reception. I could've been there, but I'd missed it.

'How d'you feel about your mum and Nathan?' I asked after her reminiscences.

Callie shrugged again as she retrieved more beer bottles from the fridge. She was doing that far too often. 'Mum deserves to be happy. She's found someone who doesn't ignore her or treat her like shit. That means a lot.'

Ouch! Bitch-slap received and understood.

'What happened to that other guy who had it bad for your mum? What was his name? Sonny?'

'He wanted to marry Mum too, but in the end she chose Nathan.'

'What made her pick one over the other?'

'You'd have to ask Mum that,' said Callie. 'And just between you and me, Mum's pregnant.'

'You're joking!' Then I frowned. 'Isn't she too old for that?'

Callie burst out laughing. 'That's just what I said!'

thirty-six. Callie

I'd only found out Mum was pregnant a few days ago. I'd come home from school and headed straight to the kitchen to get myself a drink. Mum was already there, making herself a cup of lemon and ginger tea. She looked me up and down and frowned. 'What's wrong with you? You've got a face like a slapped arse.'

I raised an eyebrow. 'Nicely put, Mum.'

'Well? You still haven't answered my question.'

'I'm fine,' I lied.

'Are you still having your party this Friday? Have the arrangements gone wrong? D'you have to cancel it?'

'Of course not.'

Mum smiled wryly. 'Worth a try!'

'Mum, you promised that you and Nathan would disappear for the night and I expect you to keep your word.'

'OK. Calm down. Nathan and I are going away for the weekend, not the night, so, when we come home on Sunday night, I expect to find this house exactly as we left it. D'you hear?'

I nodded, exasperated. How many more times?!

'So, if you're not worrying about your party, what's got you looking so constipated?'

'Again – nicely put!'

'Oh God, it's that boy Tobey again, isn't it?' said Mum, rolling her eyes.

'Why d'you say that?' I frowned. 'Maybe I just had a bad day at school.'

Mum gave me one of her patented looks, her eyebrows raised as she waited for me to speak.

'OK, so I'm still waiting for Tobey to explain why he dumped me,' I admitted. 'I've been dropping all kinds of hints that I'm ready to listen but he hasn't said a word.'

Mum sighed. 'That guy! He doesn't have a clue, does he?'

Mum was not Tobey's biggest fan. She still blamed him for me getting shot, even though I'd told her umpteen times that it wasn't his fault.

'He'll tell me eventually, I guess.' Knowing him, probably around about the time I'm pregnant with our third child. The random thought brought instant heat to my cheeks. Mum's gaze was speculative as she studied me. I always hated it when she did that. My mum didn't miss much. 'Callie, just be careful, OK? Tobey isn't on the same page as you relationship-wise.'

'Where am I?'

Mum considered this, picking her words carefully like they were delicate flowers. 'It wouldn't take much for you to think of Tobey as your one and only soulmate, if you don't already. You feel things too deeply.'

'Is that a bad thing?'

Mum shook her head. 'You're too much like me, Callie. When someone hurts you, it's hard for you to just shake it off.'

A moment's silence as we both acknowledged the truth of her words.

'And what page is Tobey on?'

'Tobey isn't as mature as you. No man is!' Mum added dryly. 'He thinks he's still looking for a bedmate.'

'That's not fair,' I protested. 'Tobey isn't that shallow. He—'

'Callie, you misunderstand me. He cares about you. Deeply. Always has done. Is he trying to rush you into bed?'

My cheeks burn. 'Mum!'

'Oh please,' she said, dismissing my embarrassment. 'If he is, it's because he believes it's the only place he can really show how he feels about you. He's scared of his feelings, and his way of dealing with the aftermath of you getting shot was to deny that he feels anything. And what's more he'll do anything to prove it.'

'He has nothing to prove to me—'

'He's not trying to prove it to you, love,' said Mum. 'He's desperate to prove it to himself. His head is all over the place and the best thing you can do is stay out of his way until his head stops spinning. And if the two of you do decide to be . . . intimate, make sure he wears a condom. No glove, no love.'

'Mum! For goodness' sake!'

'What?'

The front door opened and closed. Nathan was home, thank goodness. This conversation was setting my cheeks on fire.

'Hey. How are my two favourite ladies?' he asked.

Mum headed over to him and the two of them had a prolonged snog. *Ewww!*

Nathan put his arm round Mum's shoulder. 'Have you told her yet?'

Told me what? Puzzled, I looked from Mum to Nathan and back again. Mum put her hand on her abdomen. And then I knew.

'You're pregnant?'

'Nathan! For Shaka's sake! We agreed that I'd tell her,' Mum grumbled.

'I never said a word!' Nathan raised both hands in surrender, making me giggle.

'Callie, you're going to have a brother or sister,' Mum confirmed.

I looked at Nathan who was watching me closely.

'Well, you two didn't hang about!' I teased, genuinely happy. 'Congrats. That's fantastic news. Can I choose his or her name?'

Nathan grinned after what looked like a sigh of relief. That soon faded as he contemplated my last question.

'That depends. What name did you have in mind?' he asked warily.

'Something unique and special. Let me think about it,' I said.

'Oh Lord!' Nathan was worried – and rightly so.

Laughing, I walked over to give him a long hug and Mum a longer one. 'I'm really happy I'm going to have a brother or sister. I can't lie though – it's kinda nasty to think of the two of you going at it at your age. Aren't you too old for that? I mean, you might've put your backs out or something.'

'Well, thanks for the congratulations at least,' said Nathan, eyebrows raised. 'I'm not quite sure what to say to the rest.'

'What d'you mean – too old?' Mum said with indignation. 'I'm thirty-five, not dead. And I didn't exactly find you under a lilac bush, you know.'

No, you had to have me alone because my dad was officially murdered, hanged before I was even born. The thought slipped unbidden into my head, dimming my smile. Mum raised my chin to kiss me on the forehead, before hugging me again.

And I loved it. Hugging Mum was still new enough to be cherished. We'd spent too many years together but apart. It had taken the death of my Nana Jasmine to bring us this close together, and that fact still made me sad. So much time and love wasted. That's why I was grateful every day for Mum, Nana Meggie and now Nathan.

And Tobey.

Nathan joined us in the hug and, as I stood there, breathing them in, I was happy for the family we were, for the family we were going to be and for my new dad, but couldn't help feeling a moment's wistfulness for the dad I never knew.

Dad, if you're up there somewhere, I'll make you proud of me. I swear I will.

NOW

Daily Shouter Online

Nought terrorist laughed as he massacred five in a church

Alexander Gleeson, Nought, 40, butchered five Crosses who were attending a morning prayer meeting at the Redeemer Church, Blackfields Village. It has been confirmed that Gleeson is a paid-up member of the extremist separatist group Nought Forever. Witnesses say he entered the church and immediately started firing. 'People were toppling over left and right,' said Grace Jennings, a church attendee. 'My husband fell onto me and we both crashed to the floor. All around us came the sounds of rapid gunfire and screams. It was awful, like being picked up and dumped in hell. My husband is still in intensive care. The doctors have told me to hope for the best but prepare for the worst.' Another witness, who wished to remain anonymous, told the *Daily Shouter*: 'The shooter was shouting all kinds of racist s**t when he burst into the church. He had murder in his head and murder in his heart. We didn't stand a chance.'

THEN

thirty-seven. Tobey

Callie had a faraway look in her eyes. She got like that sometimes. There were moments when memories immobilized her and she wore her sadness like a crown, usually when she was thinking of her dad. She'd never got to meet him, but that didn't mean she didn't profoundly feel his loss. I knew her expressions, her moods, her myriad states like I knew my own. I was her. She was me. It was that simple.

'Callie, I—'

The front doorbell rang.

'Hold that thought,' Callie replied with a smile, now back in the present.

Frowning, I waited as she went to the front door. We still weren't quite right. If I didn't know better, I'd say that Callie was . . . uneasy around me. Maybe uneasy was overstating it. She was tense. Yes, definitely tense. Why wouldn't she look at me? *Really* look at me like before? It was almost as if—

Callie came back into the kitchen carrying a large box. 'The decorations I ordered have arrived. I'll put up the streamers. You can help blow up the helium balloons. The canister is in the garage.'

I rushed forward to take the outsized box from her and placed it on the central island.

'You should've called me to carry this for you,' I told her.

Callie moved to stand before me.

'I have been calling you,' she said, looking straight at me for once. 'You just haven't been listening.'

Silence. We weren't talking about party decorations any more.

'I'm sorry. I'm listening now,' I said.

'Promise?'

'Promise. I've missed you, Callie,' I admitted.

'Whose fault is that?'

'Mine.'

'I still don't understand what I did to make you end things between us,' Callie said.

I hated hearing the hurt in her voice. How could I make it up to her? I did the only thing I could think of: I kissed her, pouring apology and caring and a plea for forgiveness into that kiss. And, after a moment's stillness, Callie kissed me back, her tongue licking against my lips.

That was all it took for my body to ignite. Wrapping my arms around her, I ran my tongue along her bottom lip. Callie's gasp opened her mouth for me and that was all the invitation I needed. God, I'd missed this. So much. There weren't enough words in the Zafrikan Official Dictionary to describe how much I wanted Callie at that moment, needed her. Not just sex. This was about far more than sex. I needed to be close to her again. Connected again. There was hardly any air between us as my tongue played over hers and I held her even tighter. But then she stiffened in my arms and pulled away. I let her go at once.

'No,' she whispered.

'Callie, what's wrong?' I asked, trying to bank down my frustration.

'Tobey, you know how I feel about you, but—'

'But?'

'I'm not ready for this. After everything that's happened between us recently, I'm not going to jump straight into bed with you.' Callie's attention was entirely focused on her hands, which were fluttering like restless birds before her. 'We need to talk things through first.'

I took her hands in mine, willing her to look at me. After a moment, she did, though there was something I couldn't quite decipher in her eyes.

'Callie, you know how I feel about you,' I said. 'If you've changed your mind about me or can't feel the same way, then you need to tell me.'

'But that's just it,' she argued. 'I don't know how you feel about me, not after how you've treated me. I haven't a clue. Tobey, I'm not a chess piece you can sweep off the board and then reinstate whenever the mood takes you.'

'My feelings haven't changed.' That's all I was willing to admit to.

Callie's head tilted to one side as she studied me. 'I don't know what that means.'

'It means I want to be with you.' There! I'd said it.

Callie pulled her hands away from mine.

'You don't feel the same way,' I realized. 'I've really messed things up between us, haven't I?'

'It's not that—'

'Then what is it?'

From the tightening of Callie's lips, I knew she'd heard the note of what sounded like exasperation in my voice. It may have sounded like that, but panic would've been a better description. I'd been so wrapped up in how I was feeling that I hadn't appreciated until now what I was doing to Callie. Now, though she was standing still, she was pulling away from me.

I'd hurt her badly and she wasn't eager to give me the chance to do it again.

'Tobey, you are disappointing me so much right now. I thought you volunteered to help me so that we could have a proper talk, but you're not interested in that, are you? What's the plan? A quickie before our friends arrive?' Callie gave me a mocking conspiratorial wink.

'Godsake! It wasn't like that.'

She tilted her head to the left, then the right as she studied me, as if trying to figure out what it was she was looking at. It was like being under a microscope – and I didn't like it.

'Look, it wasn't as strategic as you're making out,' I denied, running a hand through my hair. 'I wasn't up all night, planning how to have sex with you.'

'So you're not interested in having sex then?'

'I never said that,' I countered. At Callie's raised eyebrows, I amended, 'What I mean is, can't we do both?'

'And I bet I know which one you'd like to do first,' she said.

Hellsake!

'OK, what d'you want to talk about?' I asked with impatience.

Callie blinked at me, disbelief writ large on her face. 'Oh, I don't know. How about we discuss the decorations? Or the pattern on your socks? Or maybe we could talk about me getting shot and what you did afterwards. You can tell me about your friend Rebecca and how she died, and about you and Dan. I could tell you about the terrible nightmares I've been having and how loud noises, even raised voices, make me panic. I might even tell you what it's been like not having my best friend to talk to. How about something along those lines? Or would you rather just stick to inanities about the weather?'

How was I suddenly the bad guy? Was it so wrong to want to forget all the bad things that had happened in the past year?

'Why rehash all that? The past is something I'm trying to forget, not relive over and over,' I replied, exasperated. 'I just want to go back to the way things were.'

'But we can't,' said Callie. 'We're not the same people we were a year ago – and we never will be again. Don't you get that?'

I stared at her. Everything I'd done since she came out of her coma had been to try and get us back to what we were and what we'd had before. Until this precise moment, I really thought it was achievable. But Callie was right: we weren't the same people. To try and go on as if nothing had happened in the last year except school and homework would be to live a lie. God knows I'm not into touchy-feely or all that heart-on-my-sleeve stuff, but over the last year I'd learned the hard way that just because I didn't believe in displaying my emotions didn't mean I didn't have any — or that they weren't capable of kicking my arse.

'You just don't get it, do you?' Callie shook her head.

I was beginning to. 'You're right. We do need to talk. A lot has happened—'

'Tobey, spare me, please.' She wasn't buying what I was dishing up. 'I'm not stupid. Stop pretending. You and I have always had honesty between us, if nothing else. Don't spoil that too.'

Inside, I went very quiet. Very still. I swear even my heart stopped beating. Just for a moment.

'Didn't you know, Callie? That's what I do — I spoil things. It's what I'm good at,' I said quietly.

'I didn't mean it like that,' she said, her voice growing ever quieter. 'I just meant . . . you hurt me when you ignored me, Tobey. I'm not going to lie about that. Now I don't know who we are any more.'

'Feel free to miss me with this soap-opera bullshit,' I said, dredging up a bucketful of scorn.

Callie flinched as if struck. 'Tobey, you've gotta stop this. Seriously. You can't keep pulling me to you with one hand and slapping me away with the other.'

'Is that what I'm doing?'

'You know it is,' she shot back. 'Or is this you throwing your toys out of the pram because I didn't immediately drag you upstairs to bed?'

'Or is this you being a dick tease?' I threw back at her.

A gasp followed by a stinging slap to my left cheek. A slap so hard I tasted blood in my mouth. My cheek was red-hot and smarting. Callie glared at me. I glared right back at her. Now I'll put up with a little from most people, and I'll put up with a lot more from Callie – but not that. Not that from anyone.

'Callie, don't you ever, as long as you live, raise your hand to me again,' I told her, chips of ice in every syllable.

She inhaled sharply. 'Don't you ever call me a dick tease again. Apologize for that remark.'

I said nothing.

'You know what? Something is very wrong when all we do is tear each other to pieces like this,' said Callie. 'Is that why you wanted a break?'

'I didn't say that.' Not once.

She sighed. 'Tobey, I don't know what's going on with us, but I do know it's not healthy.'

The tightening band around my chest was making it tough to speak, difficult to breathe. I swallowed hard. 'You know, my friend Connor warned me you'd wake up to the fact that you could do better than me. After all, I'm a Nought and—'

'Don't go there, Tobey Durbridge. Don't you dare,' said Callie ferociously. 'This has nothing to do with you being a Nought and everything to do with you being an arse.'

'Wow, Callie, you're determined to trample every bit of my ego into the dirt, aren't you?'

And she was making a first-class job of it too.

Callie looked me up and down with careful deliberation. 'Tobey, I see you ignored Sammi's advice to pull your head out of your arse. When you finally do that, I'll be right here waiting to talk. Until then, perhaps you could help me set up for my party?'

'Or maybe I should just leave?' I challenged.

'That's entirely up to you.'

But I wasn't ready to leave. Not yet.

'What would you like done first?' I asked with venom.

'Could you fill the buckets on the patio with ice, please, and then put these beers on top of the ice – if it's not too much trouble.' Callie was all icy politeness.

We stood in the kitchen, glaring at each other, neither of us saying a word, neither of us moving. I couldn't understand it. Recently, no matter our starting point, this was always where we seemed to end up.

And I didn't have a clue what to do about it.

thirty-eight. Callie

Just when I thought my evening couldn't get any worse . . . Who the hell invited her?

'Why on earth did you invite Misty?' Sammi asked me, her brown eyes wide with disbelief.

'I didn't,' I objected.

'She invited herself,' said Jen with disdain. 'You know she's taken to following Tobey around like a lapdog.'

'D'you want us to get rid of her?' Sammi asked in all seriousness.

I shook my head. 'She's not bothering me. Let her stay.'

Besides, if I chucked her out, that would mean I felt threatened by her and I didn't. Misty stood in the sitting-room doorway, looking around and striking a pose. And, I have to admit, she looked good. Her brunette hair with dyed blonde highlights was cornrowed above both ears and gathered up in a thick braid at the back. She wore a tight blue strapless dress that would've made someone only slightly larger a fine belt. From the seamless way it fitted her like a second skin, Misty obviously hadn't bothered with a bra or pants. Skank!

'God, she's so obvious,' said Sammi, shaking her head.

Jen nodded. 'Men like that. They think it means they know where they stand.'

'Where's Tobey?' I couldn't help asking.

'Sitting out on the patio, getting steadily sloshed,' said Sammi. 'When he's ready to go home, someone will have to wheel him out of here.'

'Look at her.' Jen wrinkled her nose with distaste. 'Misty's moving like she owns the place.'

I glanced across the room. Misty was now dancing, her arms waving in the air which – oops! – pulled her dress up even higher. Any further and she'd need an 18-certificate rating.

'Are you sure you don't want me to throw her out 'cause my earrings are clip-ons!' said Sammi. Her hand was already rising to pull them off so she'd be ready to do battle.

'No, Sammi. Leave it. I'm going to rise above it and get more burgers out of the oven.'

I headed for the kitchen before my instincts got the better of me and I marched across the room and pulled out Misty's hair extensions before stuffing them down her throat.

thirty-nine. Tobey

Callie's birthday party, and everyone was having a great time. But not me. I wasn't feeling the party mood. At all. Neither was Callie, if the expression on her face was anything to go by. Oh, she was doing her best to hide it, but I knew better. I knew her. In spite of the constant smile on her lips, Callie was sipping on her fruit punch like she suspected it was poisoned. Was she as miserable as I was? I could only hope so. Sammi and Jennifer were flanking her like hellhounds guarding Hades. Three times already I'd tried to get Callie on her own, but her friends were marking her Olympic-style and the moment I got close one of them got in my way, while the other whisked her off to another part of the house. Callie's friends were doing my head in.

'Tobey, come and dance with me,' Misty asked for the umpteenth time that evening.

Misty, bugger off!

I shook my head and tried to move away from her, but my every step was matched by one of her own. Why couldn't this girl leave me alone? Trying to shake her off was like trying to shake off swine flu. Every time I made a move, I tripped over her. It was my own fault. A couple of months after the reading of the will, in which Callie's nan had left me a whole heap of currency, I'd made the mistake of asking Misty out on a date. It was when Callie and I were on our break from each other. It was my way of proving to myself that I was my own person, that I wasn't hung up on Callie or anyone.

Maybe a cosmic ray had zapped my head and fried a common-sense pathway in my brain. Maybe it was just a brain fart. What it had definitely been, however, was a colossal mistake. Since our date, Misty had been love-bombing the hell out of me with texts and emails running close to, if not into, three digits. As far as I was concerned, going out with Misty wasn't an experience I was in a hurry to repeat. For one thing, we had absolutely nothing in common. She'd rabbited on about fashion and music and becoming a model, and I'd tried not to make it obvious that I was sleeping with my eyes open. All Misty did was talk about herself and, as a subject, she's not that riveting. When I reckoned I'd spent more than enough time with her to depart without seeming rude, Misty had leaned in for a kiss and, I have to admit, she knew what she was doing. But she wasn't Callie, so I'd stepped back and called it a night.

She hadn't left me alone since. And tonight was obviously going to be no different.

The music at Callie's party was blasting, the bass vibrating right through my feet and up through my body. I vaguely recognized the semi-famous DJ spinning the turntables in Callie's living room. The tunes were playing throughout all the downstairs rooms thanks to Callie's state-of-the-art sound system. Multicoloured lights spun and strobed in the living room and spilled out of the open French windows onto the patio where half the party had congregated now that the rain had stopped. The place was packed. Had Callie invited the whole of the upper sixth to her house? When she used to live next door to me, I'd felt like her home was my home, her life was my life – and vice versa. But in this house, left to her family by her Nana Jasmine? Not so much.

Since Callie's Nana Jasmine left me that money in her will, all my friends envied me. How many times had Connor and others told me how lucky I was, that I'd got it made. Made in the shade. Each time they said that, I smiled and uttered a few noncommittal comments and they took that for agreement. None of them, not even Callie, could see that I wasn't waving but drowning. Was it any wonder I was giving it away just as quickly as I could?

Callie headed for the kitchen. A quick look around showed that Sammi and Jenny were, for once, nowhere in sight. No time like the present. I made a beeline for the kitchen. There were three other people already in there, chatting around the central island. Callie was getting a bag of ice out of the freezer.

'Callie, we need to talk.'

She straightened up, her dark eyes narrowing. Silence dropped like a rock in the kitchen before the others in the room suddenly found other places to be, and scarpered. I didn't blame them. The temperature in the room had dropped to match the bag of ice in Callie's hand.

'What d'you want, Tobey?' She headed for the central island and dropped the bag of ice from a height to break it up. She picked it up to drop it again. And again. The noise was abrasive. Jarring.

'Could you stop doing that for a second—'

Callie chucked the ice down so hard I was surprised the bag didn't burst open on impact. 'You know what, Tobey? I don't need to be dropped on my head several times to get the message. Once or twice will do.' She dumped the contents of the ice bag into the two huge pitchers of punch in front of her. 'I'd have more respect for you if you just came right out and said you'd moved on instead of playing these games.'

'I'm not playing games—'

'Then what the hell are you doing?' Callie asked, exasperated.

How did I begin to tell her what was going on in my head? How did I explain that I just couldn't find my way out of the whirlpool of guilt I was drowning in? Too much remorse about my part in getting Callie shot in the first place. Too much shame about what I'd done when I went after those responsible. Turning my hatred on all those I deemed liable was just a pathetic attempt at masking the fact that the person I blamed most was myself. When Callie's Nana Jasmine died and left me all that money, it was as if the fates were mocking me, rewarding me for detaching my soul from my body.

And for what?

My actions didn't fix anything; they didn't make anything better. Callie getting shot was still down to me. When people started dying, my thirst for revenge had finally been slaked, but at what cost? I'd told Callie most of what I'd done while she was in hospital.

Most but not all.

No one but me – and my mate Dan – knew just how low I'd allowed myself to sink in my quest for vengeance. If it wasn't for Dan, I'd almost certainly be six feet under. Saving my life had destroyed his. He was still on the run. Every so often TV programmes like *Crime Watch* would remind the public that Dan Jeavons remained at large and if anyone saw him they should contact the police immediately. He was considered armed and dangerous. So what did that make me? If Callie found out the truth, she'd want nothing more to do with me. Every day, I'd mentally braced myself, believing that sooner or later she would find out the truth. It was exhausting. So I made up my mind: Callie wasn't going to push me away, because I was going to walk away first. That was my logic. In my head, it made perfect sense.

'No more bullshit, Tobey,' said Callie. 'Do you want to be with me?'

I shrugged. 'Of course I want to be with you.'

I didn't think it was possible, but Callie's expression grew even colder, freezing by degrees. 'Once more with feeling! Why don't you grow a set and tell the truth for a change? You couldn't even be honest about dating Misty.'

My jaw dropped. Hellsake! *She knew about that?*

'Listen, it was one date. One. And nothing happened, I swear.'

'You went out with Misty and you didn't tell me.'

'Because nothing happened. There was nothing to tell.' Why was she making such a big deal out of one lousy date?

'And if you and I were meant to be together and exclusive,

and I went out with your friend Connor, you'd be OK with that?'

I didn't answer. What was I supposed to say?

Moments passed as Callie looked at me, then her whole body slumped like a balloon slowly deflating. 'You know what, Tobey? Do what you like. Be with who you like. Just leave me alone.'

So it was like that, was it? Well, screw Callie and the way she made me feel. I was so tired of always feeling guilty around her, of feeling *less*. Even before she got shot, that's how I felt being with her. Well, I wasn't *less*.

'Fine. I'll do that. I'll do us both a favour and stay the hell away from you.' I strode out of the kitchen, meaning every word.

If Callie didn't want me, I knew someone who did.

forty. Callie

The bass of the song playing was vibrating through my skull. My head was throbbing in time to the music and what had started off as a headache was threatening to morph into a full-blown migraine. Everyone else at this party was having a great time, if the noise level and the laughter were anything to go by. From the look of it, the whole of the upper sixth form had turned up, even those who hadn't been invited. It was my day, my birthday party – and I was feeling wretched.

'Sammi, have you seen Tobey?'

Sammi had trouble looking me in the eye.

'What?' I frowned. 'What is it?'

'Last I saw, Tobey was making his way to the summer house,' she said reluctantly. 'That was a while ago though.'

'Why would he go there?'

Sammi shrugged. 'Maybe he's not enjoying the party?'

'In which case, he could just go home,' I said pointedly. 'Who was with him? Connor?'

'No one was with him as far as I could tell. To be honest, he didn't look like he was in the mood for company.'

Without saying a word, I headed out of the open kitchen doors and along the lit path towards the summer house.

Some of my other friends were on the patio, dancing or sipping at their drinks and chatting. I would've paid good money for everyone to just go home.

Our summer house was like a large detached conservatory set at the bottom of the garden – all glass and tall plants and soft furnishings. Nana Meggie used to use it for painting her landscapes and animals, but she hadn't picked up a brush in months. The summer house consisted of a couple of wicker sofas, Nana Meggie's art supplies and a gateleg table that seated six comfortably when extended. Sammi fell into step with me as I walked towards it.

'Callie, don't do this. If Tobey wants to act like a douche canoe, that's down to him, but don't let him rub your nose in it.'

I looked at her. 'He's not alone, is he?'

Sammi's lips tightened and I had my answer.

'Callie, Tobey's head is all over the place,' she said.

Funny, that's what my mum had said.

'With you on one side and Misty on the other, he probably doesn't know which way is up. And you know what Misty's like. She's good at ego stroking if nothing else. Guys always fall for that kind of thing. They don't have enough blood in their bodies to keep both heads working simultaneously. You know that.'

'Tobey isn't like that,' I protested, though I think it was more for my benefit than Sammi's. 'And he loves me. He told me so.' Once. Just once.

In just under a minute, we had reached the summer house. A deep breath later, I opened the door and stepped inside, switching on the light with Sammi a mere step or two behind me. What I saw froze me solid. Tobey was in the summer house all right. But he wasn't alone. Misty was with him. Or, to be more specific, under him. Tobey sprang up, grabbing at his trousers. Misty sat up, taking her time to smooth down her dress. And me? I just stood there with Sammi beside me. Silence reigned for several moments before Sammi shattered it.

'You sorry son of a bitch! You're supposed to be going with Callie and you'd rather be with this cheap skank? God! Misty's the school bike. Tobey, I thought you had more class. Callie's much too good for you, you skank lover. You come near my girl again and I'll personally put you in a chokehold . . .' Sammi's voice grew louder and more outraged as she spoke.

I mentally turned down the volume on her rant. Bless her, she had my back, but she was letting the whole neighbourhood know it. Misty was still smoothing down her dress while glaring at me defiantly. I dismissed her with a scornful flick of my eyelashes, but Tobey? He was different. I couldn't take my eyes off him. He, on the other hand, was looking everywhere but at me.

'Tobey?' I whispered.

And still he wouldn't look at me. A sad stillness settled over me. This was Tobey. This was me. This was us. After everything Tobey and I had been through together, this was all that was left. At last he did look at me. Sammi was shouting at Misty and Misty was screaming back, but I couldn't hear a word. Tobey and I went into freeze-frame mode, the rest of the world around us just an indistinct blur. Though Tobey's dark eyes held a world of regret, that world was not enough. Though it was quiet I couldn't hear or even feel my heart beating. No wonder. There was an excruciating pain in my chest where Tobey had reached in and ripped it out. I needed to get away from there.

'Really, Tobey. You're gonna stand there and not say a word?' Sammi ranted. 'Aren't you even going to try to explain—'

I placed a hand on her arm to stem her tirade. 'Sammi, let's go.'

I turned round and left the summer house. There was nothing more to be said.

'He was never yours,' Misty called after me. 'You're a Cross, he's a Nought. Nuff said.'

Sammi turned, blood in her eye. She was about to run at Misty and muck her shit up. I grabbed her arm, shaking my head.

'She isn't worth it,' I said quietly. 'Neither of them are.'

'You got that right,' Sammi sniffed, only slightly mollified.

We headed back to the house in silence, though others were now standing outside the summer house, watching the unexpected entertainment. By Monday morning, Tobey and Misty's antics would be all round the school.

'Callie, listen. I know you won't want to hear this right now, but I'm going to say it anyway. Misty is so jealous of you she can't see straight. I knew she'd try some shit like this from the moment she started wearing the same perfume as you and styling her hair like yours. You wear your hair in braids? A day later, she does the same. You wear cornrows on one side of your head? Give it a day or two

226

and she'll be copying. That's the main reason she went after Tobey – because you had him. If she could get him, then she'd be more like you. D'you understand?'

I barely heard Sammi, and what I did hear didn't make any sense. All I could think about was being alone. I was desperate to be by myself, crawl into bed and curl up in a ball until the pain stopped. I walked back into the house and straight up to the DJ, about to tell him to stop the music and announce the party was over. Sammi grabbed my arm, pulling me to one side.

'Don't you dare, Callie,' she said fiercely.

'Samantha, I'm not in the mood to smile and dance and pretend nothing's wrong.'

'Which is precisely why that's exactly what you're gonna do,' she argued. 'Don't give either of them the satisfaction of ruining your party.'

It took a moment or two, but I realized she was right. So that's what I did. I danced and laughed and flirted like it was the best day of my life instead of the worst. And inside? Inside I wished the bullet that had put me in a coma all those months ago had hit me just one centimetre lower.

forty-one. Tobey

I'm not stupid. It was just . . . a moment of madness. The sex meant nothing. It was nothing. Instantly forgettable. An itch that was scratched and that was all. So different to when Callie and I were together . . . Well, that had meant everything, and more now that I had something to compare it to.

I sat in the classroom with my eyes firmly planted on Mr Pike and the whiteboard, knowing that I was the subject of all the whispers around me. The afternoon sun was blazing through the classroom window, each ray battering at my head. It was already splitting and the light wasn't making it any better.

This was all Misty's fault.

The flare of white-hot anger aimed towards Misty vanished almost as soon as it had appeared. I hung my head. My predicament was just as much my responsibility as Misty's. I'm not stupid. I knew how she felt about me and that she'd have no objections if I made a move on her. I had no intention of doing any such thing, I really didn't. Turns out I didn't have to: she'd got in first. She followed me into the summer house when I'd just wanted to be alone for a few minutes, and started kissing and touching me. The huge mistake I made was to close my eyes and pretend it was Callie flinging herself at me, Callie kissing me, Callie wanting me.

I take that back – I *am* stupid. I knew what I was doing and did it anyway.

I can still feel Callie's eyes laser-burning holes straight through me. Come the break, I'll find her and try to explain. If I have to grovel, so be it. She's the best thing in my life.

I can't lose her.

I won't.

forty-two. Callie

I sat down on the lid of the toilet in the closed cubicle and seriously considered bunking off school for the rest of the day and heading home. The mid-morning break had barely even begun and I'd already had enough. Five weeks after my party and I was still getting stares and pitying looks and snide smirks. Five weeks since Tobey and Misty had got together. Why does it still hurt like it was yesterday, like it was five minutes ago?

Let it go, Callie.

Easier said than done. Sammi in particular was such a true friend, squaring up to anyone who tried to get into my business, but I couldn't expect her to act as a buffer for me for the rest of the term. Sooner or later, people would find something else to talk about, that's what Sammi and Jen kept telling me. Even Maxine, my classmate, who I must've shared two sentences with all year, had taken to giving me a hug every time she saw me, which had grown old real fast. I had important exams coming up, the most important of my life if I was to get into law school, and every day I struggled to concentrate on my work and my revision.

But I wasn't going to let Tobey or any guy make me a failure. Never again.

As for Tobey and me, well, whatever it was we'd had together, it was now officially dead in the water. The fact that he could get with Misty, of all people, had made what he and I had together tawdry. And it had taken Tobey too long to get that message. He'd tried to tell me he was sorry, that being with Misty was all a huge mistake. How do you mistakenly screw someone?

He'd initially inundated me with texts, asking me to forgive him. What difference would that make? Forgive him, don't forgive him – it wouldn't change what he did. I was glass and he'd dropped me. Now I'm shattered into a million pieces. I'll truly forgive him when he can put me back together again as good as new, with no visible joins or seams. I'll truly forget when he reaches into my head and erases the images I have of him and Misty together.

I took out my phone to read his last text message to me. Why didn't I delete it? I had no idea. Reading it was like pressing my tongue on an exposed nerve in a tooth cavity. But, in spite of all my self-reproach, I read it anyway.

> Callie, please talk to me. I made a mistake.
> I'm only human. I'll keep saying sorry till you
> believe me, till you forgive me. Please don't
> hate me. Just let me tell you face to face
> how truly sorry I am. Tell me what I can do
> to make things right between us. I love you.
> Tobey

How could he? If I believed each letter of every word he texted me, that just made it worse. He loves me? How could he love me and sleep with someone else? That made no sense. I texted him back.

> Tobey, I don't know what you feel for me, but it isn't love or you wouldn't have had sex with Misty. I don't hate you. I wish you only good things, but you and I are over. Now please stop messaging me. Don't force me to block you. Callie

That was three days ago. He hadn't texted me or tried to talk to me after that. Had he finally got the message? It looked like it. So why did I feel more miserable than ever? I never thought I'd be one of those girls who sighed over guys. What the hell was I doing in this toilet cubicle, feeling sorry for myself?

I stood up and went to take my bag off the hook on the door when someone rushed into the cubicle next to mine and retched, throwing up violently. I wrinkled my nose. God, I hated the sound of vomiting and the smell was already hitting me. Well, nice to know I wasn't the only one having a lousy day. I left the cubicle and went to one of the sinks to wash my hands. The sound of vomiting had died down. The lock on the toilet cubicle clicked open and Misty stepped out, wiping her mouth with the back of her hand, her eyes watering. She froze when she saw me, her eyes widening like she was caught in headlights.

'Are you OK?' I asked.

Misty's hand flew to her abdomen, only to immediately drop to her side. Too late.

Ohmigod! 'You're *pregnant*?'

Her mouth opened, but the only sound that came out was a strangled gasp. 'I . . . I . . .'

My jaw dropped. Maybe, if Mum hadn't been pregnant too, I wouldn't have recognized the signs and symptoms, but I did. Misty was *pregnant*. And there was no doubt in my mind about who the father was.

'Please don't tell anyone. Please,' she begged.

She wasn't even going to try to deny it.

'How far gone are you?' Stupid question. I knew exactly how far gone she was. Five weeks, two days and several hours. 'Never mind.'

But Misty *did* mind. She burst into tears. I stepped forward and, before I knew it, I was hugging her. Within moments, my shirt was soggy. It was like a dam bursting.

'I'm so s-stupid. What am I going to do?' she sobbed.

'Are you going to keep it?'

'I don't know.'

'Have you told Tobey yet?' I asked.

The door to the girls' toilets opened.

'Bugger off!' I snapped before getting a proper look at who was entering.

Without a word, three Year Four girls beat a hasty retreat. Misty straightened to wipe the back of her hand across her face.

'Are you OK, Misty?'

'No. Not even close,' she replied miserably.

'Does Tobey know?'

'No one does – except you.'

Oh. My. God!

Misty's pregnant.

Tobey's going to be a dad.

I felt like I'd been dropped down a mineshaft and was still falling. But this wasn't about me. Not any more.

'Misty, you need to tell him,' I said. 'He has the right to know.'

Misty's tears were flowing faster now. 'He'll think I did it on purpose.'

Didn't you?

A stab of bitter anger impaled me. In that moment, I loathed Misty. Despised her. She had to know Tobey had only got with her to get back at me. Why didn't she just say no? Didn't she have any pride? And now she was a bomb thrown between Tobey and me, blasting us so far apart, it felt like no force on earth could put us back together again.

Another look at Misty's unhappy face and the anger didn't die, but it did take a step or two back. Her misery was real. Whatever it was she'd set out to do, this wasn't it.

'Whatever you decide to do, you should tell Tobey,' I said. 'He'll stand by you.'

'No, he won't.'

'Well, he won't if you don't give him a chance,' I said. 'You can't go through this alone, Misty. You've got to tell him.'

'He'll hate me.'

He wouldn't be alone. I closed my eyes briefly and swallowed hard to bank down the roil of desperate hatred I felt inside. Only when I trusted that I had my true feelings under control did I open my eyes.

'Tobey needs to know. He deserves that much.'

A moment, then Misty nodded. There we stood, Misty and I, watching each other. And what I felt about her in that exact moment scared me. Actually scared me.

forty-three. Tobey

The moment the end-of-lesson buzzer sounded, Callie had been one of the first out of the classroom. I was the last. Two days ago, Sammi – Callie's good friend – had taken me to one side and put me straight. 'Listen! If you want Callie to forgive you, you need to back off. The more you push, the more she'll dig her heels in. Give her a chance to cool off and miss you.'

'Why're you offering me advice?' I couldn't help asking. 'You're not exactly my number-one fan.'

Eyes narrowed, Sammi looked me up and down, confirming my words. 'My girl is hurting, and if the only one who can stop that is you, then I'll do whatever I can to get you back together.'

For the first time in weeks, I felt a spark of hope.

'You'd do that for me? Really?' I asked.

'I wouldn't do a damn thing for you, Tobias Durbridge. You're a twenty-four-carat ass hat. I'm doing this for Callie.' Sammi was as blunt as ever. 'She might eventually forgive you, she might not – but you've got to back off. No more text messages or trying to speak to her. OK? All that's doing is pissing her off.'

'You think?'

'I know,' said Sammi. 'You two are good for each other, much as it pains me to say it, but it's not gonna happen if you don't stop with the crazed-stalker act.'

'Consider it stopped.'

And I meant it.

Two of the longest days of my life had passed since then. I could only hope that Sammi knew what she was talking about and was really on board with Callie and me getting back together.

'Tobey, I need to speak to you.'

I looked up, then sighed. For Shaka's sake, couldn't this bitch leave me alone?

'Not now, Misty.' I gathered up the last of my things, stuffing them into my rucksack.

No, I didn't want another date. No, I didn't want to hook up. It wouldn't bother me if I never spoke to Misty again. Shouldn't she have got the message by now? I really didn't need any drama today. And, besides, if I were to stand any chance of getting Callie to forgive me, I needed to stay away from Misty. After bolloxing things up so badly already, I wasn't about to do it again. That was a hard lesson I'd finally learned. I headed for the door.

'Tobey, I'm pregnant.'

All the clocks in the world stopped. The earth stopped orbiting the sun. Time itself ceased to exist. My blood was dry ice in my veins. I turned slowly. 'What?'

'I'm pregnant.'

I stared. My mind began to whirl though I stood absolutely

still. Frozen. I must've misheard, right? I was asleep and dreaming – no . . . having the worst nightmare of my life. Did Misty say she was *pregnant*?

'You're what?'

'I'm pregnant.'

'Whose is it?' I asked.

Misty's eyes widened. 'It's yours, Tobey.' At my sceptical look, she repeated angrily, 'It's yours.'

'Are you sure?'

Oh God . . .

'I haven't been with anyone since you and I had our first date together,' she said.

'Why the hell didn't you use something?'

'Why didn't *you*?' Misty shot back at me.

NO! The word was an explosion in my head.

I stared at her, mere moments away from being physically sick. My stomach was churning; my heart hammered at my ribs for release. Saliva filled my mouth. I was actually going to vomit.

Misty was pregnant . . .

I swallowed hard, then again. And again. My plans, my world, my whole life was circling round the plughole.

'You're going to have an abortion, right?'

Misty's eyes narrowed. 'I haven't decided yet.'

'You can't seriously be thinking of keeping it,' I argued.

I knew I was being a douche sack, but the shock of Misty's revelation was still pummelling me. Hell, I didn't know what I was saying. I just wanted . . . I wanted to get back my life as of five minutes ago. Five minutes ago was pretty shitty, but it was *la dolce vita* compared to now. Oh hell, I just wanted Callie as my girlfriend again. I wanted my old life back and to reclaim my sanity. All those things were floating away from me like helium balloons.

'Tobey, couldn't we . . . I mean, couldn't the two of us try to make this work? We're going to have a child. We could maybe try living together—'

'And live off what?' I asked. 'I don't have the money to look after you and a child. Are you kidding? All my money is gone, if that's what you're banking on. And I have plans. I'm going to university. I'm going to be a lawyer. Nowhere in that scenario is there room for a baby.'

Oh God . . .

'Then you should've used a condom,' Misty said bitterly. 'I can't believe you're talking to me like this. Have you even taken a second to think about how I feel?'

I stared at her. Truth to tell, no, I hadn't. But there was no room in my mind for what she might be going through. Oh my God! What was Mum going to do? She was going to kick my arse, that's what. Misty had to have an abortion. Didn't she see that it would ruin both our lives if she didn't? No. All she could see in front of her was some stupid fantasy she'd built up in her head. A fantasy where she and I skipped off into the sunset, hand in hand, and played happy families. Wasn't gonna happen. Ever.

'Who . . . who else knows – apart from you and me?' My words were as sharp as knife points.

'No one,' said Misty, dropping her gaze.

I breathed a sigh of relief.

'I can't . . . I can't deal with this right now.' Slinging my rucksack over my shoulder, I headed for the door.

'Thanks for nothing, Tobey,' Misty called after me. 'I don't know what was going on between you and Callie, but, whatever it was, you used me and now I've been caught in the crossfire.'

Though her words made me start, I left the room without looking back. My heart was still trying to drill its way out of my chest. Control over my life was whirling like confetti in the wind.

Callie . . .

Oh God! What would Callie do when she found out?

I remember when I was seven or eight Mum told me about split-aparts. Some Jurassic philosopher or other reckoned that each person only had half a soul, having been split apart from its other half for some reason or other that I can't recall. This philosopher reckoned each person spent their life searching for their other half, not feeling truly whole till they'd found the person who possessed it. Some people settled for 'close enough', unable or unwilling to keep searching till they found their true other half.

'Don't ever settle, Tobey,' said Mum. 'Find someone who has the same values, the same principles, the same interests. Someone who will treat your heart right. Even if you have to wait a long time, don't settle. Believe me, it'll be worth it.'

I didn't have to settle. I didn't have to search. When Mum told me that story, it was like cogs clicking into place in my head. Right then and there, I knew who was my split-apart. She was living next door and her name was Callie Rose. Never doubted it for a second; never said anything to anyone about it. As if! But I *knew*.

And now Misty was a grenade between us.

Misty was pregnant – and she was actually making noises about keeping it. Think. I needed to think.

What was I going to do?

forty-four. Callie

It's been a while now since Tobey and I last spoke, but it's not just me he's singling out for the silent treatment. As far as I can see, Tobey's not talking to anyone. Not even his best mates Connor and Tauren, who'd just come back to school after having his appendix removed. Tobey came to lessons, head down, talking to no one, then disappeared at break and lunch. At first I thought he was spending time with Misty, but I soon realized I'd got that one wrong. She hung around with her friends, not Tobey. Misty had obviously told Tobey her news, but as far as I could tell she hadn't told anyone else. If she had, it would've been the talk of the whole school.

What was Misty going to do? Keep it? Have an abortion? Put her child . . . their child, up for adoption? Why did I even care? Misty wasn't my concern. But Tobey was.

Where is he? What's he doing?

I was worried about him. There! I'd admitted it to myself.

The lunch break had started, I was in the common room and Tobey had pulled his disappearing act again. Was he scared? Feeling alone? Well, I wasn't about to abandon him.

I needed him to know I was still his friend – if nothing else.

'Sammi, I don't suppose you've seen Tobey recently, have you?' I asked, trying to sound nonchalant.

Sammi's eyes narrowed. She wasn't buying my act for a second. 'Last I saw he was hiding away again in practice room three, where he always goes at lunchtime.'

I frowned. Why was Tobey in the piano practice room? He wouldn't know middle C from the Sea of Tranquillity. I sprang up and headed off. Was he OK?

'Where're you going?' Sammi called after me.

'I'll see you later,' I replied. And I was out the door.

forty-five. Tobey

My head was splitting. I'd had a constant headache for the last few days and, no matter how many painkillers I popped, nothing was shifting it. Just one of the reasons why I wasn't in the food hall or the sixth-form common room. Any kind of noise went through my head like a giant spike.

So here I was in the music practice room – just a piano I couldn't play and me. The practice room was tiny, a shoe-box containing a full-size digital keyboard and two piano stools. A shelf on the adjacent wall held sheet music and a few piano practice books. This had become my bolthole during school breaks. And this would be where I stayed until lunchtime was over. I didn't want to see anyone, speak to anyone, look at anyone.

My life was a mess. I didn't need to see the confirmation of that in the eyes of every person who looked at me. Everyone knew I'd slept with Misty. No one but Misty and me knew about the consequences. But, if Misty had her way, they soon would. Even if she said nothing, her abdomen would soon be talking for her. My life was already a gossip cake that everyone in the school was snacking on. When word got out about Misty's pregnancy, my life wouldn't be worth living. Frustrated, I slammed my fists down on the keys before me. I'd been doing that a lot over the last few days, playing how I felt.

The door opened. I turned, ready to tell whoever it was to sod off. The words died in my mouth. Callie. She entered the room, closing the door quietly behind her.

'Tobey, can I talk to you?'

I shrugged, not trusting myself to speak. Swinging my legs round, I turned to face her. No doubt she was going to tear into me for sleeping with Misty. Call me out for the mess I'd made. Yet Callie didn't know the half of it. Didn't she realize she couldn't slap me with a single negative label that I hadn't already applied to myself? Straightening my shoulders, I braced myself for the onslaught.

'How're you doing?' she asked.

Oh, so we were playing that game, were we? Callie was assuming the role of Lady Magnanimous. And me? What was my role supposed to be? Serf Grateful?

I shrugged again. 'I've been better.'

'Aren't you hungry? You're missing lunch.'

'Couldn't eat a thing.'

Callie nibbled on the corner of her bottom lip, a sure if surprising sign that she was nervous.

'I've got some biscuits in my pocket. Want one?' she asked.

I shook my head.

'I don't mind getting you a drink if you fancy one.'

I shook my head again.

How many more trivialities was she going to throw at me? I ran my hand over my hair, unsure how much of this small talk I could take.

'You still taking your exams next term?' asked Callie.

I frowned. 'Of course. I'm still going to uni to study law.'

Callie and I had applied to study law at the same university. We'd spoken of sharing a flat or a house at some point, maybe after the first year. The same subject in the same university in the same town in the same world in the same lifetime. That had been the dream.

Callie cleared her throat. 'I just wanted you to know that . . . that I know about Misty being pregnant.'

No! Mayday! Mayday . . .

My heart plummeted down, down, down, out of my body towards the centre of the earth, taking the last remnants of the hope I had left with it. The moment I'd been dreading had arrived. How had she found out? Misty said . . .

Misty *lied.*

I should've known. Closing my eyes briefly, I stood up and looked straight at Callie. 'Well?'

She blinked in surprise. 'Is that all you have to say to me?'

'What d'you want me to say?'

What the hell was she waiting for? Like the earth orbiting the sun, what Callie was about to do next was inevitable. I was about to get shot down – and all I could do was stand before her and wait for the bullets to fly.

forty-six. Callie

Tobey had straightened up to his full height, and, though he tried to hide it, he was hurting. Badly. And, because he was hurting, so was I.

'I'm here because I thought you might need a friend.'

Tobey's eyes narrowed. His lips twisted into a sneer. 'And that would be you, would it?'

'Yes, it would,' I replied. Why was he being so bloody? 'I just wanted to say that if you need someone to talk to, or if there's anything else you need, I'm here for you.'

'That's it? That's all you have to say?'

'What would you like me to say, Tobey?' I asked, exasperated. 'I'm *trying* here, OK? Misty is pregnant with your child and . . . and I'm trying to be supportive, but you're not the only one hurting. You've taken what you and I had and stomped it into dust. And for what? For *Misty*. You and her – that just has "fuckery" written all over it. Was she worth it?'

Silence.

'No.' Tobey's voice was barely audible, but I heard him.

'Then why did you do it, Tobey? Why did you sleep

with the one person you knew would hurt me the most?' I asked.

Misty had been trying to get with Tobey for years. Even when he and I became an item, I could feel her breathing down my neck, just waiting for an opportunity to take my place. Once Tobey had even tried to use Misty to make me jealous. Tried and succeeded. I clenched my fists, the resentment, the bitterness I'd tried to bank down rising up like lava in an erupting volcano.

'It wasn't like that—'

'Yes, it was,' I interrupted. 'You deliberately tried to hurt me, and you know what? You succeeded. I want to be your friend, but part of me hopes you and Misty are miserable together. I hope you're both as miserable as you've made me. I hope your child *dies*.'

Tobey and I stared at each other, my poisonous words echoing between us. Oh God!

'I'm sorry, Tobey,' I said, appalled. 'I didn't mean it.'

'Yes, you did,' he said quietly.

'Tobey, I—'

'Don't say any more, Callie. I think you've said enough. You took aim and your aim was true. You can go now.'

It was only when I felt salt water run over my top lip and into the corner of my mouth that I realized I was crying. I dashed my hand across my cheeks, but the tears didn't stop. I looked at Tobey, waiting for him to crow at my tears, but, to my shock, he too had tears shimmering in his eyes. Unlike me, however, he wasn't even trying to hide them.

We stood less than a metre apart. All I wanted at that moment was for Tobey to open his arms and hold me. I wanted to wrap my arms around him and never let him go. The two of us against the world.

Neither of us moved.

'Just go, Callie,' Tobey sighed, turning to sit down on the piano stool, his back to me. 'There's nothing left for us to talk about.'

Our moment had come – and gone. Regret tore at my flesh. I turned to leave.

'Callie, wait.'

My hand froze on the door handle. Slowly, I looked over my shoulder at Tobey.

'For what it's worth, I'm sorry.'

I replied, 'For what it's worth, so am I.'

Sorry. One of the most inadequate words on the planet. A small word that stood between us like a giant sentinel from hell. If Misty had her baby, Tobey would be a father whether he decided to hook up with her or not. If she wanted an abortion, Tobey will still have slept with her as a way of hurting me. That left us precisely nowhere.

I left the room, quietly closing the door behind me.

forty-seven. Tobey

When Callie left the room, I buried my head in my hands. I knew what she was thinking. That we were irrevocably broken. If she gave me half a chance, I'd spend the rest of my life trying to put us back together. I knew I could, given time. She just needed to give me a second chance.

But that was never going to happen.

How could it, with Misty in our way? If she insisted on keeping her child, then, with each day that passed, Callie would see my mistake getting bigger and bigger. How would I ever persuade Callie to trust me again?

The hatred I felt for Misty in that moment scared me. Actually scared me. Even though on some level I knew that I shared responsibility, it didn't make any difference. If she had been standing in front of me at that precise moment . . .

This was what I got for caring. Caring about people made you soft and stupid. Caring made you *weak*. I closed my eyes, giving in to the coldness creeping over me. Rejoicing, revelling in it. My heart was freezing, like water turning to ice. I straightened up and took a deep breath. A dark quiet descended upon me, calming my mind.

It was time to change and rearrange my life. No more soft and stupid for me. No more weakness.

It didn't work.

It didn't pay.

NOW

Daily Shouter Online

Journey from loving son and dutiful husband to mastermind behind the Leopold Day Centre outrage

Marcus Dupont, 34, has been remanded in custody for the deaths of nine Noughts at the Leopold Day Centre yesterday. Described by those who knew him as a loving son and dutiful husband, he published his three-page manifesto on his social-media channels before leaving home with two automatic handguns, intent on causing misery and destruction.

Dupont, a member of the TVA (Traditional Values Alliance), stated in his rambling, three-page manifesto document that he was 'working for the good of Crosses everywhere. Noughts breed like flies and within a generation if we're not vigalent [sic] we Crosses will be outnumbered and overrun. We Crosses need to protect our own and send a message to Noughts everywhere that they are not wanted and should go back to whatever Arctic circle godforsaken country they came from.'

Marcus attended Ocampo High School, where he was described by a teacher as a straight-A student. 'I can't understand how Marcus could get involved in something like this. He was always popular with both teachers and other students. I hope he gets the mental-health care he so obviously needs.'

forty-eight. Libby

'Your dad is Tobias Durbridge?' Troy says, stunned.

'Yes,' I admit. 'The one and only.'

'But your surname is Jackman.' Troy states the blooming obvious.

'Mum and Dad weren't married when they had me and, as Dad wasn't present when my birth was registered, I couldn't officially take his name. I looked it up.'

'Your mum is Misty Jackman.' Troy takes his time over the words, blinking like a giant lightbulb had just switched on over his head. 'That explains so much. I didn't put the name and the person together until now. I just knew your mum as Miss Jackman.'

'Well, now you know.' What difference does knowing my mum's full name make?

'My sister knows your dad,' says Troy. 'They went to school together.'

I frown. I didn't know that.

'In fact, your dad and Callie, my sister, were an item before he hooked up with your mum.'

I didn't know that either. I digest Troy's news in silence.

'What else do you know about your dad and my sister?' he asks.

'Not much,' I admit. It's galling to find that Troy probably knows as much, if not more, about my dad than I do, courtesy of his family.

'Your mum is a card-carrying Cross hater. Is your dad one too?' asks Troy.

'No! Of course not,' I state with indignation. 'He's not like that.'

I can't know that, not for sure, but, from what I've seen and read about my dad on the news, I'm sure he doesn't think that way. Besides, if he and Troy's sister once dated, doesn't that prove it?

'But you and your mum are,' Troy declares. The way he looks me up and down makes me bristle.

'I am *not*. My beliefs are my own. I'm not my mum.'

'Aren't you?'

'No, of course not.' The thought burns straight through me.

'Sounds to me like your mum has spent her whole life jealous of my sister and she can't get past that,' Troy says slowly, his voice overflowing with disdain. 'And you're too lazy to do your own thinking so you let your mum do your thinking for you.'

Troy's words are a slap across my face. And the way he looks at me. Like I'm nothing, worse than nothing.

'You're a fraud, Libby,' says Troy. 'You talk a good game about how you make your own decisions and run your own life, but you lie like a rug! You're so desperate for your mum's love that you've let her turn you into an exact copy of her.'

'Fuck you, Troy.' He has no idea what's happened these last few weeks.

'No, fuck you first, Libby. My mum told me all about it, about how Misty went after Tobey even though she knew your dad and my sister Callie were meant for each other. How Misty got pregnant and broke my sister's heart. And, after all that, your dad *still* wanted to be with Callie. Not your mum but my sister. That's why Misty can't stand my sister or any Crosses – because she knows your dad could never love her the way he loved my sister. I remember what you told me in Year Seven about some of your mum's messed-up shenanigans. You even look like your dad – another reason for your mum to resent you with her screwed-up logic. Are you really so stupid you can't see the blindingly obvious?'

The slaps just keep coming, each sentence a backhander, full force, with sharpened knuckles.

'I'm not my mum,' I insist again. Was that a little less conviction in my voice?

'Your comment about us Crosses only looking out for our own? Is that really what you think or is that one of your mum's planted ideas?' asks Troy. 'And what you said about how us Crosses can't be trusted – your view or your mum's? Enquiring minds would love to know.'

He is playing my own words back to me. Words I'd said in the sixth-form common room to get more votes. But I just copied some of the antics the proper political parties had got up to during the last general election. I'd figured that maybe a third of those eligible to vote wouldn't bother because it's a school election – who cares? And a third would vote for Zane and Meshella because, well, they were Crosses, but the votes would be split between the two of them, meaning neither would win. OK, so Zane is biracial but he's still darker then me. And maybe, just maybe, I could mop up the other third and a little bit more by playing the separate-but-equal card. That's what the current government of Liberal Traditionalists had done at the previous election years ago, allowing them to bring in the confirmed residency bill. The bill may have brought them a ton of bad publicity, but it also brought them a shitload of votes. The bad publicity didn't stop them booting out of the country Noughts who were elderly and disabled, Nought criminals, Noughts too ill to work and all those Noughts who didn't have the proper paperwork to prove they weren't illegal immigrants. Never mind that most of the Noughts kicked out of the country had been born here or had come to Albion when they were infants. Never mind that they had worked and paid taxes and fought for their country. That was no longer good enough. Noughts were still getting booted back to the nearest Fenno-Skandian country. Mum says that's why we Noughts will never be accepted as a true part of Zafrikan society. Not when any ruling government can pass arbitrary laws to kick us out whenever they like. Mum says that's why we shouldn't even try to belong, but should set up our own state and should only care about our own first, last and always.

Mum says . . .

Mum says.

If such tactics were good enough for the government, why weren't they good enough for me? Only the government didn't get half the flak I'm taking from Troy.

How is that fair?

forty-nine. Troy

Libby is looking at me, stricken.

Yeah, that hit you where you live, I think sourly.

I mean, come on! I didn't need to be a rocket scientist to figure that one out. Despite every cutting remark Libby has ever made about her mum, she's still doing her damnedest to be just like her. What's that about? And, now that I know who her dad is, the resemblance is unmistakable. Uncanny even. Libby is still blinking at me like a stunned owl, like I've said something insightful. Hardly.

'I'm not getting into a blinking contest with you, Libby,' I tell her straight.

And I can't take being down here a moment longer. I'm about ready to start climbing the walls; either that or start banging my head off one. There has to be a way out of this basement. There just *has* to. Deciding on the direct approach, I start up the stairs.

'What're you going to do?' Libby asks from behind me, trepidation in her voice.

'Make a nuisance of myself,' I reply.

'Because making a nuisance of yourself is a sure way to win friends and influence people.'

Really? 'What's your plan then?' I turn to ask. 'To make yourself as small as possible in the hope they'll forget all about us?'

Even in this dim light, I can see Libby's cheeks begin to redden. Bullseye!

'Not gonna happen, Libby. You're the one that wanted to be up and doing,' I remind her. 'If we want out of here, we'll have to do it ourselves. If there's only one person out there, then we might stand a chance.'

'There are three of them – at least. The tiger, the rabbit and the fox.'

'But it doesn't take three people to babysit a locked door,' I point out. 'If we're very lucky, there'll only be one or two out there, not all three.'

'You think the two of us stand a chance against grown men?'

'Libby, we stand no chance at all if we don't try. You want to be a coward and do nothing? Go for it. Me? I'm gonna do something.'

For Shaka's sake! Libby is a real dead weight around my neck. It's like having to fight our assailants and her at the same time. Heading up the rickety wooden staircase, I'm aware that my tone is unnecessarily brusque, but I'm not sure how much longer I can stay in this cellar without losing it completely. I'm not a fan of confined spaces at the best of times – but this? This is like someone has reached into my head and extracted my idea of hell.

Fists clenched, I pound on the door. 'LET US OUT OF HERE! LIBBY HAS COLLAPSED! SHE NEEDS HELP!'

'I have not—' Libby calls after me.

I glare at her. 'Shush!'

'Oh!'

Bloody idiot.

'PLEASE! LIBBY NEEDS HELP! SHE'S HARDLY BREATHING!'

I keep pounding on the door and shouting until my throat protests and my hands and wrists are red-hot and aching, but I'm not going to give up. I can't. If I give in to the despair flooding over me, then I'll drown.

fifty. Libby

Troy is making far too much noise. The last thing either of us wants or needs is to accelerate whatever plans our kidnappers have for us. Troy is right about one thing though: I do just want to make myself as tiny as possible until we're rescued. How does banging on the door and demanding to be let out because I'm supposedly ill help us? Like suddenly the ones who grabbed us off the street will listen to Troy and think, *One of them is sick. We shouldn't have abducted them like that!* and then they'll let us go?

'Troy, you're giving me a headache,' I state softly for his ears only.

He glowers at me, incredulous.

'Are you kidding me, Libby? Is your home life with your mum so awful that you'd rather stay down here and rot?'

Now he's not the only one who's scowling. He has a whole repertoire of low blows when it comes to me.

'How is demanding to be released getting us anywhere?' I ask, exasperated. 'All you're going to do is piss them off.'

'Good. Then they'll open the bloody door and—'

The sound of the bolt being drawn back is unexpected, jarring. Troy and I both freeze until we hear the sound of the key turning in the lock. Troy quickly beckons me up the stairs before he takes a step back, ducking to his right to stand just behind the door as it slowly opens.

Oh God! My heart is inflating inside my chest, pushing against my ribs, my spine, till there's a tight band right round my torso. I walk halfway up the stairs. The man wearing the rabbit mask appears.

'Water. Aspirin. Stay there.' His voice is deep and gruff, but there's something not quite right about it, as if he's trying to disguise his voice. He bends to place two large bottles of water, what looks like a packet of biscuits and a blister pack of tablets on the floor. His head turns to look at me. I see the frown in his narrowed eyes behind the mask. 'Where's your friend?'

Oh, Troy, don't do anything stupid—

Too late!

Troy shoves the door forward. It smashes into Rabbit Man just as he's straightening up. A yell of surprise and the man falls to the floor on all fours, his bare hands thudding against the quarter-space landing at the top of the stairs. Troy pulls back the door, slamming it forward again on the man's head. Not even a groan. The man in the doorway drops like a stone. Troy leaps out from behind the door and charges through it, jumping over the guy now lying spark out on the floor. I race upstairs in full panic mode. I have no idea what Troy is up to, but I don't want to get left behind. Being stuck in this cellar with Troy is bad enough. Stuck down here on my own would be far worse. When I reach the doorway, to my dismay I see Troy battling a tall, thin man in jeans and a black leather jacket, wearing a fox mask. The driver. The fox leaps onto Troy's back and is trying to put him in a chokehold. Troy pulls at the fox's arms, spinning round and backing into the nearest wall at speed to try and dislodge him.

I jump over the rabbit guy, looking about for some way to help Troy. A frantic glance around gives me a better grasp of where we are. It's definitely a house, with stairs running up to a first floor, and a basement. On the ground floor, through the closest doorway, I can see two old, collapsible wooden chairs and some empty, discarded pizza boxes on the floor – that's it. The rest of the room is empty. The hall is bare floorboards with protruding nails and discoloured walls. We're in an abandoned house that shrieks neglect. A second to take it all in. My only thought now is how to get out. Troy manages to dislodge the fox man on his back who falls to the floor. I leap out of his way as he lands. Immediately the fox jumps up, launching himself at Troy, his gloved hands round Troy's throat. Troy lashes out. The fox only just manages to dodge his flailing blow. I take a step forward, ready to make my own dash for the door. One of us . . . one of us has to escape this house. A hand grabs at my ankle. Instinctively, I kick back, smashing my heel into the rabbit's face. *Tuck into that, you bastard!*

'Ooof! You little bitch!'

An icy frisson of recognition runs through me. That voice . . . Where have I heard it before? No time to stop and think. I run for the door just as Troy manages to land a blow to the fox's chest, which floors him again.

'Stop them!' calls out the rabbit, scrambling to his feet.

That voice . . .

Troy is only a step or two behind me. This might be our one and only chance to get away. I wrench open the door — and we *run*.

fifty-one. Troy

A street. Evening by the feel of it. The air is filled with darkening blues and sodium orange. The shock of the outdoors. I'd lost track of the time of day down in that basement without my phone, and now being outside makes me stumble and pause, but only momentarily. Now that the sky is my ceiling, the thought of being dragged back to the basement sends a chill down my spine.

RUN!

We're out of the door and sprinting along the road faster than I've ever run before. We're in a street of terraced houses, all boarded up and dilapidated. I don't recognize the houses, the area – nothing about this place is familiar. And the worst thing? The whole area is quiet. Eerily quiet.

We run – like the devil himself is chasing us. Libby is racing along beside me, matching me step for step.

Where are we?

I look around for a road sign, a recognizable landmark – but there's nothing.

Keep running.

Behind us a car engine starts, the sound ripping through the quiet. Already it's in motion. I didn't think it was possible for my heart to roar any harder. I was wrong.

'Troy . . .' Libby's terrified whisper echoes in my head.

'Don't look back. Keep going.'

We need to get off the road. There's a corner up ahead. I pray there's some place to hide, some bolthole nearby. We round the corner, only to pull up abruptly at the sight before us.

The docks.

Huge pallets, shipping containers and crates the size of lorries fill the view. All shapes, sizes, colours, and so many of them they go on for kilometres. At least I know where I am now – roughly. East Gurendah Harbour. But there's no one in sight. Shouldn't this place be heaving?

There's no time to ponder that. A quick glance over my shoulder shows the car behind us getting closer. There's at least one hundred metres of scrubby wasteland filled with debris and junk between us and the nearest dockside pallets. Not enough debris to hide behind, but hopefully enough to slow down a car. Whoever's driving will have to get out and follow us on foot.

No time to think.

'That way!' I point towards the harbour.

We take off.

If the car behind us isn't going to drop us where we stand, we need to run like the wind. Fail, and we won't get a second chance. If we're caught, we'll both end up decorating the bottom of the harbour.

The answer is simple.

Don't fail.

RUN!

fifty-two. Libby

My mouth is open, dragging air down into my lungs as I run. My lungs are red-hot, burning inside my chest. The throat-catching stink of shit, rotting food and fish pummels at my senses. Troy is only a step or two ahead and he keeps slightly twisting his head to the left to make sure I'm still at his shoulder. Shouting comes from behind us, but no more car engine noises. The two men who'd kidnapped us are obviously on foot now, chasing after us, shouting obscenities. I choose not to focus on what they're yelling. Troy and I sprint past the nearest pallet and keep running, turning left, right, right, ducking round the vast shipping containers.

I'm not going back to that basement.

Troy pulls me down behind one shipping container, a finger to his lips. We both listen. Silence. Our captors have obviously stopped running too, doing the same thing, listening out for us. Troy points to the low harbour wall and nods. I frown. Why is he pointing in that direction? The only thing beyond the wall is the river.

'Once we're in the water, we'll swim across to the other side and contact the police,' Troy whispers.

My heart nosedives. I shake my head. 'You go. I'll hide here until you can bring help.'

'Don't be stupid.' Troy frowns. 'I'm not leaving you behind.'

'You must. You swim across the river and get help. OK?' *Don't make me say it. Please.*

'No. Not OK. We both go or we both stay,' Troy insists.

'Troy, I can't swim,' I admit.

fifty-three. Troy

You have got to be shitting me. I search Libby's face for a sign that she's pulling my leg. There is none. 'Please tell me you're joking.'

'I can't swim,' she repeats.

'Well, we can both just hide out in the water. You can doggy paddle, and when the coast is clear I'll swim across and—'

'NO! I can't get in there. I won't. You can't make me.'

What the hell? Libby's voice is rising as she stares at me. No, it's more than a stare. Her eyes are wide like she's forgotten how to blink. And her lips are pressed so tight together as to be bloodless. I've never seen her like this before.

'Keep your voice down, Libby. And you need to get real. We have to jump in. It's our only chance.'

'I'm not being a diva. It's not that I d–don't fancy getting my hair w–wet or s–something.' Libby's talking so quickly that her words start to trip over themselves. 'I can't be in the water.'

'For Shaka's sake! Why not?'

'*It's just a joke. Just for a laugh. Ha ha. Where's your sense of humour, Libby?*' Libby's eyes are wild, and she looks through me as she speaks. I haven't a clue what she's saying. *'Where's your sense of humour, Libby?'* she repeats.

What the hell? What's she playing at?

'Troy, I'm afraid of the water. No, it's more than fear, it's a phobia. Rivers or lakes or the sea – makes no difference. Hell, standing in a puddle gives me a panic attack.'

If that last statement was an attempt at humour, then I'm not feeling it.

'You'll just have to get over it,' I say dismissively. 'It's the river or the basement – those are our only two options.'

'There they are!' The shout comes from the end of the row of shipping containers we're crouching behind. Two men, one with a tiger mask and the one wearing the rabbit mask, are sprinting towards us.

'Libby, come on.' I grab her hand and pull her towards the harbour wall. She struggles to get out of my grasp but I'm not letting go. If I have to, I'll pick her up and jump. I look over the harbour wall. The river, a good two storeys below us, undulates with dark grey-brown eddies in the evening light. Our captors are yelling at us, getting ever closer.

'Libby, trust me. Hold my hand and jump,' I order. 'I won't let you drown. I've done life-saving!'

'No. I can't. You go. Leave me. Get help.' Libby is clawing at my hand, which is still holding her other wrist. Her nails dig deep, drawing blood.

'Libby, move your arse.' I pull her forward, swinging one of my legs over the low wall.

'NO! LET ME GO! I CAN'T. LET ME GO.'

Our two captors are less than ten metres away, screaming

abuse, closing fast. Libby is screeching in my ear, still clawing at my skin. She's twisting and coiling, trying to pull free. She's bending my fingers back like she's trying to break them. Jesus! The man in the tiger mask is carrying something in his right hand. A torch?

'Stay where you are!' he yells.

'You're gonna be fucking sorry!' shouts the other.

'Libby, please trust me.' Desperation laces my words.

'Troy. Go!' Libby manages to pull away and sinks to the ground, sobbing like her heart is breaking. Our kidnappers are almost upon us.

Jump, Troy. You might never get another chance . . .

Heartsick, I swing my leg back over the wall so I'm on the same side as Libby. I see what the man in the tiger mask is holding now. A gun.

'You fuckers better get your arses back to the house. Now. Or your bodies will be found floating in that river behind you.' Tiger Man is beyond pissed. He sounds like he's a hair's breadth away from shooting us anyway, just for the hell of it.

'You don't want to test us,' adds the man in the rabbit mask, sounding equally pissed off.

Libby's head jerks up. I see the shock on her face as she stares at Rabbit Man. What did she expect? That he'd give us both a hug for trying to escape?

'Put your hands in the air. Move!' the tiger barks, waving us back the way we came with his gun.

Taking Libby's hand, I help her to her feet. Why on earth didn't I jump? The opportunity was within my grasp and I threw it away. And for what? For Libby. Even now, she still looks terrified. Haunted. A split-second decision not to leave her in that state might end up costing both of us our lives. At the very least, our best chance at escape has vanished. We're heading right back to where we started.

The walk back is excruciating. Every time I try to lower my arms, the tiger guy jabs the barrel of his gun in my back – hard. I get the message. I guess ensuring our hands are in the air as we walk keeps us off balance. Hard to run with your hands up. I can't even look at Libby. How can anyone be afraid of water, for Shaka's sake? That's like . . . that's like being afraid of the air we breathe or the food we eat. She was probably just too chicken to jump. If we'd taken a run at it and we'd tucked our legs up as we jumped, I'm sure we would've been just fine. We could've been halfway across the river by now, instead of on our way back to that dank, rank basement.

I can't bear the thought.

Maybe Libby feels about bodies of water the same way I feel about dark, enclosed spaces. When I told her we should jump into the water, she looked like she'd rather saw off her own leg than follow my suggestion. And the way she kept insisting that I should go and leave her behind . . . I glance at Libby. She's staring straight ahead. I think she really meant it about me going without her. Did the river really bother her that much? Stupid question. If it didn't, we'd both be all the way across it by now.

Oh hell! There's the house we escaped from. The only one where the bottom windows aren't boarded up. I slow as we approach it. The gun jabs into my back again, pushing me forward. In their rush to come after us, they left the front door wide open.

'Where is she?' the tiger asks the rabbit, his voice gruff.

She?

Who are they talking about? Libby's right here beside me.

We enter the house, back in this prison that smells of piss and old food. A single dim bulb provides the only light in the hall. I hate this place. Tiger and Rabbit push Libby and me forward, past the living room, towards the basement door. I can't do this. Go back down to that basement? I can't do it. I won't. I'm about to turn and take my chances when footsteps sound behind us. I look round. The man in the fox mask emerges from the sitting room – but he's not alone.

Three men – all Noughts – follow him out, each armed with a gun. None of them is wearing a mask. One Nought has curly red hair and a matching trimmed moustache and beard. The second Nought wears his blond hair in locks tied back and extending down past his shoulders. The last Nought guy is bald and wearing black jeans and a black short-sleeved T-shirt revealing upper arms each the size of one of my thighs. I stare, thrown at the sudden sight of them.

'Libby!' the fox calls out urgently.

The person in the fox mask isn't a man, but a woman. I blink in surprise. How did I miss that? Shocked, Libby spins round and utters one bewildered word.

'Mum?'

I recognize her voice straight away. '*Mum?*'

The fox stumbles towards me, still wearing her mask. The rabbit steps in front of me, reaching out to her.

'Misty? What the hell—?'

His voice . . . Ohmigod! I was right. Back at the harbour wall, when Rabbit Man threatened us, I thought I had to be going crazy, that my ears were deceiving me. The voice had sounded so like Pete's but I dismissed it as my imagination playing tricks.

It all clicks into place now. Mum – and Pete . . .

'Libby, run!' Mum calls out.

Without warning, I'm hauled backwards and pushed to the floor.

BANG! BANG! BANG! BANG!

The sound is explosive. Deafening. Like the end of the world. Troy's body covers mine as the guns go off. Ears ringing, heart pounding, I struggle to stand back up. I have to get to Mum.

'Libby, for Shaka's sake! Stay down,' Troy hisses, his breath warm in my ear. His voice is coming at me through cotton wool. I can barely hear him over my thundering heart and the continuing sound of explosions over my head. I turn my head, the only part of my body I can move. The fox is looking down at the blooms of red spreading out across her light grey hoodie. Mum pulls off her fox mask as if to get a better look, her expression pure shocked surprise – and bewilderment. Such bewilderment.

'MUM!'

Mum drops to her knees, her eyes now on me. Then she pitches forward – and is still. Behind her, Pete is already on the floor, his mask lying beside him as he looks out of the front door, staring out into nothing for all time. His gun still in his hand, Tiger Man is lying next to him. His mask is still on but he isn't moving.

I stare at Mum's body, both of us frozen in the moment. It's so clear now. My own mum and Pete snatched me off the street and kept me in a basement, just to get money out of my dad. No explanation or confirmation required. I know Mum and I know the reason why she did it. The moment both Pete and I found out who my dad was, it was inevitable that she'd pull this kind of stunt. Maybe Pete put her up to it. Maybe he didn't. Was it my threat to go through my trust-fund bank account that prompted Mum to try and rinse Dad for more cash? Or maybe it was my promise to ask if I could go and live with him instead. My own mum did this to me, put me through all this, and for what?

For money.

Lousy, stinking money.

The man in the tiger mask. I didn't know him. One of Pete's lowlife friends who agreed to help for a slice of the pie? Probably.

My mum . . . My own mum did this to me. That knowledge carves its way through me, slicing and dicing. This house, this situation is a monument to just what Mum thought of me. I was a means to an end, nothing more.

'You two, get up.' Combat boots fill my vision as the men who emerged from the living room stand before us. Troy shifts off me, then gets to his feet before grabbing hold of my hand to pull me up.

'Keep your hands where we can see them.'

Mum . . .

I turn to go to her, but Troy pulls me back, frantically shaking his head.

'That's my mum!' I cry out. 'She needs me.'

'Stay where you are, unless you want to join her,' the massive bald guy sneers. The other two men peel away from him, one heading up the stairs, the other down into the basement.

'Sh-she's dead?' I whisper, my eyes on Troy.

Grimly, Troy nods at me.

I dig my nails into my palms. Not enough. The pain isn't enough. I dig harder, raking so deep I draw blood. And still it isn't enough. I open my mouth – and a howl rises up from the very depths of my soul. It erupts from my mouth, the cry of a wounded animal.

'Shut the hell up!'

I can't stop. Even when the bald man takes a step towards me, his arm raised, I can't stop. Out of the corner of my eye, I see Troy move forward, but he isn't fast enough. The bearded man slaps my face so hard I stagger and fall. My cheek burns. I can taste blood in my mouth. The whole world tastes of blood. Troy is at my side in an instant, kneeling down to cradle me in his arms.

And me? I just want to die, but my scream dies before I do.

I clutch at Troy's arm, trying to merge his flesh with mine. If I let go, I'll sink, my mind pulled under by ragged, jagged, scrapping thoughts of my mum and what she'd done. If I let go of Troy, I'll surely sink, never to rise again. I glance over at the bodies on the floor. Yes, one of them really is my mother. I'd thought . . . I'd *hoped* . . . Mum lies still, eyes closed, entirely too motionless to be asleep.

I need to wake up. Please let me wake up.

The words are a prayer in my mind, constantly repeated.

Let me wake up.

Mum . . .

I don't dare let go of Libby. She's trembling so much that if I move she'll melt into a puddle on the floor – and I'll be only a second or two behind her. Baldie takes a step towards us. I pull Libby closer, my arms tightening round her.

'Don't hit her again. That's her mum, arsehole. You just killed her mum.'

'Then keep her quiet,' says Baldie. 'And that goes for you too.'

I can't believe I just shouted at the Nought thug waving his gun around, but I had to shout, otherwise the words would've died of fright in my mouth. Beads of sweat prickle like pin jabs all over my body. My heart is revving up so fast I expect it to burst through my ribs at any moment. I'm still having trouble absorbing it. Libby's mum was the one who abducted us. But *why*? And why me? What did she want with me? Libby's mum didn't know me from a hole in the ground. We'd only met once when I was eleven, and even then she could barely look at me. So it had to be Liberty who her mum had wanted. But then why didn't she just grab her from her own home? Why grab her from school? It made no sense. Speculation, however, would have to wait. The fact was, Libby's mum was dead, shot full of holes along with her accomplices, but by whom?

Who are these Nought men?

Libby is trembling for the both of us. I've never seen anyone killed in real life, yet here I am less than a couple of metres away from three dead bodies. My arms tighten round Libby. The rust-iron smell of blood fills my nostrils. The pools of blood beneath the bodies are no longer spreading outwards. Proof that their hearts aren't beating? Guns that have been recently fired have a very distinctive smell. A bit like fireworks but so much stronger. Is that cordite? I'm not sure, but it's a smell I know I'll never forget. My ears are still throbbing from the sound of gunfire. All the time the guns were going off, I didn't dare raise my head. At any minute, I expected to feel a bullet rip into my flesh or explode my skull. Each moment could've been my last. The gunfire has died away. My terror hasn't. Libby and I are alone with three dead bodies and three armed brutes who'd shoot us as soon as look at us.

The bald guy kicks the gun out of Tiger Man's hand, then picks it up. He twists it this way and that, examining it, then sneers, 'A replica – and not even a good one.' Dropping it on the floor, he studies me and Libby like we're specimens under a microscope.

'Is that Liberty Jackman?' The bald man's quiet voice is gruff. Chilling.

My heart begins to thump hard. Why does he want to know? Asking Libby's name is ominous. I nod slowly.

'Ding, ding, ding! Jackpot! Now listen to me, Troy. In fact, both of you, listen up,' he says. 'Amateur. Hour. Is.

Over. One word or step out of line and it'll be your last. Do as you're told and you might just make it through this.'

I look up at the bald guy towering over me. This lot have no problem showing their faces. I know what that means.

'Who are you? What do you want? Are you Nought Forever?' I ask. 'Is this about politics or money?'

'What's the difference?' The bald guy's silky smile chills my blood. 'We want something only your sister and Liberty's dad can deliver.' The bald guy winks at Libby, the mocking smile never leaving his face. 'When word reached us of what your mum was planning, well, we just had to follow them and step in when the time was right to take over. If your mother, her pathetic lover and his equally pathetic brother were still standing, I'd thank them for making our job so easy. Getting hold of both of you at the same time is a lovely bonus. My boss will be very pleased.'

'Who's your boss?' I ask.

Baldie raises an eyebrow. Yeah, it was unlikely he'd answer the question, but I had to ask.

'That's Pete's brother?' Libby whispers, indicating the man in the tiger mask lying on the floor. She's still clinging to my arms like they're a flotation device. She isn't the only one in danger of drowning.

'Yeah, that piece of shit in the tiger mask is him,' sneers the bald guy. 'Or rather it was. He came to my boss for help in return for five per cent. Five per cent? Why settle for a little when you can have the lot? His thinking was too small. We have bigger and better plans in mind for both of you.'

A shiver runs down my spine. Libby clutches at my arm that much tighter.

The other two muscle-heads come into view.

'Boss, the cellar is secure. We can stash them down there,' says the bearded guy.

'No! Don't put us back down there. Please . . .' Libby's nails are now digging into my skin. I wince but hold on to her like my life depends on it – which it probably does. The man in front of me knew my name. He had to confirm Libby's. The shoe is now on the other foot. They're here for me, not her. She's a bonus – and bonuses are expendable.

'Shut the hell up and get down there,' the blond Nought with locks hisses at Libby.

'The upstairs is deserted, but the doors don't have locks and some of the floorboards are rotten,' says the bearded guy. 'Those shitsticks lying over there obviously weren't planning on a long stay.'

'Who'd want an extended stay in this craphole?' says the blond guy.

'On your feet, you two. Get down in the basement,' says Baldie.

It takes a few seconds to untangle my arms from Libby's. I stand up, helping her to her feet. A surreptitious look around. Can we make a break for it? Two of the three thugs stand between us and the front door. The only way I could make a dash for it is if I picked up Libby and hurled her at them first. There's no point in trying to run anywhere with Libby in tow. She can barely stand up, never mind run for her life. And there's no way I can leave her behind. Plus the heavies have guns. Big frickin' guns. Real ones. Pointing straight at us. Now I'm a fast runner, but not fast enough to outrun a bullet.

My heart plummets as I realize we're going nowhere – except back to the basement. Libby snatches for and finds my hand. With guns pointing the way, we reluctantly stumble through the door and onto the stairs that lead down to our dungeon. The air smells slightly fresher due to the fact that the door has been open for a while – but only slightly. The room is still uncomfortably warm, the air still stale. We've only taken a couple of steps when the door slams shut behind us and there comes the sound of bolts being pushed shut, top and bottom. We make our slow way back down the stairs. Libby and I turn as one at the bottom, staring up in dismay at the now bolted door. Our last chance of freedom has slipped through our fingers.

'I'm sorry, Troy,' Libby whispers. 'I should've tried harder to jump, but I . . . Mum used to pull on my legs when I was having a bath to drag my head under the water. I can't bear the thought of being underwater. I'm so sorry. My mum . . . she did this. My mum and her pondscum boyfriend Pete and his equally lowlife brother.' Libby's voice is barely audible. 'Now we've gone from the frying pan into the raging fire.'

'I don't understand. Why would your own mum do something like this?'

'For money. What else?' says Libby sombrely. 'Mum blitzed through the trust fund Dad set up for me. I found out, so I guess this was her way of trying to get more out of him.'

Frowning, I scrutinize her. I don't like the way she's speaking – in a monotone. And she looks so calm. Too calm. I mean, Shaka wept! Libby's mum would do that to her? *Really?* She'd set all this up just for money? Well, Libby has no doubt about it. And, if that is the case, then her mum has paid for it. I will never forget the way the blood spread across her fleecy jacket when she was shot, or the look on her face when she realized.

I sit down on the nearest crate near the stairs, unwilling to get too far away from the door.

'What d'you think this lot are after?' whispers Libby, sitting down next to me.

'The same thing as your mum and her boyfriend, I expect. Money – if we're lucky.'

'What does that mean?'

I shake my head. What's the point of making Libby even more anxious than she already is? Something tells me that those men above want more than mere money. This has something to do with my sister defending Tobey Durbridge. Do they want her to dump him as her client? Back off? Deliberately throw the case? What?

The problem is, I know my sister. She can be led but not driven, as Mum says. And someone trying to blackmail Callie into giving up or losing this case? Never gonna happen. Callie has never allowed, and will never allow, anyone to bully her. So where does that leave Libby and me?

In the middle of nowhere.

'We're going to die, aren't we?'

I glare at Libby. 'What the hell kind of question is that? No, we're not going to die. Bollocks to that. Those dickheads upstairs need us alive.'

Libby looks at me and nods once. Once is enough. Maybe

she believes me. Maybe she doesn't. Maybe her mind is still on her mum. But, in that moment, *I* believed me. That is enough. We're going to find a way out of this.

Libby bows her head. Tears run down her cheeks, picking up the pace with each passing second. But she's quiet. Sobbing silently. I place a tentative arm round her shoulder, giving her every chance to tell me to back off. Instead, she turns into my body and her tears become a waterfall. Hugging her to me, I hold her tight while she cries for her mum and what might've been and what was.

THEN

fifty-six. Tobey

The studio lights were blinding, casting everything behind them in shadow. I closed my eyes, gathering myself while the host of *Guest of the Week*, Kennedy Coughlan, had powder applied to his brown forehead to reduce its sheen.

'Thank you for agreeing to be tonight's guest,' Ken said to me as the make-up artist buzzed round him with her brushes, dabbing at this and brushing at that. 'But, let me tell you now, I think it would be a disaster if you became Prime Minister. You Noughts are responsible for most of the problems in this country and your own political views are naïve at best—'

'Five!' announced the studio manager.

'And wilfully ignorant and out of your depth at worst,' Ken continued.

'Four!'

Ken smirked at me while I regarded him, momentarily stunned. But only momentarily. So it was like that, was it? Good to know. If he was going to come at me, guns blazing, I needed to be ready to spike his guns and no messing. Eyes narrowed, my mouth snapped shut. It wasn't the first time an interviewer had tried to knock me off my stride just before a live interview and it sure as hell wouldn't be the last. It was a common tactic to put me on the back foot. None had been quite as blatant as this, but it was nothing I couldn't handle.

'Three!' The studio manager counted down the last two numbers on her fingers.

'Welcome, ladies and gentlemen, to *Guest of the Week*. Tonight's guest is Tobias Durbridge, MP, who has ambitions to become this country's first Nought Prime Minister after the general election next month. The mind boggles!' Ken raised his eyebrows as if sharing a private joke with his viewers before he turned to face me. I acknowledged him with a professional smile, ignoring his last snarky remark.

'So tell me, Tobey, how does it feel to be the first Nought to stand a real chance of becoming this country's Prime Minister?'

Yawn-snore! How many times was I going to be asked that unimaginative question? Jesus, it was so boring to be asked that over and over. 'How does it feel to be the first Nought blah–blah?' Pfft! As I am, was and always will be a Nought, how the hell can I compare it to being anything else? And the thing that pissed me off the most? I really couldn't remember any Cross political candidate being asked how it felt to be a Cross doing the same job. No Cross was asked what it was like to be the Cross anything. That was just taken as the default position. It was as if the rest of us who were WAME – white and mixed-ethnic – were aberrations. And how much did I hate that acronym? How insulting was that? Crosses were one group and everyone else got lumped into the WAME category like we were all one big, homogenous mass and not worthy of distinct categorization. We Noughts were always being accused of playing the race card. If the Crosses would stop dealing it, I would be more than happy to stop playing it.

'I would deem it an honour to be elected Prime Minister of our great country. It would mean the electorate had faith in my abilities and my determination to get the job done.'

Dan and his battalion of media trainers had taught me that, far from trying to downplay my Noughtiness, as they mockingly called it, I should use it, abuse it, lean into it and make sure it was in everyone's face.

'I believe the people of this country are ready for something new. A new perspective, a new vision. I hope they see me as the new broom that will sweep away the old complacent, stagnant practices.'

Ken, move on, you tosser.

Like a heavyweight boxer training for a title fight, I'd trained for these media sharks. Trained hard. I'd had mock interviews running into double figures to get me ready for people like Ken Coughlan.

Years ago, when Dan and I decided that I'd run for Mayor of Meadowview, we'd had a conversation I'd never forgotten. It had taken place in his penthouse when I was a lot more naïve than I am now.

'The press is gonna come at you like an express train,' Dan told me. 'They'll use and abuse you as clickbait and to sell advertising. As the media won't think twice about exploiting you, you need to return the favour.'

'How d'you mean?'

'If the press lies about you, shout it out long and loud.

Let everyone know they're lying. If they tell the truth, shout out longer and louder that they're lying. Whatever they say, they're lying. Shout false information. That's how to win the mayoral election.'

At my puzzled look, Dan gave a long-suffering sigh, like he was talking to an idiot. I admit, it pissed me off.

'You want to get not just your supporters but everyone not believing a word the press says about you. That way, when the press realizes you can't be bought, taught or manipulated and they come at you with the truth, no one will believe them.'

'And you reckon that will work?' I asked, unconvinced.

'It has in the past,' said Dan. 'Most of the media in Albion stopped reporting the news years ago. Now it's opinion and soundbites taken from social media. That's going to be their downfall. Too many modern reporters think that presenting the news is all about giving opposing views equal airtime. I say the sky is red with green stripes; you say it's purple with pink and orange spots. Lazy journalists will present both our views as the story of the sky. Smart journalists stick their heads out of the window and check the facts for themselves before reporting back on what's accurate and what's not. Luckily, there aren't too many smart journalists around these days.'

'Jesus, that's cold, Dan.'

'No, that's accurate,' he shot back. 'If reporters are too lazy to do their jobs properly, we're going to exploit that. If the view of Joe Nobody from across the road is given the same weight as an expert with a PhD in their field, we can use that to our advantage.'

'What makes you so smart about this all of a sudden?' I asked.

'It's not all of a sudden,' said Dan. 'It's thanks to Eva. She got me educated and encouraged me to think, to find out facts and figures and the truth for myself.'

His eyes took on a soft, kindly light that had me blinking in stunned amazement. I'd never seen that kind of light in Dan's eyes when he was talking about anyone else. This woman – whoever she was – seemed to be his one and only weakness.

'When will I get to meet this paragon?' I said.

'We'll see,' he dismissed.

Why was he so keen to keep me away from her?

'Now I reckon the media will build you up and indulge you while they think you don't stand a chance, but the moment it looks like you might actually win? That's when the knives, bullets and poison will come out,' Dan continued. 'They'll ridicule you, they'll drag up your past, they'll make up stuff about you or slant the truth. You've got to be ready for all that and you've got to grow a hide thicker than a rhino's. If you don't think you can do that, say so now. Don't waste everyone's time, especially mine. I don't back losers.'

'I'm not a loser. And I'm not a quitter. I can do this,' I insisted.

And here I was, just scant weeks away from fulfilling my ultimate dream, but I had this interview to get through first.

'Tobey, isn't it true that Dan Jeavons, the notorious underworld figure, bankrolled your campaign when you ran for Mayor of Meadowview?' asked Ken.

'May I remind you that Dan Jeavons is a legitimate businessman. Yes, he has served time in prison, but he's put his past behind him. Or rather he would, if the press stopped throwing his past actions in his face. He and I were at school together. We're friends. I don't turn my back on my friends. This attempt by the opposition to paint me guilty by association is beneath contempt. Now perhaps you'd like to ask me some questions regarding my politics and policies rather than my friends and associates?'

Ken nodded, satisfied that by mentioning Dan he'd done enough to sow a few seeds of doubt in people's minds about the type of person I called friend.

'OK, Tobey, let's talk about your political failings to date,' said Ken, bringing me back to the present. 'You were Mayor of Meadowview for almost five years before you became a Member of Parliament for the opposition. During that time, Nought-on-Nought crime in Meadowview increased from ten deaths a year at the start of your tenure to five times that by the time you left office. The number of pupils excluded from Meadowview schools more than doubled each year you were Mayor. The number of homeless in Meadowview quadrupled. Based on that track record, why on earth should anyone vote for you to become this country's next Prime Minister? So that you can do to the entire country what you did to Meadowview?'

There was a silky smile on his lips as he let that land.

Breathe in.

Breathe out.

This was live TV. No re-dos. No second chances.

'How interesting that you refer to crime in Meadowview as Nought-on-Nought crime,' I began. 'Statistically, crimes tend to happen within the same communities, whether it's within a family unit or any narrower section of the community. For example, over ninety per cent of all murders in this entire country are perpetrated by Crosses against other Crosses. Yet these are never referred to as Cross-on-Cross crimes. They're just referred to as crimes. It's interesting that crimes are never colour-coded in this country unless they're committed by Noughts. But, to answer your question, during my tenure as Mayor, the government saw fit to cut all funding to Meadowview by over forty per cent. Forty-three per cent to be exact—'

'That's as may be but—'

'You asked me a question, please allow me to answer it.' I interrupted Ken's interruption, adding just enough steel to my voice to make him shut up. 'No other region in the country had to suffer the swingeing cuts that Meadowview was forced to endure. Youth centres and libraries had to close. Social care for the elderly, the very young and the vulnerable also had to be severely cut back. We had to shut our parks at six in the evening and close them completely on Sundays. Home-building schemes had to be abandoned. Now some people have speculated that Meadowview had to endure such draconian funding cuts as the price for electing their first Nought Mayor to office.'

'You can't be suggesting—'

'I didn't say me, Ken, I said "some people". It's interesting that when I became an MP and the next Mayor of Meadow-view took over – who happened to be a Cross, affiliated with the current government – all Meadowview's funding was not only reinstated but increased on top of that by twelve per cent. Don't you find that interesting?'

Ken's smile had fallen off his face and found its way onto mine.

Suck on that, you bastard.

'I can honestly say that, if I am elected Prime Minister, I'll ensure that regional funding is allocated based on need and nothing else.' I mentally sat forward, though I remained upright and relaxed in my chair, as had been drilled into me by my media trainers.

It was on.

Isabella Monroe, my full-time executive assistant and part-time lover, had insisted that I couldn't duck out of doing *Guest of the Week* any longer. Kennedy Coughlan had even started making snide comments on social media about me constantly turning him down. I wasn't. I just couldn't stand the man. Ken was a Cross presenter of unshakeable reputation. He wore his famous black suit and gold tie like a suit of armour and, along with his manicured moustache and trim beard, he was instantly recognizable and revered. He was below average height, a number of centimetres shorter than me, and had a deep, melodious voice. A voice that whispered subliminally in a dulcet tone – *trust me*. And most people in the country did. Very few knew what a womanizing, dodgy scumbag Ken Coughlan truly was. The *Guest of the Week* programme was his personal weekly platform to annihilate his enemies. And, lucky me, it was my turn.

I addressed the rest of his points, taking each in turn and making sure not to appear flustered or peeved. That wouldn't do at all. Ken allowed me to make my points, but stated when I'd finished, 'Aren't these just excuses to try to cover up your incompetence?'

'Kennedy, you don't need to be a genius or even particularly good at maths to appreciate that, with forty per cent less money between one year and the next, services are inevitably going to suffer. If I'm making a coat and you take away almost half my material, you can't expect me to make a coat of the same length and quality.'

'Well, I'll leave it for our viewers to decide whether or not your excuses are even remotely valid,' said Ken directly to the camera.

'Way to be impartial, Ken.'

'I'm totally impartial,' he bristled indignantly.

Damn! This man wasn't even trying to hide his antagonism towards me. Good! What I needed to do now was make him even angrier.

'I understand your need to defend the current government.' I shrugged. 'After all, your sister was Secretary of State for Education, your brother-in-law is a top civil servant and your daughter Yasmin did a year-long unpaid internship with the Minister of Justice. How lovely that Yasmin can afford to work for an entire year with no pay. I can't think of many twenty-two-year-olds in Meadowview who could afford to work so long for so little.'

'We're not here to talk about my daughter,' said Ken furiously.

'True, but, Ken, you did just say you were impartial, which is a blatant lie.'

'I beg your pardon—'

'Well, you're best friends with Felu Farjeon, the Chancellor. Felu has one of the top three jobs in government. How can you be impartial?'

'Felu and I may be friends, but that has no impact on how I do my job,' Ken argued.

'None?'

'Absolutely none.'

'So he never tells you how or who to interview?'

'Of course not,' Ken dismissed. 'And, if you don't mind, this is my show. I ask the questions here.'

I studied Ken, feigning puzzlement. 'You had lunch with Felu on Wednesday. Are you saying my name wasn't mentioned throughout your entire meal?'

'We had better things to talk about than you,' Ken said, not even attempting to hide his abject contempt.

That was what I was waiting to hear. I pulled my phone out of my jacket pocket and pressed an icon on the screen before laying it down on the table between us. A conversation recorded two days ago immediately began to play.

'*I'm interviewing that jumped-up blanker bastard on Friday. The ex-Mayor of Blanker Town.*'

Ken's voice played out loud and clear. He prided himself on his distinctive tones. Let him try to deny that was him.

'*Tobias Durbridge?*' said a male voice in answer to Ken's statement.

I turned to the TV camera, addressing the viewers directly. 'This was recorded two days ago, on Wednesday at lunchtime. The voices you can hear are Ken having lunch with the Chancellor, Felu Farjeon, in case any of you are wondering about the second male voice.'

I turned back to Ken, faux relaxing in my chair. Ken leaned forward to snatch up my phone. I got in first. I held it in my hand, swiping to turn the volume up to its maximum setting.

'Where did you get that? That's an illegal recording,' Ken said furiously.

'*Don't worry about Durbridge,*' said Felu, his tone over-flowing with disdain. '*By this time next week, his own kind will have voted him out of office. Blankers don't know a damned thing about loyalty.*'

'*Don't underestimate the stupidity of the public – or Durbridge,*' said Ken. '*He's tenacious. The little weasel has had a taste of power now. He won't give it up easily.*'

'*He won't have any choice. All you need do is hit him with the decline in Meadowview services under his reign. Five years of minimum funding took their toll. Make sure the blame is laid at that blanker's door and don't let him try to place it elsewhere.*'

'*Well, the blanker has finally agreed to appear on my pro-gramme.*' Ken's laugh was distinctive. '*Crucifying him is going to be the highlight of my month. Hell, my year! And, when he's down and can't get up again, I will shake his hand. I wouldn't want it to appear that my attack on him is personal.*'

As the two of them laughed heartily, I stopped the audio broadcast. That was enough. Ken and I sat in silence, watching each other. He stared at me, his brown eyes sparking with fury. The clapback from this would mean both he and Felu Farjeon would lose their jobs – and we both knew it.

Did I feel sorry for him?

Did I bollocks! I was a master of the deeply satisfying art of not giving a damn.

'How did you get that recording?' asked Ken at last.

'It was emailed to me,' I replied. 'The person who sent it signed their email: "a concerned Meadowview citizen". Maybe it was someone at an adjacent table? Or perhaps a disgruntled waiter or waitress you neglected to tip? But like I said — and as you and your friend the Chancellor of the Exchequer have just confirmed — my budgets were deliberately slashed in an effort to drive me from the political arena. The government might hate my guts, but they had no right to make the people of Meadowview suffer because of it. All I can say is, roll on the general election so that the people of this great country can let the current government know exactly what they think of such tactics.'

Waves of animosity washed over me as Ken stared a hole right through me. I met his animosity with a slight beatific smile. Let the TV viewers see me in all my unthreatening glory. The contrast between Ken and me would be even starker.

The rest of the interview was anticlimactic. Ken continued to ask me questions, which I answered fully and evenly. Once the interview was over, he leaned forward, his hand held out. I looked at it, then at him and shook the proffered sweaty object.

The moment the producer announced we were no longer on the air, I snatched back my hand, making a show of wiping my palm on my trouser leg.

'You son of a bitch!' Ken announced.

I leaned forward, one hand over the radio mic on my jacket lapel, and said for his ears only, 'Do unto others as they would do unto you, only do it first.'

'You'll pay for this.' Ken's dark brown eyes were almost black with rage, his face set in an ugly snarl.

'Now, Ken, should I turn on my camera phone and record this too? I'd be more than happy to put it on my website.'

'Fuck you, Durbridge.'

I took out my phone and held it up between Ken and me. 'Could you repeat that, please?'

'Fuck. You. Durbridge,' Ken obliged.

What an arse!

One of the many satisfying things about power was seeing the bodies of your enemies float by on the river of life while you watched from the bank, eating popcorn.

'And a merry Crossmas to you too,' I replied, even though we were only a few months into the new year.

Switching off my phone, I removed my radio mic and headed off the set. There, waiting for me, was Dan Jeavons – my campaign manager, chief backer and friend of old. Next to him was his second in command, Jarvis Burton. Jarvis, a particularly nasty piece of work, wore his wavy brown hair styled in a top plait with buzz-cut sides, military style. He looked every centimetre the hard man he was. Dan took particular delight in telling me some of the things Jarvis had done on his behalf. Tales to frighten children and adults alike. Dan had chosen his lieutenant well. Jarvis didn't say much, but he didn't miss a thing, and I had it on good authority that he was not just vicious but ruthless when crossed.

'So how did I do?' I asked Dan softly.

He grinned at me. 'That was a masterclass.'

'It should be good for a couple of days' headlines at least.'

'Yes, Minister,' Dan agreed with a smile. 'Or should I say, yes, Prime Minister?'

We exchanged a smile. It hadn't happened yet and I didn't believe in counting my chickens, but we both knew the job was all but mine. I didn't know how Dan did it and I didn't particularly care, but he always managed to winkle out all the dirty little secrets that everyone in the public eye tried to keep hidden. And everyone had them. Many an incompetent, failing MP had stayed in power because of the secrets they knew. Those personal, potentially explosive details that others in power tried so desperately to keep buried.

Including me.

There was one secret in particular . . . And, if it ever saw the light of day, I didn't doubt for a second that I'd be banged up and doing time until my hair had turned grey. There was nothing I wouldn't do to protect myself. Absolutely nothing.

And both Dan and I knew that.

fifty-seven. Callie

As I waited for the kettle to boil, I looked out of the kitchenette window, watching the world scurry by while the afternoon took its time. I hadn't grown out of my habit of people watching. It was like a hobby, making guesses about the lives of those coming into and leaving our offices, seeing what I could tell about them from their clothes, the way they carried themselves, the way they moved in relation to other people. Where I had the chance to check my suppositions, I didn't do too badly. In fact, nine times out of ten my observations were spot on.

Watching Tobey on *Guest of the Week* the previous evening was a case in point. From the time Tobey was introduced by Ken Coughlan, I could tell by the way he was sitting and the smile on his lips that came nowhere near his eyes that he could smell blood in the water. I wasn't even going to watch the programme until I heard who the guest would be. Seeing Tobey on the TV was as close as I'd got to him since university. And even then it wasn't as if we'd exactly hung out together. Too much lay unresolved between us. But, I have to admit, I was glad I wasn't Ken Coughlan as I watched *Guest of the Week*. It'd been brutal. The news headlines this morning had been full of analyses of the programme. By the end of the week, I fully expected to hear that Ken had resigned – if he had any sense.

Once the kettle had boiled, I made my way back to my office with a black coffee for me and a herbal nasty for Stacy, the Nought temporary secretary who'd been working for me for over a year. With Sol's blessing, I'd offered Stacy a permanent position – and more than once – but each time she'd turned me down.

'I make far more money working freelance,' she told me. 'And if you piss me off, I'm out the door with no notice and no goodbye. Why would I want that to change?'

Which was fair enough!

I passed Stacy her herbal mess. 'Any calls or letters I should know about?'

She shook her head. 'The important correspondence is on your desk or attached to the notifications on your electronic notepad. The rest is just the usual nonsense from a couple of Nought Forever pinheads threatening you with all sorts for prosecuting one of their members last year.'

'Oh, boohoo!' I exclaimed, unimpressed. 'God, that lot need to be dropped down a deep mineshaft.'

'Amen to that,' Stacy agreed. 'They're worse than the Liberation Militia, and God knows the L.M. were bad enough.'

'Yeah, but Nought Forever have denounced violence,' I quoted, deadpan.

'My arse!' Stacy said at once. 'They've just put a suit and tie on it, is all.'

I nodded and headed into my office behind Stacy's desk. Funny, I didn't remember closing the door. I very rarely did that during the day; only when making confidential phone calls or conducting sensitive interviews, neither of which I'd done. It was only as I sat down at my desk that I noticed him sitting on my sofa, which he'd pushed back against the wall.

Jon Duba – who had the uncanny knack of turning up unexpectedly, alarm systems and secretaries be damned. I shook my head as he winked at me. This was exactly the way we'd met two years ago, with him turning up at my office unannounced and uninvited.

There he'd sat, a middle-aged Nought guy with close-cut, salt-and-pepper hair, wearing round glasses, black trousers, a dark brown polo shirt and a black leather jacket. I'd stared in shock. Behind those glasses, lime-green eyes watched me, unconcerned. Then he'd smiled.

'Who are you and how the hell did you get into my office?'

'Hello, Miss Hadley. I'm Jon Duba, rhymes with tuba. Employ me as your covert investigator and I'll tell you anything you want to know.'

'How about I phone for security and have your arse arrested? Then you can tell the police how you got in here.'

Jon shrugged. 'Feel free. By the way, I'm an ex-copper. You'll find that useful when I work for you.'

I stood up slowly and started edging towards the door. This was obviously a nutty-nut, and the sooner I took myself out of arm's reach, the better.

'I took early retirement due to injury on the job. After that, I did a few courses. One was in computer science, and now there's not a computer on the planet that I can't hack into. You'll find that useful also,' said Jon.

'And why should I take you on?' I couldn't help asking.

'Because you need me. You just don't know how much yet,' he said. 'I'll tell you what – I'll work for you for free for the rest of the month. If you then decide that you can do without me, I'm gone with no hard feelings.' He dusted off his hands as he spoke to emphasize his words. 'However, if you decide to keep me, you pay me for my first month's work. Deal?'

'No.' Was this man for real? 'I don't know you from a hole in the ground.'

'How about I prove to you right here and now how good I am?'

'How d'you propose to do that?'

'Ask me three things about you, your work, your life that you think I won't know,' said Jon. 'If I answer all three correctly, you give me a job.'

OK, I admit it. I was intrigued. I stopped edging towards the door and eyed Jon speculatively. He smiled, knowing he had me.

'All right. I'll play. What was my dad's middle name?'

'Ryan.'

I stared. How the hell . . . ? My dad's middle name was a matter of public record: after all he'd had to give his full name when he appeared in court. But the fact that this man before me had done enough research to know that . . .

'OK, OK. Second question.'

'This is fun,' said Jon, settling back in his chair.

'What's the love of my life?'

'The law.'

'Too easy.'

'You asked it,' Jon pointed out.

'Right. Third question.' I racked my brains for some obscure question to which only I knew the answer. Then this nutjob would be out of my office, hopefully without ructions. 'What's the biggest regret of my life?'

Jon studied me, his eyes narrowing like he was trying to read my mind.

Ha! Got him. 'Don't let the door hit you on your way out.' I made my way back to my desk.

'Do you mean your biggest regret or your greatest regret?' asked Jon.

'What's the difference?'

'Your biggest regret would be defending Iain Seagrove and him being found not guilty when he was charged with murdering his wife. He was as guilty as sin. Two years later, he murdered his girlfriend and you've always felt . . . responsible. Your greatest regret, however, is telling Tobey Durbridge that you hoped his child with Misty Jackman would die.'

My mouth fell open and stayed that way. No one knew that. No one. Only me and Tobey, and I sure as hell hadn't told anyone. I was too ashamed. Who had Tobey told that this man should get to hear about it? I stared at Jon. Who *was* he?

'Do I have the job then?' he asked.

'I should have you thrown out on your ear.'

'Probably,' he said. 'But do I have the job?'

That was my introduction to Jon Duba, my covert

investigator, my friend and the greatest pain in my ass. To this day, he hasn't told me how he knew so much about me.

'You enjoy sneaking into my office, don't you?' I said, eyebrows raised. 'What d'you do? Wait for Stacy to pop to the ladies and then make your move?'

'I could tell you, but then I'd have to kill you.'

'Then, by all means, keep it to yourself.' I sat down, sipping my coffee. 'So are you here for a specific reason or just to be a general nuisance?'

'Charming!' said Jon, unfazed. 'I come bearing news.'

'Oh yes?'

'Solomon has put your name forward to become a circuit judge in the current round of selections and it looks like it might just happen.'

I stared, astounded – which was my default mode when talking to Jon. And, what's more, he loved it! 'How on earth do you know that?'

Jon tapped the side of his nose. 'I have my sources.'

Which is what he always said when I asked him how he knew stuff.

Solomon was my head of chambers as well as my friend, but he'd never said anything about putting my name forward for such a prestigious position.

My eyes narrowed. 'Hang on. Don't I have to be a district judge before I can be considered for the role of circuit judge? I'm just a barrister.'

'They brought in a fast-track scheme for exceptional barristers with a number of years' court experience.'

'I know that, Jon, but only one barrister has ever been fast-tracked that way, to my knowledge.'

He shrugged. 'Well, you're more than qualified. And you win far more cases than you lose. There's another reason – but you won't like it.'

Uh-oh! 'I'm listening.'

'All the current circuit judges are Crosses,' said Jon. 'If you're appointed, the fact that you're half Nought won't hurt.'

'I see.'

Already I was bristling. When was this BS going to stop? Years ago, I'd watched others on my course with lower grades get offered pupillage way before I found a law chambers prepared to take me on. That was part of the reason why I was so grateful to Sol for giving me a chance. And I'd worked my arse off, determined to make sure that he never regretted it. On one of my first independent cases as a green barrister, a Nought court official, Martin Morris, refused to let me enter a courtroom through the officials' entrance until he'd fully checked my credentials. Other Cross barristers, however, were allowed to swan past me, completely unchecked. It'd been intensely humiliating. To this day, Mr Morris and I kept it strictly professional; no pleasantries were ever exchanged.

'I have issues with being a political appointee. If they're looking for a diversity poster girl, they can fuck off and look elsewhere,' I said, rearing up on my high horse. 'I've had it with people looking down on me because one of my parents was a Nought.'

'Cool your jets. I said it's another reason, not the only reason,' Jon pointed out. 'You're not the problem; you're the solution. Besides, you're one of the best barristers in the country and you know it, so don't get sniffy.'

'Hmmm.' I was only slightly mollified.

Jon pursed his lips, raising his chin as if issuing a challenge. 'I should congratulate you on your forthcoming promotion, but I'm not going to.'

'Excuse me?'

'If you become a circuit judge, you won't need my services any more. You'll be presiding over cases, not investigating the facts of them.' Jon sighed. 'It's taken me two years to train you up and get you used to my way of working. Now that's all out the window. This displeases me.'

'Whoa! Can we roll back a bit? Are you sure about this?'

Jon drew himself up, his shoulders back. 'My sources and resources are impeccable. I don't open my mouth unless I'm sure. You ought to know that by now,' he said haughtily. 'As long as you don't drop a heavy object on the Chief Law Chancellor's foot, it's a done deal.'

'Why hasn't Sol told me this himself?' I asked.

'You'd have to take that up with your boss, not me.' Jon shrugged. 'But, if you want my advice, wait for him to bring up the subject and then act surprised and grateful. He won't like it if he knows we're ahead of him on this.'

Which was sage advice. Solomon already thought Jon was dodgy AF.

Circuit judge . . . It was what I'd hoped for, but I didn't think it'd happen for at least another eight to nine years at the earliest. To become a circuit judge at my age would be the stuff of dreams.

'Meanwhile, back down to earth, your current case has a major problem,' said Jon.

'How so?'

'Beatrice Fairley, the innocent client whom you're so vigorously defending? The woman accused of killing her sister? She's as guilty as sin. What's more, I can prove it.'

Son of a bitch!

'How? Beatrice has an alibi. She was captured on CCTV filling her car with petrol.'

'And she paid at the pump, didn't she?'

'So? Are you saying the footage was doctored?' I frowned.

'Of course not. The woman driving Beatrice's car and wearing Beatrice's clothes wasn't Beatrice. It was Lily, her seventeen-year-old daughter, who passed her test three months before the murder. The CCTV footage shows a blonde woman wearing a cap and Beatrice's distinctive T-shirt and ripped jeans. Beatrice's daughter kept her head down the entire time she was at the petrol station so the camera couldn't get a close-up of her face, but she forgot to mask her hands.'

'What about them?'

'Even though Beatrice is a widow, she still wears her wedding ring. Her daughter Lily's fingers were all bare. Plus Beatrice is left-handed and Lily is right-handed. You can clearly see her using her right hand to fill the car's tank and to pay at the pump.'

'Hardly conclusive evidence,' I pointed out.

'But enough for the prosecution to establish some doubt,' said Jon. 'And, as the prosecutor is your ex, you know he's going to do everything he can to win, especially as it's against you.'

Which was true. There was no love lost between Gabriel and me. He still couldn't believe I'd kicked him to the kerb for being an ass hat to my brother.

'Once you let Beatrice Fairley know that you have proof she wasn't driving her car that night, she'd be a fool not to change her plea.'

I shook my head. 'Jon, why d'you insist on doing that? My client pleaded not guilty. By telling me that you can prove she's a liar, you've effectively scuppered my case.' And not for the first time either.

Jon shrugged, unconcerned. He knew full well that, as a barrister appointed by the state, I was not allowed to knowingly deceive the court. I either had to advise my client to change her plea or find a new lawyer, or I'd have to tread very carefully to ensure I didn't put someone else on the hook in my efforts to get my client off it.

'If you insist on defending the guilty, this is what you get.' Jon was unrepentant.

'Jon, I've told you before, I can't pick and choose like that. Under the law, everyone is entitled to a fair trial.'

'Oh, spare me, please!' he dismissed. 'Your client bumped off her sister Rosalind so she could hop into bed with her sister's husband, Carl.'

'She what?' I said, stunned.

'Beatrice and her sister's husband have been having an affair for over a year now. He wouldn't or couldn't leave his wife so your client decided to make up his mind for him. He's been crying big crocodile tears about losing his wife, but she was barely cold before he was back in bed with Beatrice.'

'How d'you know?'

'Something smelled wrong about this case so I followed him for a few days. I thought he might've hired someone to kill his wife, but, when I found out about his affair and his alibi was solid, I turned my attention to the victim's sister. You've got to stop defending these lowlifes, Callie. It's beneath you.'

'The guilty are just as entitled to a legal defence as the innocent,' I argued. Again. It wasn't the first time we'd had this conversation.

'Guilty or innocent, my job is to find out the whole truth,' said Jon. 'Not bend it, shape it or present you with the edited highlights.'

'All right.' I sighed. 'Show me everything you've got.'

'You can thank me later.' Jon smiled, breaking out his tablet to show me the footage he'd duplicated.

'Thank *you*? Pfft!' I derided. 'Jon, you've just made my case and my life that much more complicated.'

He winked again. 'You're welcome!'

fifty-eight. Tobey

Dan wasn't alone when I entered his penthouse. Jarvis was behind the bar, pouring himself a ginger ale. A Nought woman wearing the tightest, shortest red dress I've ever seen lounged on the sofa, long legs crossed and flicking through a fashion magazine. I'll say one thing for Dan, he had taste. The woman wore her red hair braided and decorated with painted beads. Blood-red varnish adorned both her toes and fingernails. She was stunning – and what's more she knew it.

'Honey, why don't you go and wait for me in the bedroom?' said Dan.

The woman smiled at him, dropped the magazine and immediately did as she was told, but not before giving me an appraising look. I turned to Dan, annoyed.

'Godsake, Dan. This was supposed to be a meeting between the two of us. I don't want your side chick listening in.'

'Who? Abby?' he chortled. 'I trust her before I'd trust you.'

I raised an eyebrow but bit back my retort. If that's how he felt, I wasn't inclined to argue. If he didn't know by now that women couldn't be trusted, he'd learn sooner or later.

I toyed with the idea of taking Abby away from Dan, just to disprove his words about who could and couldn't be trusted. I didn't doubt for a second that Abby would be happy to swap Dan for me. I recognized the look she gave me – I'd seen it enough times. Power was the greatest aphrodisiac on the planet. But then what? I was within arm's length of getting everything I'd ever dreamed of. Not only was I predicted to keep my parliamentary seat, but the smart money was on my party, the Democratic Alliance, winning the upcoming election and I was on track to be voted the next Prime Minister by the electorate. It was such a headrush. A constant buzz. Tobias Durbridge, Prime Minister. God, I loved the way the words sounded in my head. Saying them out loud would be even better. Even ten short years ago, a Nought Prime Minister would've been unthinkable, yet here I was with my eyes on the prize that was within my grasp. And it was all thanks to the man in front of me. Dan was useful. Now wasn't the time to antagonize him. I walked over to his oversized windows. Dan moved to stand beside me.

'Jarvis, go and keep Abby company,' he ordered.

Without a word, Jarvis headed for the bedroom. The door closed with a barely audible click. That was Jarvis. He did everything with silent precision. He could sneak up behind you and slit your throat, and the first thing you'd hear was the sound of your own blood gushing out. Dan had taken great pleasure in recounting a couple of times when Jarvis had to do exactly that – on Dan's orders of course.

'Ken Coughlan resigned a couple of hours ago and was threatening to sue you. Just so you know.'

I frowned. 'Sue me? For what? For revealing what a racist scumbag he is?'

'His lawyers called it prejudicial disclosure.'

My snort of derision was instant. Hellsake! Lawyers! The spawn of vampires and vultures. 'I'm assuming you handled it?'

Dan smiled. 'Of course. I threatened to broadcast the rest of the covert recording where he boasted about his affair with his producer, and his wife being too stupid to realize. Surprise, surprise! The lawsuit was withdrawn.'

'Yeah, I bet it was,' I said dryly. 'Ken's no fool. Losing his job is one thing. Losing half of everything he owns if his wife divorces him is something else entirely.'

'Tobey, be careful. Playing that recording on Coughlan's show has made both of us a lot of powerful enemies.' Dan's voice held a warning. 'They'll be waiting in the wings, biding their time.'

Tell me something I didn't know.

'Pfft! Let them bring it,' I dismissed. 'Thanks to you and your sources, I have the dirt on a number of officials and politicians and, if they decide to come at me, I'll make sure they know it. Ken Coughlan got off lightly.'

Dan and I stood in silence, side by side, looking out of his window. I gazed out across the city nightscape. Tower blocks and office complexes had sprouted ever higher like weeds searching for limited light. Vast shopping centres had devoured all but the hardiest local shops. There was a time when the sheer scale of the view, the urban majesty of it, would've stolen my breath away.

Not any more.

'Look down there, way down on the ground, at all those people scurrying like ants to get home, to go to work, to lead their trivial lives. Like Eva says, for every ten stupid people in this world, there are another hundred stupid people.' Dan's lips twisted into a sneer. The utter contempt seeping from his every pore was disturbing. 'Sometimes I stand here and feel that, with the sweep of my arm or the stomp of one foot, I could eradicate them all.'

Dan's words clanged like a great bell in my head. He turned to me with a sudden laugh, his expression clearing. 'Don't mind me. The view from this window is sometimes . . . intoxicating. This is a city ripe for the taking, if you have the balls to step up.'

Where was Dan going with this?

'What do you see out there, Tobey?' he asked.

'I see the best city in the world,' I replied.

'Damn right. And soon it will be all yours,' he replied silkily. 'This world is full of sheeple, not people, all longing to be told what to do, how to think. Sheeple who are lost without someone to follow. And you know the best part? Even when most of them know they're being led over a cliff, they'll still follow because it's less effort than thinking for themselves. It's the human condition.'

Silence. I let Dan's cynical words sink in, recognizing them for what they were. The thing that gave me pause was that I agreed with them. I was a man now, not an idealistic boy. The truth, no matter how excruciatingly painful, was still the truth. It'd taken me a long time to understand that.

Unbidden, Callie Rose Hadley crept into my mind. I

shook my head, mentally slamming the door in her smiling face. She had a nasty habit of doing that, creeping up on me and entering my thoughts before I could check myself. And she never came alone but dragged a whole world full of longings and regrets with her. Stop it! Time to return to the matter at hand.

Dan moved over to the bar, pouring himself a quality single malt whisky. No cheap blended stuff for Dan.

'I'll have one of those.' I stepped away from the window.

We sat down opposite each other on the plush cream leather sofas placed before the floor-to-ceiling windows. Drink in hand, I contemplated Dan's love of this penthouse. It was understandable. The view alone was enticing. The building, the location, the view made it much too easy for him to feel the master of everything he surveyed. I turned my attention back to Dan. Seventeen years ago, a lifetime ago, we used to be mates. Real buddies. What were we now? Acquaintances was too tame a word. Colleagues? Associates? Ah, I had it — collaborators. That's what we were, collaborators. We'd hooked up to get me elected Mayor of Meadowview and we'd been together ever since. Working together for the good of us both.

And the rest of the world be damned.

One year ago, Dan and I had been seated in this room, in this fashion, drinks in our hands as we both agreed that I should run for Prime Minister, despite all the odds being stacked against me.

'Those upper-class, private-school, elitist Cross bastards like to pretend there's some kind of magic to succeeding in politics that only they can access. It's not magic; it's just a set of learned rules. Wanna know what they are?' Dan took my silence to be assent. 'Here's how you succeed as a politician in five easy steps. One. When you're campaigning, pick two or three big ideas and stick to them. Research the hell out of them, get behind them and promote the hell out of them.'

'How do I pick the two or three ideas?'

'Simple. Just read the room, Tobey. In this case, read the mood of your constituents. What most concerns them? Makes them angry? Makes them march? Makes them want to throw things at the TV? You need to tap into that, even if you don't agree with the policies you're supporting and promoting. And, if someone or an organization comes at you with hard facts and statistics, don't back down. Just accuse them of not caring about the wants and needs of your constituents.'

'Fair enough,' I said.

'Two,' Dan continued. 'Pick a fight with the media and then win it.'

I sat back. 'Are you kidding? How on earth do I do that?'

'Accuse the media of being soft on crime, soft on immigration, soft on holding the opposition accountable, then hammer home the point whenever you have the chance. Three. Give the impression that you know all about and even share the lives of the sheeple. Cry with them. Make them think you're one of them, when you obviously aren't. They'll believe what they want to believe, and what they want to believe is that you're working for them, rather than the other way round.'

And I thought *I* was cynical. 'Jesus, Dan, that's cold.'

'But true. You need to practise your smile and moderate how you speak so you'll appeal to more people and you won't come across as a smarmy, entitled Nought arsehole who's forgotten his roots.'

I didn't imagine the censure in Dan's voice as he said that. My lips tightened as I regarded him. Now was not the time to call him out on how he truly felt about me. Whether I liked it or not, Dan was giving me gold. I'd be foolish to let my ego get in the way of accepting it.

'Four. The Cross opposition will choose to use euphemisms wherever they can. Your job is to challenge them with real language that everyone can understand. That way the working class will resent the hell out of those who hide behind the status quo and will see you as their champion.'

'For example?'

'For example, your opposite number will talk about people who live with the challenge of food insecurity. That's when you come back at them hard and fast and call it what it is – people are starving. They want to talk about the challenges of household fiscal management? Come back at them hard on cuts to welfare leading to people being unable to pay their rent or their utility bills or put food on the table. Keep it real. Don't let the bastards patronize or get away with flowery language.'

I was impressed – and curious. 'How d'you know all this stuff?'

'A very special woman taught me,' Dan replied.

Eva again.

I knew who he was talking about without him even

saying her name. That woman had to be very special indeed. Yet, in all these years, I'd never even met her. Dan spoke about her only rarely, but always with reverence. I'd suggested enough times that we should all get together for a meal, but Dan had never acted on my hints – subtle or otherwise. I couldn't help wondering why.

'And last but not least,' said Dan, when he knew he had my full attention again, 'seize big moments and control them. Don't be afraid to pass someone else's good idea off as your own. But, if you say or do something which brings you negative clapback, then you palm it off on someone else asap. Never admit liability. It's a sign of weakness. Get it?'

'Got it.'

'Good. Any questions?'

Plenty. Starting with – when will I get the final bill for your services? What's your help going to cost me – and not just in money? Questions danced in my head to the sound of warning bells.

'If you've finished staring a hole through me,' said Dan dryly, 'I repeat – any questions?'

'Just one. What do you get out of all this?'

'You, in the palm of my hand.' Dan smiled like a fox in a barn full of chickens. 'Can you live with that?'

I considered but not for long. 'Yeah, I can manage that.'

Could I though?

I banished the question from my mind as we shook on the deal. Dan might think he owned me, but I was my own man, my own boss. Always had been. Always would be. But could it be that I was just deluding myself? Was I using Dan while he was still useful? Or was he using me? I found it hard to tell any more. Besides, what was wrong with both of us using each other if it was to our mutual benefit?

'I'm having a dinner party soon for movers and shakers and useful moneymakers. Can I count you in?'

'Would this happen before or after the election?' I frowned.

'Before of course. I need to remind a few people that I know where the bodies are buried – literally in a couple of cases.' Dan smiled. 'People who will be useful to both of us.'

'And a dinner party is the best time and place to do that?'

'Tobey, it's the only place,' said Dan. 'It'll be a scratching party.'

'A what now?'

'A scratching party. A quid-pro-quo event. A "you scratch my back, I'll scratch yours" occasion,' he expounded. 'I'll have something on every person at the dinner party, and what's more they'll all know it. I'm owed some favours and it's time to collect. I'd like you to be my star guest.'

I regarded Dan, donning my poker face. His star guest, or his star puppet?

Time would tell.

fifty-nine. Callie

'Mum, are you OK?' I'd been speaking for the last ten minutes and the faraway, troubled look on Mum's face told me she hadn't heard a word. 'Mum?'

'What, dear?' Mum finally took in my worried look. 'I'm sorry, Callie. I just have a lot on my mind at the moment.'

'Care to share?'

She regarded me, contemplating my request. Something was definitely wrong.

'I've been invited to a dinner party on Friday and I'm trying to find a way to duck out of it,' she said at last.

'And you can't say you're busy or unavailable?'

'The man hosting this dinner party isn't good at taking no for an answer,' Mum replied.

'Anything I can do?'

She smiled. 'No, love. I'll sort this. It's just annoying, that's all.' She regarded me thoughtfully. 'Callie Rose, you know I love you, right? Very much.'

'Yeah, Mum, I know.' I frowned.

Where was this coming from? Something was definitely amiss—

'Um-hmm?' Troy cleared his throat.

Mum smiled. 'I love you too, Troy. Don't you ever forget that.'

'Not likely to with you telling me every day,' he said.

'You'd soon miss it if I didn't,' said Mum. She turned her attention to the home-made seafood linguine before her and resumed picking at it. I looked at Troy, who just shrugged at me and carried on eating his dinner, his attention wholly taken up by the mobile phone in his left hand.

'Troy, you know Mum doesn't like phones at the dinner table,' I pointed out.

'Look at her,' said Troy. 'She's miles away. If she's not bothered today, why should you be?'

My brother was right. Mum was once again off in a world of her own and, if her expression was anything to go by, it wasn't a happy place. Mum wasn't just worried: there was something else, something more primal in her expression that it took me a few seconds to decipher. Something I hadn't seen on Mum's face in a long, long time.

Fear.

NOW

sixty. Troy

'I've made a mess of your shirt.'

I glance down at the wet patch of material over my right shoulder and the right side of my chest. 'You didn't snot, did you?'

Libby gives a hiccup of a laugh. 'I don't think so. I can't guarantee it though.'

I raise an eyebrow, but then we both smile, though Libby's is faint and quick to evaporate.

'Thanks, Troy.'

'For what?'

'For the use of your shoulder.'

'Any time.'

Silence.

'Troy, I wish . . . I wish you'd jumped without me. I wish you'd escaped.' Libby's voice is barely above a whisper.

'We escape together or not at all,' I tell her.

'I hope you don't live to regret that,' she says.

She's not the only one.

'You OK?'

'Not even a little bit.'

I take Libby's hand in mine and give it a squeeze. I can't even begin to imagine how she must be feeling. How would I feel if I learned my mum had grabbed me off the street and scared me shitless, all so she could get money off my dad? It doesn't bear thinking about. And what Libby had said about her mum pulling on her legs in the bath so that her face would go under the water . . . What kind of sick bastard does that to their own child? What kind of sick bastard does that full stop? Libby's home life must've been worse than hell. I can't even imagine what it must've been like to live with a parent like that, or, rather, I don't want to imagine it. All at once my mum's endless hugs and constant fussing around me don't seem that bad.

'Troy, I want you to promise me something,' says Libby.

'What?'

'If the chance comes to escape again, I want you to promise that you'll run and not look back. You won't wait for me or anyone.'

'I can't—'

'Please. Promise. That's all I'll ever ask you to do for me.' Libby looks up at me, her blue eyes huge and pleading. 'Please.'

She really means it and she isn't going to back down.

'I promise,' I state reluctantly.

'Thank you. And I know you're a guy of your word, so I'll expect you to keep it.'

'Libby, this is all academic,' I point out. 'I doubt if this lot will fall for the same trick.'

She looks at me. 'I may have a way to get us out of here, but it's dangerous.'

Hmm. I don't like the sound of this. 'I'm listening.'

THEN
The Party

sixty-one. Tobey

I read the email again. I'd already read it so many times I almost knew it by heart.

Liberty . . .

It was from my daughter, Liberty, forwarded on to me by Jade, my new personal assistant. My ex-lover and ex-employee Isabella and I had come to a parting of the ways. My decision, not hers. Here I was, sitting in the back of my chauffeur-driven WMW, being taken to Dan's dinner party where I'd need all my wits about me. What a shame my thoughts were now all over the place. I didn't know what to think, how to feel.

The first time I held my daughter in my arms and looked down at her, I knew her name like I knew my own. It sprang into my head and refused to budge. Liberty Alba. Unfortunately, her surname was Jackman. If there was some way I could've given my daughter my name without having to marry her poisonous bitch of a mother to do it, I would've done so in a heartbeat, but it didn't work like that. Looking down at Liberty in that moment had been a revelation. I didn't believe it was possible to fall in love at first sight until then. Looking into Liberty's blue eyes, I knew otherwise.

If only she'd had brown eyes, then she would've been perfect.

I felt ashamed of that thought, but that didn't make it any less real – or honest.

Liberty Alba.

The path I'd taken since Callie and I broke up for good and I left school was so different to the one I originally envisaged. It was the new path that had inspired my daughter's name.

In the months that followed, for Liberty's sake, I tried to make it work with Misty, I really did. Misty and Liberty moved in with my family. Less than six months later, it was obvious that Misty and I were water thrown on burning oil – a total disaster. I was at uni and trying to make that work. Misty couldn't understand why I had no money left from my legacy windfall from Callie's Nana Jasmine and she hated that I was studying all the time instead of hustling to replace all the money I'd given away. After six months, Misty moved back to her mum's house, taking Liberty with her. Because I didn't go running after her, she refused to let me see my daughter. And, I admit, I didn't put up much of a fight about that. At that time, I had nothing to offer either of them. It wasn't until years later, when I finally managed to find my feet, that I set up a trust fund for my daughter. And even then Misty still refused to let me see Liberty.

'She doesn't know you. Your sudden appearance in her life would just confuse her,' she told me.

I didn't argue. Not like I should've done. I told myself that Misty was right. One year turned into five, turned into ten. I paid more money into Libby's trust fund so she wouldn't go without, but that's all I did for her. And now my daughter had written to me.

Dear Dad,

It feels a bit strange to write that word when I've never been able to call you that to your face. I've only just learned that you're my dad. Mum always told me that my dad couldn't care less about us. I only found out the truth because I intercepted a letter the bank wrote to me about the trust fund you set up for me. Mum has spent all the money, but I don't even care so much about that, not if it means that you and I can finally meet and get to know each other. I know you're a very busy man, but I'm hoping you'll be able to find time for me in your life. My email address is above and my mobile number is below. I'm crossing my fingers that you'll get in touch.

Your daughter,
Liberty

Daughter . . .

That word meant something completely different now than it did when I was still a teenager. Then it had meant worry and despair and fear, and an intense sense of being tethered to the ground. Hell, not just tethered but staked. Now it meant . . . hope. Hope that I could turn some of my focus without rather than within. Hope that I could grow bigger to meet her expectations rather than shrink and shrivel to fulfil my own. Dangerous word, *hope*.

Liberty. She might just live up to her name and set me

free. Free of my cynicism and misanthropy. Wouldn't that be ironic? Of course I'd get in touch with her. What was she like? Did she take after me? Her mum? Both of us? Neither? Was she popular at school? I bet she was. I shook my head, acutely aware in that moment of how little I knew about my own daughter. That bitch Misty had told me Libby wanted nothing to do with me. I'd sent birthday and Crossmas cards and a number of letters over the years. None of them had ever been so much as acknowledged. This email made me think Libby hadn't received a single one of them. And all the trust-fund money was gone? My lawyers could deal with that and Misty later. Right now, I wanted nothing more than to get to know my daughter.

I was already in full planning mode. During the next couple of days, I'd get in touch with Libby and arrange a meeting. Then we'd take it from there. I needed to make up for lost time. Almost eighteen years of lost time. But, before that, I had to get through this bullshit evening.

'Would you like me to wait for you, sir?' asked Ben, my driver, as he pulled up in front of Butler's Wharf.

I looked up at the riverside apartment building before me – all twenty storeys of it – and was sorely tempted to say yes. I really wasn't in the mood for socializing. With less than one week to go before the general election, I had more productive things to do with my time. For Shaka's sake, I had three interviews – two radio and one TV – lined up for the following morning, all before 11 a.m.

'No, Ben. That's OK. You go and get yourself some dinner,' I replied.

Ben, a Nought in his late fifties with white-blond hair

and a trim matching moustache, nodded his head. 'Just phone when you're ready to be picked up, sir.'

How many times had I asked Ben to call me Tobey rather than sir, but I was still waiting for that to happen. Getting out of the car, I made my way to the apartment-block entrance. Dan's penthouse occupied the whole of the top floor of this exclusive block. In the centre of the city, with the east aspect overlooking the river, it must've have set him back several million – conservative estimate! To think that, only a decade ago, I'd been visiting him in prison. Now look where I was visiting him. I pressed the button of the video entry system to his apartment. Almost immediately the tempered glass doors clicked open. I made my way inside.

Up on the twentieth floor, I stepped out of the lift to find Dan's door was already open. A deep breath later, I entered his apartment. I wasn't the first to arrive, but, from the look of it, I wasn't the last either. Others had already taken up position around his lounge. Kellan Bruemann, the Cross CEO of a worldwide construction company, stood at the floor-to-ceiling window. The view wasn't the only thing he was drinking in, to judge by the huge glass of cognac in his hand. He was starting early. It was barely seven o'clock. What was he doing here? I knew for a fact that he detested Dan.

To my surprise, Isabella Monroe, my ex-PA and ex-lover, was also present. Hellsake! What had she been saying to Dan about me? The way we parted meant she wasn't exactly a paid-up member of my fan club. Not any more. She stood by a lamp where the light could best show off her gold sequined dress. I have to admit, she looked stunning. Bella caught sight of me, held my gaze for a moment, then looked away with a scornful flick of her eyelashes. I sighed inwardly. She was still bearing a grudge, that much was obvious.

'You're dumping me? You're actually *dumping* me?' Isabella couldn't believe it when I told her.

'Bella, I told you I'm not looking for anything serious or permanent, but you're picking out baby clothes,' I replied. 'I told you when we started this affair that all I was looking for was occasional companionship. Nothing else. Nothing more. And you agreed.'

'I thought . . . I hoped what we had might develop into something deeper,' Isabella admitted.

I shook my head. 'I can't help what you hoped.'

God, I sounded like a callous bastard, but it was time to nip this in the bud. *Tout de suite.*

'That's it? That's all you have to say?' Isabella was incredulous.

I sighed. 'I'm hoping we can both behave like adults about this. We can still be friends and you're a damned good PA—'

'You think I'd work for you after this?' Then Isabella proceeded to tell me where to stick my job and what to do once it was firmly wedged. I know I had it coming, but it didn't make it any less unpleasant.

I beckoned for the security guards standing in the office doorway to come forward. Bella left the office with her few possessions and her head held high as the guards escorted her from the building. She finally got the message.

I hadn't seen her since. Now here she was – her and my business secrets in Dan's living room. Should I be nervous? This smelled suspiciously like some kind of set–up – and I didn't like it. I'd need to keep my wits about me. I headed over to Kellan. Him I'd met before.

'What's what, Kell? How are you?'

'Good evening, Prime Minister.'

'I haven't won yet.'

'But you will. Dan's tied it all up for you with gift wrapping and a pretty ribbon.'

'I like to think that, if I do win, I had a little something to do with it,' I ventured.

'Maybe not as much as you think,' said Kellan. 'Do you know what we call your friend?'

I shook my head. Kellan looked me up and down before answering his own question. 'Mr Stain Remover.'

I was taken aback. 'What?'

'Dan Jeavons makes all your problems, all those annoying little stains in your life, disappear.' Kell unfurled one hand in a sudden explosive movement to emphasize his point. 'And Dan doesn't charge money. Nothing as vulgar as money. No, your friend trades favours. He does something for you, and maybe next week, or next month, or next year, he'll ask you to do something for him. But he only asks once. I learned that the hard way.'

'What does that mean?' I frowned.

'It means that Dan Jeavons doesn't like to be disappointed. I didn't take his threats seriously, and now I've lost everything. My wife left me. My children hate me. My friends have deserted me. All I have left in the world are my connections.' There was barely disguised scorn in Kell's voice. He might need Dan, but he certainly didn't like him. I didn't know Kell's history and, to be honest, I didn't particularly care. I already had ninety-nine problems. He wasn't going to be added to them.

'You want some advice?' he said, lowering his voice slightly. 'Walk away. *Run* away. Get as far away from Dan Jeavons as you can. He's the devil and he enjoys collecting souls.'

Dan walked into the room from his study. He made a beeline for us, an easy smile on his face. 'Talking about me, Kell?'

'I was just telling your friend here to get as far away from you as he can,' said Kellan.

His honesty startled me. I expected obfuscation in response to Dan's direct question. Kell didn't even try to dissemble.

'Well, Tobey, are you going to take Kell's advice?' Dan issued a direct challenge.

'Not today,' I replied.

'Ah! At least I tried,' said Kell, taking another sip of his cognac.

Dan regarded him as he slowly swirled his cognac in its glass. Neither of them took their eyes off each other. Then, without warning, Dan backhanded Kell across the face. The cognac glass went flying, smashing against the adjacent wall and raining glass.

'Just business, Kell,' said Dan. 'Just business.'

Blood trickled from the corner of Kellan's mouth. He wiped at it with the back of his hand, studying it for a moment before turning back to Dan, his mouth twisting into a facsimile of a smile.

'As you say, Dan, just business,' he said quietly.

The tension in the room could've been cut with a cotton bud. But then Dan started discussing the latest election-poll figures, and Kell and I joined in the conversation as if nothing awkward had happened. George, Dan's butler, was already tidying up the glass on the floor. Soon afterwards, Dan and I disappeared into his study for around ten minutes to discuss the finer points of some last-minute campaign strategies. By the time we emerged, more guests had arrived. Most I recognized.

Jarvis, Dan's deputy, stood at the window, talking to Dan's brother, Tom. Jarvis was loyalty personified, as many of Dan's enemies had found to their cost when they'd tried to buy him off or get to Dan through him. Tom was a completely different proposition. He was young, not just in years but in outlook, and had no poker face to speak of. His every thought, emotion, feeling was writ large on his face. Did he even know how far his brother's empire had expanded? Did he know all the legal and not so legitimate ways in which Dan had made his vast fortune? I doubted it. Tom looked like a younger, fresher version of Dan, before life had pummelled him and he'd started fighting and hating it right back. How long, I wondered, would it take for Dan to corrupt his younger brother just like he tainted every other person who got too close to him?

Standing behind the bar, pouring himself a glass of champagne, was Patrix Ellerman, Cross lawyer for hire to the rich and famous – but mostly the rich. I'd never met him but felt as though I knew him, though by reputation only. Patrix was a good-looking man in his early forties, with a ready smile and a keen intellect. He was a very successful lawyer, but, if you lacked the funds to pay his exorbitant fees, you'd best keep moving. It made him easy to bribe and he was as easily bought as a morning cup of coffee. Hell, if I couldn't find a friendly face, I'd settle for a familiar one. Seated on a bar stool watching him was a middle-aged Nought woman whose hair was more silver than its original colour. This woman was definitely looking at sixty in the rear-view mirror. Patrix said something to her, one eyebrow raised, which immediately had her tilting her head up to laugh. Well, at least someone was enjoying themselves. I continued to look around.

What the . . . ?

Was that—? Oh. My. God! It was!

Persephone Hadley. Callie's mum. What on earth was Sephy doing here? She was speaking in low but urgent tones to Owen Dowd of all people, who was sitting at the grand piano in one corner of the room. Between them, Alex McAuley and the Dowd family used to run every illegal enterprise in Meadowview. After Callie got shot, I'd made it my business to get revenge on both fraternities. Thanks to me, Alex McAuley had been shot and killed and Gideon Dowd was still languishing in prison. I'd helped Gideon's younger brother Owen onto the Dowd family throne. The king was dead. Long live the king. And Gideon's younger sister Rebecca? Her blood was on my hands too. Dan knew all my dirty little secrets. Owen Dowd knew some of them. He ruled Meadowview with an iron fist and his reputation for ruthlessness wasn't just talk.

Since when did Sephy know Dowd? From across the room, I couldn't make out what they were saying, but they were obviously doing more than just discussing the weather. Owen shrugged and said something to Sephy that she obviously didn't like. What the hell could the two of them have to talk about? Whatever it was, it was obvious that, though the volume wasn't rising, the temperature of their quarrel was. Sephy was getting more and more irate and Owen wasn't far behind. With a face like thunder, Sephy spoke more earnestly to him. She said something which made Owen leap to his feet, his finger waving in Sephy's face. Then Sephy hauled back and slapped him so hard my own teeth rattled. Damn! There was obviously some slapping gas or equivalent in the air tonight. The room went deathly quiet.

'Say that again. I dare you,' Sephy challenged, her quiet words echoing around the room.

Owen's eyes darkened with rage, setting his expression like it was carved in stone. Hell! He was going to retaliate. Not if I had anything to do with it. I started towards them, but Dan got there ahead of me.

'Owen and Sephy, I think you've forgotten where you are and that you both have an audience,' he said silkily.

A moment, then Sephy looked around the room. Her eyes alighted on me and narrowed. I guess I still wasn't her favourite person.

'Dan, if you'll excuse me, I believe I've outstayed my welcome. I'll be leaving now.' Sephy headed over to one of the cream leather sofas to retrieve her handbag.

'Persephone, please stay.'

Three words from Dan. Three seemingly innocuous words, but they froze Sephy in her tracks. She turned to look at Dan like they were the only two in the room. What was going on between them? A person with half an eye could spot Sephy's loathing for Dan, and yet here she was in his apartment, and all he had to do was ask her to stay and it looked like she was actually going to do it. What hold did he have over her?

'Owen, I believe the lady might be more inclined to stay if you were to apologize,' said Dan.

'Apologize? Are you s-serious?' Owen spluttered.

Dan turned to look at him. 'Apologize. Now.'

Owen's eyes narrowed. He turned to Sephy and said, 'I apologize if my words offended you.'

'*If?*' said Sephy with scorn.

Dan favoured Owen with a hard stare.

After a petulant huff, Owen said reluctantly, 'I apologize for offending you.'

'See! We're friends again.' Dan was all smiles now, as fake as a wooden credit card.

Owen and Sephy continued to scowl at each other, before Owen finally sat back down at the piano and started playing a jazz classic. And, to my surprise, he was good. I guess even lowlifes like Owen Dowd needed a hobby. Sephy continued to glare at him. There was something going on here, some subtext that eluded me. It was unexpected enough that Sephy should be at one of Dan's dinner parties, but that both she and Owen Dowd were here?

What was Dan up to?

'Ladies and gentlemen,' announced George, Dan's butler. 'Dinner is served.'

He made a sweeping gesture towards the dining room, indicating that we should all take a seat. The first things I saw when I walked into the dining room were place name cards on the table. Godsake! Who had Dan stuck me next to? As long as it wasn't Bella. I really wasn't in the mood for ex-lover drama this evening. I moved round the table, trying to find my place. On one of the place cards was written the word *Eva* in cursive script. That had to be the elderly Nought woman who'd been with Patrix at the bar. Was this the famous Eva at long last? It had to be. I was finally going to meet her properly. I continued round the table, checking the cards. So Jarvis was going to join us for dinner, was he? Was Dan expecting ructions? He'd arranged the seating so that Jarvis was literally his right-hand man.

At last I found my place card.

My heart dropped, then sank even lower. So much for that then.

I'd been placed at one end of the table, directly opposite Dan, but I had Bella to my right and Owen Dowd to my left. And Bella was already throwing serious shade my way.

Godsake!

Something was very wrong with this set-up. Unease wrapped round me like an ill-fitting polyester suit. Dan was playing a very dangerous game, a game where only he knew the rules, but, if he wasn't careful, someone could end up getting hurt.

Or worse.

NOW

sixty-two. Callie

My blood had turned to ice water in my veins. I couldn't believe it. There had to be some kind of mistake. 'My mum was there? At Dan's house?'

'That's what I said.'

The look Tobey was giving me held a blatant challenge that I chose to ignore. He was dressed in a dark blue suit and a light blue shirt with no tie. His dark brown hair fell almost down to his collar. Most Noughts in politics kept their hair short, but everything about Tobey proclaimed his difference from the norm and he revelled in it. From the moment he walked into my office, I felt like I was standing on shifting sand. His appearance, his voice, everything about Tobey made me strangely self-aware. And, from the moment he sat down, he kept giving me knowing looks, like he knew exactly what effect he was having on me. But now it was his words that had my full attention. I regarded Tobey, not even bothering to try and disguise the frown clouding my face. 'What the hell was Mum doing in Dan Jeavons' apartment?'

Tobey shrugged. 'You'd need to ask her that, not me. You wanted me to recount what happened on the night Dan died. That's what I'm doing.'

Tobey, Jon and I were seated in my office, and every other sentence Tobey uttered just emphasized how little I knew about him now. To defend him, I needed all the facts, but Tobey was hitting me with some I could never have anticipated.

'How does Mum even know someone like Dan Jeavons?'

'I refer you to my previous answer,' said Tobey wryly.

'Was Mum present when the body was found?' I asked.

'Your mum left during dessert. Dan's body was found after coffee and liqueurs,' he said. 'As far as I know, the police eliminated her from their enquiries. I wasn't so fortunate.'

Detective Chief Inspector Dabo was in charge of the Dan Jeavons murder investigation and I knew him well. DCI Dabo hadn't said one word about my mum being involved and her name hadn't been mentioned in any of the crime reports I'd read. I didn't like hearing about it from Tobey. I should've been forewarned.

Mum had been at Dan's apartment?

I was still trying to wrap my head round that one. Was that the dinner party she'd been talking about? The one she really didn't want to attend? It had to be. Jon tapped my arm and showed me his tablet. He'd drawn out a sketch based on Tobey's account of the evening Dan was murdered. I nodded in Tobey's direction. He'd need to confirm the seating arrangements, not me. Jon scrolled down to show Tobey his sketch, but none of the accompanying notes above it.

'Is this an accurate representation of where everyone was sitting?' he asked.

Tobey reached out for the tablet. Jon pulled back slightly, making it clear that he could look, but touching was not an option. With a quirk of his eyebrow, Tobey turned his full attention to the sketch.

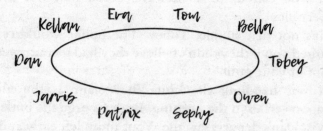

'Yes, that's accurate – as far as I remember,' Tobey confirmed.

I took another look at Jon's diagram. 'So my mum was sitting between Patrix and Owen Dowd, who she'd had an argument with earlier that same evening? Whose idea was that?'

Tobey shrugged. 'Dan and his games.'

My frown deepened. Just what did Dan think he was playing at? Had he deliberately set out to make his guests feel as uncomfortable as possible, or just my mum?

'Why was Patrix Ellerman there? How does he know Dan?' I asked.

Tobey rolled his eyes. 'Jesus, Callie, how would I know? You seem to be more interested in the motivations of every other guest present that night rather than in my own situation. I've been in office less than a week. It's only thanks to the super-injunction you took out that the press isn't crawling all over this. Can you imagine the fallout if my arrest is made public? I want you to make this disappear. I didn't do it. Prove it so I can get back to my job, where I can do some good. The country needs me. I'm the only one who can unite it after the fiasco that was the last government.'

'It's not that simple, Tobey. The police wouldn't have charged you if they didn't believe they had incontrovertible proof of your guilt.'

'I was handling the knife they claim is the murder weapon earlier in the evening. Both George the butler and Jarvis, Dan's deputy, saw me. Your mum left early and Dan was dead when I entered his study after everyone else that night. Those are the facts.'

'When did Dan leave the dinner table?' asked Jon.

'After the first course. He said he had some important personal phone calls to make, and off he went to his study, closing the door behind him,' said Tobey.

'Who apart from you went into the study?' Jon leaped in before I could.

Tobey shrugged. 'Most of us at one time or another.'

'Do you remember in what order?'

'Not really.' Tobey's eyebrows drew together as he attempted to recall. 'I think Kellan Bruemann went in to see Dan first, followed by Patrix, then Tom, Dan's brother. Then it was Owen, Sephy and Eva. Or was it Eva first? I can't remember. Jarvis and Bella didn't go into the study – at least not that I saw. I was the last to enter while we were still dining. By that time, Sephy had already gone home and Dan was still alive. We all moved to the living room and played cards and chatted for an hour or so. Patrix was the first to leave after dinner and Dan still hadn't put in an appearance. After that, others started leaving. I went into the study to tell Dan that I was going home, and that's when I found him slumped in his chair with a knife in his back.'

'Was his body facing you when you entered the room or did he have his back to the door when you found him?' asked Jon.

Tobey thought for a moment. 'He was slumped over his desk but facing the door.'

'More proof that he was stabbed by someone he knew,' said Jon. 'No way would Dan Jeavons let a stranger get behind him, knife in hand.'

Tobey nodded, acknowledging the truth of his words.

'Why did the knife have your fingerprints on it?' Jon asked.

'It was an ornamental knife Dan kept on his desk. I'd been admiring it earlier in the evening. I never denied handling it, but I didn't use it to kill anyone.'

'The fingerprints weren't smudged or obscured,' I informed him. 'It looks like you were the last to use it.'

'Obviously not, as the killer handled it after me,' Tobey shot back. He paused. 'It's not looking good for me, is it?'

'To be honest, no.'

'Are you telling me that this case may actually come to trial?'

'If we can't come up with some way to prove your innocence, I'd say that was entirely likely,' said Jon.

'I didn't do it,' Tobey insisted.

'That's what they all say,' said Jon evenly.

Tobey looked him up and down. 'Callie tells me you're an investigator. Are you any good?'

'I'm the best,' Jon stated evenly.

Tobey raised an eyebrow.

I smiled. 'He really is as good as he thinks he is. If he can't exonerate you, then you did it.'

'Then I guess my fate lies in both your hands,' said Tobey. 'Because I'll tell you this: if this case does go to court, I shall plead not guilty and defend myself vigorously. I have no intention of going down for something I didn't do.'

'I believe in you, Tobey,' I told him. 'I know you didn't do it.'

He looked at Jon, waiting for a similar assertion from him. He didn't get it. Instead, Jon regarded him steadily without saying a word.

'Reserving judgement?' asked Tobey.

'Not really,' said Jon. 'You see, I think you're guilty.'

sixty-three. Troy

The room is too warm, too small, too dim. The walls are beginning to echo again, to breathe. *Out. In.* I watch their subtle movement. Slowly and slightly bulging towards me, only to draw in again, just as carefully. Their movement is only noticeable if you watch and wait for it. Only if you sit absolutely still and—

'Troy? Troy, snap out of it. What're you doing?' Libby's voice breaks the silence.

The walls stop moving.

I turn to her, just in time to catch the concern in her eyes.

'I'm not doing anything.'

Libby shakes her head. 'You're staring at the walls like you've never seen them before. You're not freaking out, are you? Because I'll lose it completely if you do.'

I glance back at the stationary walls. 'No, I'm not freaking out. How much water do we have left?' I ask.

'Half a bottle each, if that. We should go easy on it. Conserve it until we get out of here. So what d'you think of my plan?' says Libby hopefully.

'I think it's bollocks,' I tell her straight. 'Go through with it and it's suicide for at least one and probably both of us.'

Libby had the perky idea of feigning illness again until they brought both of us out of the basement and into the hall, and she would launch herself at the heavies, taking a hail of bullets if necessary for the greater good, while I made a run for it. I mean, damn!

Libby scowls. 'Have you got a better idea?'

'Yeah. If I know my sister, she's already working on rescuing us. I say we sit tight and wait to be found.'

'That was my plan at the beginning of all this and you hated it,' Libby reminds me.

'Well, maybe I've come round to your way of thinking.'

'You don't want to do that,' she says softly. 'My way of thinking has brought me nothing but misery and a stone in my heart.'

Silence.

'It's just that I hate doing nothing,' Libby admits. 'It's like accepting our fate. Consenting to it even.'

On that at least we agree.

'Have you got someone at home to report you missing to the police?' I look around at the walls, which are holding their breath.

'The only person who might've reported me missing kidnapped me in the first place, so I'm afraid I won't be much help in getting us out of here, but your family will report you missing. That's right, isn't it? You've got someone who cares about you? Right?'

I nod, careful to keep my expression neutral. Libby is gabbling, talking fast to keep me with her. I realize with a start that she's scared I'll slip so far down into my own thoughts that she won't be able to reach in and pull me back up.

'Yes, that's right. The police are probably already looking for us,' I agree, though I have no way of knowing. 'Did you recognize any of those three men upstairs?'

Libby shakes her head.

'But you said you didn't recognize our original kidnappers and they turned out to be your mum and her friends,' I point out.

'They had masks on,' she protests. 'Mum was the driver in the fox mask so I never got a good look at her. And besides they let Pete's brother do most of the talking. I'd never met him before so how was I supposed to recognize his voice?'

Is that the truth? I eye Libby, who meets my gaze without looking away or flinching.

'Troy, I'm not lying,' she says quietly. 'I didn't know what my mum had planned and I certainly don't know who this new lot are working for. If I knew, I promise I'd tell you.'

'OK.' I believe her. Almost.

But not quite.

sixty-four. Callie

'Callie, have you lost your entire mind?'

I sighed inwardly. I'd been expecting this, but that didn't make it pleasant. Solomon, the head of my chambers, was scowling at me like it had just come into fashion. I'd been at work for less than five minutes and had barely got my chair warm when Stacy, my PA, told me that Sol wanted to see me. His scowl greeted me the moment I set foot in his office. He was sitting behind his behemoth of a desk, and not happy didn't even come close to describing his face right now.

I started to speak as I shut the door behind me, feeling it prudent to get in first. 'Sol, if you'd just let me explain—'

'Go on then,' he challenged. 'Explain to me how you took on an unwinnable case without consulting me first. A case that will bring us swathes of bad publicity and God knows what else. And now, to top it all off, this chambers has started receiving *death* threats. Explain yourself.'

I sighed. Sol was ready to exhale napalm and I was right in the line of fire.

'Solomon, I've already apologized for not clearing it with you first, but Tobey came to me directly as a friend and asked for my help, and time was of the essence if I was going to suppress his arrest. I couldn't turn him down. I've had a super-injunction slapped on this case so the press can't say a word about Tobey in connection with Dan's murder until the trial starts – if it starts. They can't even say there's an injunction stopping them from giving out more data on the case. And why're you assuming this case is unwinnable?'

Sol's eyes widened to their limit. 'Callie Rose, are you deliberately trying to wind me up? Tobias Durbridge is as dodgy and dirty as they come—'

'That's not true,' I interrupted, adding reluctantly, 'He might've bent the rules a couple of times during his election campaign, but he's not dirty.'

'Grow up, Callie. How d'you think he won in the first place? Because of his dimples and gleaming smile?' Sol scoffed.

'He doesn't have dimples,' I murmured.

'Callie, he's no good. Who d'you think bankrolled his political campaigns? Dan Jeavons, that's who. And it's an open secret how Jeavons made his money. He flooded the whole country with Prop and he has kids transporting and selling the drug up and down the country. If there's a hell, he'll surely be roasting in it. That's who your friend Tobey crawled into bed with.'

I forced myself to count to ten. It was only just enough.

'Sol, be fair. Daniel Jeavons and Tobey aren't one and the same person. Why hold Tobey accountable for Dan's actions? This case isn't about drugs. It isn't about politics either. Tobey has been arrested for murder and that's my focus. A murder he didn't commit, I might add.'

'Says who?'

'Says Tobey – and I believe him.'

'And I own a bridge across the Zambezi I'd be more than happy to sell to you.' Sol gave me the full force of his famous, patented narrow-eyed courtroom stare that had many a person in the witness box sweating bullets into buckets. 'Callie, are you sleeping with him?'

What? Say what? 'Of course not.'

If anything, Sol's eyes narrowed further.

'Oh, for heaven's sake,' I said, exasperated. 'We went to school together. He's an old friend, though I haven't seen him in a number of years. He came to me and asked for my help and I said yes. That's all there is to it.'

'Really?'

'Yes, really.' What a disappointment. I'd never had Sol down as one of those guys who found it impossible to believe men and women could be friends without sex rearing its head.

'Callie, if – and it's a big if – you take this case, you're going to open yourself up to all kinds of accusations, recriminations and general shit-stormery.'

'I know that.'

'Do you? Have you seriously thought about this?' said Sol. 'You're going to make enemies just by taking this case. It's not too late to back out.'

'Tobey's my friend. I can't desert him when he needs me most.'

Sol sighed. 'You are making a *huge* mistake. If you're determined to take this case, just make sure you disclose any and everything of relevance to me before the trial. I won't have these chambers exposed to any kind of censure or clapback. Do I make myself clear?'

I frowned. Since when did I hold anything back from my head of chambers? I'd done so in the past. Why would I start now? I didn't care for the implication.

'That's not my style, Sol,' I replied. 'I thought you knew that.'

I made sure not to look away from Sol, who was still scrutinizing me. A sense of unease began to creep along my spine.

'What're you not telling me?'

'Callie, I've heard things,' Sol began reluctantly.

'What kind of things?'

'Listen, I understand he's your friend, and believe me he's going to need all the friends he can get in the next few weeks,' said Sol. 'But I've heard some things about Tobias Durbridge, about some of the methods he employed to become Mayor of Meadowview and during his ministerial campaign. He's not above fighting down and dirty.'

'Is any politician?' I asked.

'True. But there's dirty and then there's what Tobey and his cohorts indulge in.'

'Such as? Come on, Sol, stop beating about the bush. Have you got actual proof of what you're saying or have you been listening to gossip and innuendo?'

'Callie, your friend isn't into politics to bring people together. He's into looking out for number one – and what's more, he's good at it.'

I shook my head, not recognizing the man Sol was describing.

'You're wrong. I know for a fact that Tobey was left a ton of money when he was younger and he used it to set up an addiction treatment clinic. He would've kept the money for himself if he was only out for what he could get.'

'People change,' said Sol quietly.

'Not Tobey. Not that much. I *know* him. He wouldn't lie to me.'

Sol shook his head. 'Callie, you're not thinking straight. I know you hope to be a judge one day. Take this case and there will be repercussions. Like it or not, times have changed. Judges are now political appointments. Take this case and you can kiss any prospect of becoming a judge goodbye.'

And there it was. Sol had brought out into the open my biggest concern about this case. Political trials had political consequences. This case had 'career scuppering' written all over it. Had Tobey really made so many political enemies that defending him meant abandoning my career aspirations? It would appear so. It was my dream to become a judge. Every professional move I'd made over the last ten years had been with that goal in mind. Was I really prepared to lose it all over one case? I already knew the answer.

'Sol, Tobey needs my help. I'm not going to turn my back on him.'

'Callie, I really, *really* hope you know what you're doing.'

I swallowed hard. That made two of us.

'Hello?'

'Hey, Callie, it's Tobey.'

My smile was instantaneous. I held the phone closer to my ear. 'What's what, Tobey?' I asked, playing his usual greeting back to him.

'Not much. You OK?'

My smile faded. 'I'm fine. Any reason why I shouldn't be?'

'None that I know of.'

My antennae started to quiver. 'Tobey, what's wrong? You sound . . . off.'

He sighed. 'It's just been a bitch of a week. I know it's late but I wondered if you fancied grabbing a bite to eat with me?'

I glanced at my watch. It was almost ten. Well, my brother Troy had stood me up earlier so dinner with a friend would be welcome. And as for my brother? No text, no email, no message to tell me why he was a no-show. We'd have words about that the next time I saw him.

'You haven't eaten yet?' I asked.

'I'm lucky if I manage more than a few cups of coffee a day at the moment,' said Tobey. 'But it is late. You've probably already eaten. Forget I asked. It was just—'

'I'd love to have dinner with you,' I interrupted. 'I'm just back at my office, doing paperwork that can wait. Where shall I meet you?'

'How about we have dinner at mine?' said Tobey. 'I could have something delivered.'

Pause.

Tobey sounded so desperate for company. 'But if you'd rather not—'

'No, that'd be lovely,' I said. 'I already have your address. Shall I meet you there in thirty minutes?'

'Sounds good. See you in half an hour then.'

I disconnected the call, staring down at my phone. I hadn't been alone with Tobey since . . . since we were teenagers. Damn! Had it really been that long? Racking my brains, I realized I was right.

Dinner at Tobey's.

Be careful, Callie.

Be very careful.

Callie walked into my apartment before me, then stopped. I'd met her down in the foyer, arriving as we did within seconds of each other. Part of me wondered why she'd agreed to meet me, but I wasn't about to argue or check this gift horse's teeth. Leaving two of my close-protection officers in the foyer and the other two outside my front door, we entered my apartment.

'Computer, switch on the lounge lights,' I ordered.

The lights above immediately came on.

Closing the door, I moved to stand beside her, watching as she looked around, taking it all in. I'd paid Amber and Dyson, the famous interior designers, an absolute fortune to put this penthouse together for me. The apartment had three reception rooms, one of which I used as my study, and four bedrooms, each with its own en-suite. Every time I opened the front door, I felt like I'd arrived. But now I was seeing it through Callie's eyes, with its sterile white walls and its dark oak hardwood floors. The white leather sofas were all sharp angles and straight lines. Even the artwork on the walls was geometric by design. The other rooms continued the theme of monochrome hardwood floors and furniture that was designed for effect rather than comfort. The place looked like what it was: an expensive bachelor pad, a conquest den, made for my comfort alone and no one else's.

Callie turned to me and smiled. 'It's very . . . functional.'

'You hate it, don't you?'

She shrugged. 'Well, it's not to my taste but it's your home. You're the one who has to be comfortable here.'

Though the words were lightly said, I was disappointed, like I'd failed a test I didn't even know I was taking.

'Ready to eat?' I asked.

'You got FeedMe on speed dial then?' Callie teased.

FeedMe was just one of the fast-food delivery services available in the capital. I never used them.

'Our dinner is already here.' I indicated the dining table across the room. A trolley filled with covered plates sat behind the table and a bottle of champagne was cooling in the ice bucket.

'Oh.' Callie regarded me, eyes narrowed. 'You were so sure I'd agree to your suggestion to have dinner here? Am I that predictable?'

A verbal trap. If I walked into this one, it could take my head clean off.

'No, Callie, you're not predictable at all. I was hoping, not assuming.'

'Oh.'

A lot of meaning in one syllable.

'Well, as you've gone to all this trouble, let's eat. I'm starving.'

Callie shrugged off her jacket, throwing it over the arm of my sofa as she went, like she was laying down a challenge.

She was at the table and pulling out her own chair before I'd got it together enough to follow her. Removing the named warmers from over our starters, I placed a bowl of soup in front of Callie, before setting my own plate down on the table. The name of a well-known restaurant was written round the rim of our crockery. No chance of pretending *I'd* cooked our dinner! Callie waited till I was seated opposite her, then said, 'Food from Bertollini's. I'm impressed. I didn't even know they did takeaways.'

'I asked them nicely,' I said. Plus being PM didn't hurt.

Callie waved her hand in the direction of the food trolley keeping the food warm beside us. 'This is all stuff from their current menu?'

'I asked for your favourites,' I replied. 'Minestrone soup with fresh brown rolls, petti di pollo al burro and tiramisu.'

'You remember? After all this time?'

I smiled. 'Of course.'

A moment's pause to share a smile.

Callie said, 'What're we waiting for?! Let's eat.'

Smiling, I reached for my napkin.

Our dinner conversation flowed like the champagne. It was as if all the intervening years between us rolled up, then rolled away until they were out of sight. Callie teased me throughout the meal. She teased me about getting into law school and then dropping out. She teased me about getting all that money from her nan and then giving it all away. She teased me about being a borough councillor and then becoming Mayor of Meadowview. For Shaka's sake, she even teased me about my hairstyle. My PR person and my hairdresser had got together and decided a shorter, more regimented cut would appeal to more voters than my usual unruly, wavy hair flopping over my forehead. On this one, I'd overruled them. Callie teased me like she'd been there while they were discussing it.

'You look like you're ready to join a boy band,' she said.

'You've heard me sing,' I pointed out. 'Not gonna happen.'

Callie took another mouthful of her chicken. 'So you never took singing lessons to round off your can-do-anything Superman image.'

'Is that what I have?' I asked, surprised.

'You know you do. You are Prime Minister. My God, I'm having dinner with the PM.' Callie's eyes were wide with mock wonder. 'But, seriously, look at everything you've achieved through sheer hard work, intelligence and determination. Women love you. Men admire you. Even dogs and cats adore you. You sure know how to work it, Tobey!'

'But for how much longer? I've had to hand over most of my workload while I fight this case – which is politically motivated, at least in part.'

'You believe there's some kind of conspiracy here?' Callie frowned.

I shrugged. 'It's just interesting how they came after me with so little evidence.'

'And that's going to be the downfall of this case.' Callie was all assurances.

When this was all over, I'd make sure that those involved in having me arrested paid for it. A silent vow but a sincere one nonetheless.

'If the voting public get to know about my arrest, my

career will be all but over,' I said. 'To a lot of people, being arrested is the same as being guilty. I'm a Nought, Callie. There's a whole swathe of the Cross population just waiting for me to fuck up. Godsake! During the election campaign, I wore brown shoes to a TV interview and the news that night discussed whether or not the wearing of brown rather than black shoes made me unfit to run as PM.'

Callie sighed. 'Yeah, I remember that. But look – when I get this case dismissed due to lack of evidence, I'll make sure you can pick up where you left off with not a single stain on your character. Worst-case scenario, if the case does go to trial and the judge throws out the super-injunction, you'll have to temporarily remove yourself from office until the matter is resolved. But, if that does happen, tell your deputy not to get too comfy in your chair. I don't intend for this case to take long.'

I couldn't help the smile that spread. Some things never changed. Once Callie got the bit between her teeth, there was no stopping her.

'Thanks, Callie,' I said. 'It's good to know you've got my back.'

Her hand covered mine. 'Always, Tobey. Always.'

She made to pull her hand away, but I snatched it up and kissed her palm. Her wrist was perfumed with some kind of vanilla scent. She smelled gorgeous: good enough to eat. Callie slowly pulled her hand out of mine and we went back to finishing our dinner.

'Now tell me more about the *Gentlemen's Monthly* photo spread you did last month,' said Callie. 'May I just say how devastatingly gorgeous you managed to look in the photos. Someone must've spent a good couple of weeks photoshopping the hell out of those pics.'

I pursed my lips. 'Bitch! You're loving this, aren't you?'

'You know it!' Callie laughed, barely pausing for breath before the teasing continued.

And I loved it.

It was well after midnight and into the small hours. This was the first time in forever that I'd had a conversation that didn't revolve around politics. We discussed films, music, books, and I couldn't remember when I'd been so relaxed, so able to let my guard down. We'd finished our tiramisu hours ago and had just spent the time since playing catch-up until at last Callie glanced at her watch and sighed.

'I'd best head home before I turn into a gourd,' she said, quoting a famous Cross myth about the consequences of staying up past midnight. She stood up. 'Tobey, thank you for a lovely evening, good food and great company.'

I got to my feet. 'The night is still young.'

'Yeah, but I'm not!' Callie shot back with a wry smile. 'I'll phone for a cab and be out of your hair within fifteen minutes, if you don't mind me waiting here until it arrives.'

She headed over to the sofa to retrieve her jacket, taking her phone out of the pocket. I took hold of her free hand and pulled her to me.

'What I mean is, I'd like you to stay the night,' I told her softly.

At that moment, more than anything else in the world, I wanted her.

Callie's smile had disappeared. She sighed. 'That's not a

good idea, Tobey.' She shook her head. 'I'm your lawyer. You're my client. There are all kinds of rules against that. As it is, I feel like I'm already bending enough of the rulebook for it to qualify as origami.'

'What rules are you bending?'

'My mum was at Dan's dinner party. If it wasn't for the fact that she left before Dan was killed, I would have to recuse myself from this case. As it is, Solomon, my head of chambers, will be acting as co-counsel to make sure there's absolutely no conflict of interest.'

'This isn't about Solomon or the case. It's about us, Callie. You and I belong together. We always have and we always will,' I told her. 'So I'm asking you to stay with me.' I stroked a thumb over her lips. 'We were friends first. And lovers, long before you were my lawyer,' I whispered, my lips mere millimetres from her own.

Callie drew back slightly. 'We slept together once. That hardly makes us lovers.'

'We made love together once – and sometimes once is enough to know when two people are right together. So stay? Please?'

Silence.

What was Callie thinking? Once I could read her face like a picture book, but during our years apart she'd obviously become more adroit at masking her expression. I stepped back, inwardly sighing. No more pleading. Callie was right. This wasn't a good idea. I guess only one of us was emotionally frozen in time. Stupid of me to think that she'd ever—

'It would be very unfair and downright cruel to drag

some poor taxi driver out at this time of night,' Callie told me.

The relief I felt was instant and heartfelt. 'Cruel and unusual,' I agreed. 'So is that a yes?'

'That is a— We shouldn't do this. It's such a bad idea. We'll both regret it in the morning. Maybe we should just take a minute and—'

I kissed her, effectively halting the high tide of words. Callie's phone fell on the sofa before her arms wrapped around my neck, pulling me closer, holding me tighter.

I reluctantly drew away. 'So that's a yes?' I needed to hear her say it.

'That's a hell yes.' Callie grinned. 'I've missed you so much, Tobey.'

Reaching out with one hand, she stroked her fingers over my cheek, my nose, my lips. Her touch was already melting the wall of ice I'd carefully built up around my emotions. A mutual smile and, taking her by the hand, I led the way to my bedroom. Tonight Callie was mine. I had till the morning to find a way to make one night last a lifetime.

Peace. That's what I felt for the first time in a long, long time. I was where I was meant to be, with the one person in this world who was my true other self. Hours earlier, when we'd entered my bedroom, I hadn't even bothered switching on the lights. Moonlight now flooded the room, giving it a silver glow, as if the night itself were blessing us. The room was so silvery bright, it could only be a full moon out there, the night-time clouds having moved on. Underneath the duvet, Callie's hand stroked my chest and my abdomen, slow, circular movements that increased the peace I felt. It wasn't a flash of insight or a thunderclap of reason that hit me. Rather it was the calm acceptance of something I'd kept buried so deep, I thought it must surely have died. I was mistaken. The simple truth was, I still loved Callie and I knew in that moment I always would. There was a space and a place in my heart that belonged to her and her alone.

'What're you thinking?' she asked lightly.

'That you're peace,' I said honestly.

'That I'm a piece?' Her voice held an unmistakable frown. 'Of what? Tail? Ass? Is that what this is? A booty call?'

'You've got to be kidding me—' I blinked at her in dismay. Was that really what she thought was going on here? She thought I was—?

Callie burst out laughing. 'Totally got you! Act like you know!'

I shook my head, holding her closer. 'Tell me why I've missed you so much again?'

I pulled her to me for another kiss. A long one. From the living room came the intro to the song 'Mama Says' by Freel. It was only just audible. Quizzically, I looked at Callie.

'That's my ringtone for when Mum phones me,' she explained. She swung her legs out of bed and was already on her feet. 'Computer, lights on.'

The bedroom lights complied immediately.

'Do I have my own ringtone for when I phone you?'

'Now that would be telling.' Callie winked, heading for the bedroom door.

'Where're you going?' I sat up to ask. I didn't want her away from me, not even for a minute.

'To answer my phone.' She turned to me and smiled. 'If Mum's calling me at this time of night, then . . .' Her smile faded as her eyes skimmed over my torso. Her phone rang off as she walked back to sit down on the edge of the bed. She leaned in closer to my chest. Good! I opened my arms, hoping she was going to kiss me as a precursor to another bout of love-making. God knows I wanted her again.

'Oh. My. God!' Callie breathed.

'What's the——?'

And only then did I remember my tattoo, lasered off but unfortunately still just discernible. I'd had it inked over my heart the day my daughter Libby was born.

Two words written in cursive black ink on an undulating white flag in the middle of a red heart. Laser treatment meant the flag had gone, the red heart was faint, but the black writing was still just legible – *Nought Forever*. The thing had been a pain in my arse from the time I'd entered politics. In the very few photos of me wearing swimming trunks that were in the public domain, I'd always had make-up applied over the tattoo to cover it up. Callie was looking at me like I'd sprouted two horns out of my forehead and a tail from the small of my back.

'Callie, let me explain——' I began.

'What the hell, Tobey?' She leaped off the bed like she'd been stung. She backed away from me, staring as if I really had turned into the devil himself.

'I can explain——' I climbed out of bed, oblivious to my nakedness.

'Jesus! You're a member of Nought Forever,' Callie whispered.

'I was,' I said, trying to move closer to her, but, for each step I took towards her, she took one away. 'Not any more. Not for years.'

'You belong to a Nought supremacist group, any one of whom would gladly kick my head in as soon as look at me.' Callie shook her head, still backing away.

If she left now without giving me a chance to put things right, I'd never get this evening back – and I was greedy. I wanted more, a lot more. I moved forward with determination before she could outpace me and grabbed her upper arms.

'Callie Rose, you will listen to me. I joined them the year after we split up,' I told her urgently. 'When I finally realized what I was getting into, I shook them off and left. I was angry, and joining them was a way to vent that. It was a stupid mistake, but that's all it was.'

Callie's eyes held horror as she regarded me. Had she even heard a word I'd just said?

'Oh. My. God. I'm such a simp. Why did you do it? Why did you sleep with me if you hate me and mine so much?'

'I don't hate you. I—'

Silence. God, I couldn't believe what I'd almost just said.

'You what?' Callie prompted.

'I don't hate you. This is ridiculous.' I dragged my hand over my hair. 'Why won't you believe it was just a stupid mistake?'

'Because you joined that group. You have their emblem tattooed over your heart as a badge of honour.'

'Hellsake! I've had five laser treatments to remove it. And I told you why I did that.' I raised my voice, exasperated. 'I was angry.'

Callie flinched. I struggled to bank down my frustration. I had to make her understand.

'I was drowning in anger at the time,' I tried again, moderating my voice. 'And the NF were there for me when no one else was.'

'What could make you so bitter that you'd join a Nought supremacist group?'

Silence.

Callie's eyes widened as she heard what I'd left unsaid. 'It was me, wasn't it? You hated me. That's why you joined them.'

And, as much as I might want to, I couldn't deny it.

sixty-six. Callie

I stared at the man, the *stranger*, before me. I'd just slept with the enemy. God! All I wanted to do was go home, hit the shower and scrub myself clean. The Tobey I knew would never have joined the N.F., no matter how angry and hurt he was. My Tobey loved me enough to never make that decision. My Tobey had been swapped for this . . . this doppelgänger.

'Callie, it was just a bad mistake.'

Did Tobey really believe that? No, he couldn't. No one could be that stupid.

I said scathingly, 'You want to vent your anger, you go for a run or hit a punchbag. No one but a Nought supremacist son of a bitch would get a tattoo like that.'

'Godsake, it's just ink – and ink I had removed at that. Stop making such a big deal out of it,' said Tobey.

'It's a symbol of hatred and contempt for anyone who doesn't look like you, Tobey. I can't believe I actually . . . I've got to get out of here.'

I pushed past him, gathering up my clothes and quickly putting them on.

'Callie, it's just a tattoo.'

'No, Tobey. It's a way of thinking, of *being*. Getting it is one thing. That tells me who you were. Still having the remnants of it over your heart? That says who you are, Tobey. Don't you get that?'

Oh my God. All these years, I'd held on to the memory of a guy who didn't exist except in my imagination.

'It says who I was, not who I am,' Tobey said angrily.

'It also says get yourself another lawyer,' I told him, surprised my words were so icy cold when my insides were burning, melting into a puddle of pain and betrayal.

Tobey drew himself up to his full height, his eyes, his whole expression now an unreadable mask. 'Callie, you can't quit as my lawyer. If you quit, that tells the whole world I'm guilty.'

'The whole world doesn't know about your case or that I'm your barrister – remember?'

'And that's the way I want it to stay. If it comes out that you dumped me as your client, how will it look?' said Tobey.

'That's not my problem. I'll see myself out.'

Tobey grabbed my arm. 'Callie, you're not going anywhere. You're as good as putting a noose around my neck if you abandon me now.'

'Which part of "not my problem" are you struggling with?' I blazed. 'Get one of your bigot friends to defend you.'

I pulled out of his grasp and headed for the door, grabbing my bag and phone from the sofa as I did so. I just wanted to go home and shower for a week. A month. Tobey was a member of Nought Forever. God, I was going to be sick. Why would he do it? Why would he sleep with me if he hated me so much? Was this all about retribution? Had he really been nursing a thirst for revenge all these years?

'Callie, you're still my lawyer. If you try to back out of this case, I will go to the CPS, the Legal Ethics Committee and the Bar Council and tell them all that you and I are having an affair. I may lose my lawyer, but you'd lose your career. And, if that doesn't work, I'll go to the press. I know a few rags who would love a story like that. Can't you see the headlines? "Nought PM beds Cross lawyer." That should shift a few newspapers and garner some online ads and revenue, don't you think? And if all that doesn't work, I know things about you and your family that even you don't know – and I won't hesitate to use them against you.'

Horrified, I spun round, staring at Tobey. 'You would do that? Who *are* you?'

He wouldn't. He *couldn't*.

'Don't test me,' he said quietly. 'I'm fighting for my political life here and I'll do whatever is necessary to make this go away. You will defend me, Callie, and what's more you'll get me off this charge of murder. Believe me, we'll both pay the price for anything less.'

A creeping stillness washed over me as Tobey and I regarded each other. I dropped my gaze, trying to regroup. Jon and Sol were right. I'd clung on to the Tobey I used to know as a teenager, too stubborn to see that he no longer existed. Sex with me was just his way of ensuring I remained committed to his cause.

'So it's like that, is it?' I said, looking up.

'Yeah, it's like that,' said Tobey. 'You're my lawyer. I won't allow you to desert me at this late stage.'

'The real Tobias Durbridge finally stands up. Very well. If you'll excuse me, I have work to do to prepare for your trial.' I turned and headed for the door. Inside I was crumbling, but on the outside my back was straight and my footsteps didn't falter. I could at least take comfort in that.

I opened the door, determined not to look back, only to have the door pushed shut from behind. I spun round. Tobey stood before me with just a few centimetres between us. I tried to step away, only to smack back against the door.

'Callie, don't go. Not like this,' he pleaded.

'Tobey, let me leave, please.'

'Why won't you listen?' he said, running a hand through his hair again. I recognized that habit of old. It's what Tobey did whenever he was frustrated and things weren't going his way. Glowering at each other, neither of us wanted to be the first to back down.

But then the mood between us shifted. The look on Tobey's face changed from anger to something far more dangerous. His gaze lowered to my lips. Immediately I turned my face away.

'Don't you dare! Don't think you can seduce me into staying. Let me leave this instant or our deal is off. You can find yourself another lawyer and be damned.'

A moment, then Tobey stepped back. I opened the door, resolving never to be alone with him again.

'Callie, it doesn't have to be like this between us,' he said softly.

'It is what you made it,' I turned to him to say.

'So be it. You know where to find me,' said Tobey, his eyes burning into mine.

Yeah, ruling in hell.

I slammed his door shut and pressed the button to call the lift, ignoring the two bodyguards who flanked the doorway. Only when the lift doors closed behind me did I allow myself to collapse. I sagged against the back wall, struggling to keep it together. I'd never in my life felt so . . . cheap, so ashamed.

Inside my bag, my phone rang again. Retrieving it, I saw I had a number of missed calls, all from my mum. She was on the phone to me now. A deep breath, then I forced myself to sound calm and normal.

'Hi, Mum. How come you're phoning me so late?'

'Callie, where the hell have you been? Didn't you get my texts?' Mum's voice was frantic. 'I've been trying to get hold of you all evening.'

'Mum? What's the matter? What's happened?'

'It's Troy.'

'What about him? I was supposed to meet him for dinner, but he stood me up.'

'He phoned me a couple of hours ago. Well, I thought it was him because the call was from his phone, but it wasn't him and—'

'Mum, slow down. You're not making any sense,' I interrupted. 'What's going on? Did someone steal his phone?'

'Oh, Callie, they've got Troy.'

Pause.

'What?' I said, stunned. 'Who's got what?'

'The man on the phone said he has Troy and Libby. That's a girl in his year. The man said that if I wanted to see Troy again in one piece I had to give you a message.'

'What message?'

As Mum spoke, my blood ran like Arctic waters. At first I hoped it was a bluff or someone's idea of a bad joke, but by the time she had finished relaying the message I knew this was as real as it got.

My worst fears for my brother's safety had been realized. While I'd been in Tobey's bed, Troy was being held against his will. Was he even alive?

No! I wasn't going to go there. He had to be alive, he just had to be. His kidnappers couldn't coerce me into doing what they said if they harmed him.

Calm down, Callie. Think.

'Callie, we need to contact the police,' Mum urged. 'I know they said not to, but we don't stand a chance of getting him back without the help of the police.'

'Don't contact them yet,' I replied. 'Give me forty-eight hours to find him first. After that, if I'm no closer to finding him, then we'll involve them.'

'Callie, we can't take that chance. Not with Troy's life. What can you do in forty-eight hours that they can't?' asked Mum.

'I'll get Jon, my colleague, on it. He still has friends in the police service and I can call in some favours of my own. You know Jon. He's the best at what he does. He'll find them. Mum, please. Let me handle this.'

'If anything happens to Troy and the other girl—'

Oh. My. God . . . The penny had finally dropped with the name of the girl snatched alongside my brother. 'Mum, you said the girl's name is Libby. Is that Liberty Jackman?'

'I don't know,' she said, agitated. 'I guess so. That's the only girl in his year with that name. Wait. Is that the same girl Troy told us about? The one whose mum didn't want a Cross in her house?'

'Yeah.' My mind was racing at full throttle. 'Mum, I need you to trust me. Don't worry. I'll find Troy and bring him home.'

'Troy must be so scared. If anything happens to him—' Tears were all too evident in Mum's voice. Tears that broke me.

'It won't. I won't let it,' I interrupted, my voice harsh with grim determination.

'Callie, d'you really think you can get him home?'

'I'll do whatever it takes, Mum. That's a promise.'

And if it meant making a deal with the devil, then so be it.

sixty-seven. Tobey

What had I done?

How many times had I told myself to get this damned tattoo taken care of properly? But, after the last painful laser treatment, my doctor had warned me that my tattoo was probably as faded as it would get and that any further treatments could cause irrevocable skin damage, leaving me with scar tissue and a huge blemish on my chest. As there would be no more topless photoshoots to show off how physically capable I was of doing the job, I'd decided to call a halt. The idea of scars over my chest certainly didn't appeal. Now, thanks to my vanity, my liberty was in jeopardy. If Callie followed through with her threat to dump me as her client, I'd be well and truly up shit creek with no way back. Yes, there were other lawyers, but she was one of the best and the only one I could trust with what I needed to disclose.

My head had been all over the place when I first had the tattoo done. I'd split up with Callie and had just had Libby, and my life and future were in the toilet. To my way of thinking, Callie and Owen Dowd were the primary authors of my misery – particularly Callie. What had she ever done but brought turmoil into my life?

I left school, trying to focus on what I was.

And what was I? A Nought, loud and proud. A Nought – first, last and forever.

The tattoo was my way of remembering and paying homage to that – or so I'd thought at the time. The ink on my chest was my way of building a wall between Callie and how I felt about her. For years, I persuaded myself that it had worked. Sometimes a whole day passed without me thinking of her.

When I joined Nought Forever, I lasted the grand total of six months. Within days, I knew I'd made a mistake. I'd joined a so-called organization that contained nothing but bruisers and losers. The bruisers were looking for a cause – any cause – to act as camouflage for their love of putting the boot in. Nought Forever welcomed them as long as they focused their aggression on Crosses. As for the losers, they were far more dangerous. They were desperately trying to live in a past that had never really existed in the first place. Losers blamed Crosses for everything they deemed wrong with their lives and their belief was a convenient hook upon which to hang their hatred. Even from within the organization, I kept telling myself I wasn't like them. But I'd done some things . . . Such things . . .

So I got out. Shook them off and walked away.

I sat naked on my bed, contemplating the mess I'd made of my life, and the greatest hits just kept on coming. The best evening of my adult life had turned into the worst. Callie truly believed I'd go to the Bar Council and the media if she dropped my case, and I needed her to go on believing it. With her as my lawyer, I stood a slim chance.

Without her, I stood an icicle's chance in hell of getting through this unscathed.

I wasn't going to spend the rest of my life in prison. That wasn't an option.

I'd die first.

A tap at the front door. Donning my dressing gown, I headed over to open it.

'I'm sorry to disturb you, sir, but Miss Hadley here says she needs to speak to you urgently, and as she just left your apartment—' Michael, one of my Cross protection officers, was all apologies.

Callie stood to one side, her shoulders back, her expression resolute. 'I really need to speak to you, Tobey. It's important or I wouldn't be here.'

That I believed.

'Michael, please put Miss Hadley on the list of people who may see me at any time,' I said.

'Of course, sir.'

I stood aside to let Callie walk past, closing the door quietly behind her.

She stood in the middle of my sitting room with her back to me as if she were fighting for composure. When she finally turned round, alarm bells immediately began to sound in my head. I had initially thought she might've wanted to rip into me again but saw at once I'd misread the situation. Her whole demeanour remained unnaturally stiff, like she was fighting to remain in control. I waited for her to speak.

'Mum received a call earlier from my brother Troy's

phone,' she began. 'Troy has been abducted. I need you to prepare yourself, Tobey.'

'For what? What's going on?' My tone was sharper than intended, but Callie knew it wasn't directed at her.

'I'm sorry, but they also have your daughter, Liberty.'

The bones in my legs dissolved. I collapsed down into the nearest chair. 'Are you sure? Are they all right?'

'They have to be.' Callie sat down beside me, taking my hands in hers. 'The alarm wasn't raised until both Troy and Libby failed to show up for the school head-student election result. The school tried phoning Libby's mum, but apparently they still haven't managed to contact her. Mum knew that Troy was supposed to meet me for dinner so she wasn't overly worried, but he never put in an appearance. I just assumed he had stood me up.'

'So who has them? What do they want?'

'I've been told to give you a message. They want you to go public with the charge against you and plead guilty to Dan's murder or you'll never see your daughter again. I've been ordered to drop the super-injunction and your case or my brother will be sent back to me in pieces. If either of us goes to the police or tells anyone what's really going on, Troy's and Libby's blood will be on our hands. That was the message. Mum said the man who spoke told her he was working for Dan Jeavons.'

The silence in the room was oppressive, overwhelming, when Callie finished speaking. Liberty . . . Was it true? Had someone taken my daughter just to force me out of office? No . . . this was so much more than merely wanting to see me out of a job. There was real malevolence at work here. Someone didn't want to just see me down and out, they wanted me crucified at the end of it. This was definitely worthy of Dan, but he was dead.

'D'you believe the threats?' I asked. 'D'you think someone really does have them?'

Callie nodded. 'Troy wouldn't just disappear. I tried phoning him, but his phone isn't even ringing and that thing is practically superglued to his hand. Can you check to see if Liberty is safe?'

'Hold on.' I retrieved my phone from my jacket pocket and checked Libby's email to me. Clicking on the mobile number she'd provided, I held the phone to my ear.

'Her phone isn't ringing either,' I said after a few moments.

Callie sighed. 'They've probably been destroyed so they can't be used as tracking devices. 'Who d'you think did this?'

That was just the point: I hadn't a clue. It was hard to track down someone when you didn't know who you were looking for.

'Is it someone out to avenge Dan's murder?' Callie ventured. 'Someone who is convinced that you're guilty?'

'But I'm not,' I replied. 'If it's someone who works . . . worked for Dan, they must already know that.'

Callie's eyes shimmered hazel with unshed tears. 'Oh, Tobey, what do we do?'

sixty-eight. Troy

The bolts draw back. The key turns in the lock. The bald thug appears at the top of the stairs, a phone in his hand.

'Troy, you're going to send a message to your sister,' he says without preamble. 'Tell her to do as she's told or you'll be the one to suffer if she doesn't.'

He walks down to the middle of the staircase. 'Shaka's brew! It stinks in here.'

'Then empty the bucket,' snaps Libby. 'Or let us out to use a proper toilet.'

'You two are staying right were you're at.' The bald guy's eyebrows begin to knit together at the suggestion. He trains his phone on me. 'Stand together.'

Libby takes a couple of steps to stand at my side.

'Start speaking, Troy.'

Glaring at him, I clamp my lips together while my hands flutter in front of me.

The guy lowers his phone to scowl at me. 'Speak or I'll snap your girlfriend's neck like a twig.' He raises his phone again.

'Fuck you, baldie, your two shithead friends and the grey van that brought us to this derelict dump,' I state slowly and clearly. 'Will that do?'

He lowers the phone and gives me an oily smile. 'That'll do just fine.' If I didn't know better, I'd say his smile held grudging respect.

'You got a message you want to share, princess?' he says to Libby, holding up his phone again.

'What Troy said – squared,' Libby replies. Her tone would give a lesser man frostbite, but the bald guy just laughs and stops recording. He heads back up the stairs and leaves the basement, not forgetting to bolt the door behind him.

sixty-nine. Callie

'Solomon, I need to talk to you,' I began.

Sol turned from his computer screen to look me up and down. A frown bit into his face.

'I'm not going to like this, am I?'

I raised an eyebrow. 'What makes you say that?'

'Because you never call me Solomon unless you're about to say something that's going to ruin my day. Am I right?'

With a sigh, I took a seat in front of his desk. This wasn't going to be pleasant. Now that I'd been sent proof that both Troy and Tobey's daughter Libby were indeed alive and being held captive, I had no choice but to follow the instructions I'd been given.

'Oh, dear God. Callie, what've you done now?' Sol swung round in his black, custom-built ergonomic chair to face me.

'It's about Tobey Durbridge.'

'I kinda figured it would be.'

I took a deep breath and told him everything – about growing up together, about the money Nana Jasmine had left him, about the reason we'd split up at school and about the night we'd recently spent together. The only facts I omitted were Tobey's tattoo, his threats if I dropped his case, and that my brother and Tobey's daughter had been taken and why. I didn't dare tell Sol about Libby and Troy in case it got back to the kidnappers. The fewer people who knew the whole truth, the more room we'd have to manoeuvre. By the time I'd finished, my cheeks were on fire, but I forced myself to tell Sol the sorry, sordid truth – just not all of it. When I stopped speaking, you could've heard a grain of sand drop on a beach. Sol looked at me like I was certifiable – which probably wasn't far from the truth. He closed his eyes briefly, muttering, 'Jesus, take the wheel!'

I winced. That was Sol's go-to exclamation whenever he was about to explode. I didn't have long to wait.

'Are you out of your ever-loving mind? Have you lost the little sense you were born with? You know what Tobey Durbridge is. Hell, everyone in these chambers knows exactly who and what Tobey Durbridge is. The smart money reckons that Daniel Jeavons wasn't the one heading up the biggest criminal fraternity and drug-running business in the country – it was Tobey pulling the strings.'

'Don't be ridiculous,' I retorted, frowning. Tobey the ruthless, ambitious politician, I could believe. Tobey as some kind of crime overlord? Not so much. 'Sol, he set up a drug rehabilitation centre in his teens, for God's sake.'

'That was then. This is now.' At my dubious look, Sol let me have both barrels. 'You're still unwilling to believe that your friend is corrupt, aren't you? Are you really that naïve? Callie, I'm telling you, Tobey is no good – and that's the man you jumped into bed with. I hope he was good in bed. I hope he was the best damned lover you've ever had because you're going to suffer some serious consequences over this.'

'Sleeping with Tobey may not have been the smartest decision of my life—'

Sol guffawed. 'You think?!'

'But the trial proper doesn't begin until tomorrow. There's still time to salvage this.'

'Salvage th–this?' Sol spluttered. 'Have you been taking stupid pills?'

'Now hold on a minute, Sol—'

'No, you hold on, Callie. I suggest you kiss your career goodbye.'

I leaned forward in my chair, briefly covering my face with my hands. Smoothing back my hair, I desperately tried to marshal my thoughts, but it was like herding cats and toddlers at the same time.

'Sol, trust me, OK?' I said at last. 'I need you to trust me.'

He tilted his head to one side. 'What aren't you telling me?'

'Sol, I'm not stupid, though the evidence would indicate otherwise. I'm asking you, as a friend, to let me handle this case my way.'

He shook his head. 'Are you going to continue this affair with Durbridge?'

'No,' I replied vehemently. 'That's all over. It was a one-time, huge mistake and it'll never be repeated.'

'Hmm . . . And is Durbridge likely to blab to the media about your . . . indiscretion?'

'No.' I forced myself to look Sol in the eye and lied. 'He wouldn't do that.'

'I kinda wish you hadn't told me,' sighed Sol. 'You've made me complicit in your inappropriate behaviour.'

'That wasn't my intention,' I said.

'You realize if Tobey decides to make a complaint or publicizes what you've done, there could be charges levelled against you. You could end up in prison, Callie.'

I nodded. 'If it comes to that, you can deny all knowledge. As far as I'm concerned, this conversation never took place.'

Sol steepled his fingers, resting them against his lips as he regarded me. 'You mean that?'

'Of course.' I was shocked he even had to ask. 'If I go down, I'm not going to drag you with me. We're friends.'

'You want to continue with Tobey's case?' asked Sol.

Hell, no! If I could walk away from this unscathed, then I would in a heartbeat. But I was caught like a fox in a steel trap.

'Sol, I need to see this case through to the end.'

'Even if it leads you to the gates of hell.'

'Even if it drags me into hell itself.'

'Callie, park your pride for a moment and listen. I really think you should let me take over as lead counsel. Have you filed the IDT-12 forms with the appropriate court clerk yet?'

I shook my head. 'I wanted to talk to you first.'

'Good. Leave the counsel and co-counsel sections blank and send the rest.'

'Sol, I'll do as you suggest, but Tobey wants me to defend him. How can I back out now?'

'At least give it some serious thought. OK?'

The phone on Sol's desk began to ring. He snatched it

up. 'Yes?' he barked into it. 'I'm sorry. Hold on just a moment, please.' He covered the mouthpiece with his hand. 'Callie, I hope you know what you're doing.'

I stood up, forcing a smile. 'That's what you pay me for. Don't worry, Sol, I'll fix this.'

And I walked out of his office, quietly closing the door behind me. Fix this? I hoped I sounded convincing because I didn't have a clue what I was going to do. My brother's life was slipping through my fingers like sand and the tighter I tried to hold on, the more sand escaped.

Troy, I'll get you out of this. I swear I will.

But how? How?

I'd been shown to one of the interview rooms in the basement, beneath the courts. The room was a shoebox and unpleasantly warm. There was no window, just downlighters set into the high ceiling. The headache that had started the previous night hadn't abated any. It was still kicking my arse. In one corner of the ceiling sat a security camera, no bigger than a golf ball. Callie had assured me that, though our conversations in here would remain private, they still had to be recorded.

Hurry up, Callie. I want to get this over with.

I didn't have long to wait. Callie entered the room, closing the door behind her. To my surprise, she looked the way I felt, like she'd been left out in the rain for hours and put away wet. I obviously wasn't the only one who'd had trouble sleeping. Callie sat down, only giving me a cursory glance before opening the work satchel she took everywhere.

'As you know, I've had Jon investigating our' – Callie glanced up at the security camera – 'our case. He hasn't made the progress we both hoped for and the judge wouldn't entertain my motion to dismiss the case so you will have to enter your plea for the record. When you plead not guilty, the judge will want to hear statements from both me and the prosecution outlining our case. Then she'll make a decision on whether or not there's enough evidence to commence a jury trial. I think I have enough to create a reasonable—'

'Who's prosecuting?' I interrupted.

'Gabriel Moreland with Leanne Grant as his co-counsel.'

'I heard Moreland is a piranha.'

'You heard right then,' Callie confirmed. 'Gabriel is a man who likes to win. He's looking forward to taking you on personally.'

Yeah, I bet. The world was full of wannabes who had something to prove.

'I guess this is it. We both know what we have to do, Callie. You'll resign as my lawyer. I'll plead guilty and give Dan's friends what they want, and just hope they keep their end of the bargain.' I spoke with a calm I was far from feeling.

'So that's it? You coerce me into defending you, and now you're prepared to roll over and play dead?' Callie frowned.

'What choice do I have? What choice do either of us have?' If I continued with Callie as my lawyer, they might harm my daughter. They might even come after Callie next. Causing pain to the two people I cared most about in this world wasn't something I was willing to contemplate.

'Now you listen to me, Tobey Durbridge,' said Callie, frost crackling in her voice. 'I'm your lawyer, and I'll remain your lawyer unless and until you explicitly tell the judge you want someone else defending you.'

Godsake! She wasn't making this easy, was she?

I lowered my voice until it was barely above a whisper. 'If you don't drop me as your client, Dan's friends may carry out their . . . promise regarding Troy and Libby. You want to take that risk?'

'Jon is still working on that,' said Callie. 'Thanks to Troy, we know there are three male kidnappers – all Noughts – and we have reasonable descriptions of each. We also know that Libby's mum and two friends snatched Libby and Troy off the street in the first place, bundling them into a grey van, but Misty and her friends were killed by these new thugs.'

'Misty is *dead*?'

Callie's expression was immediately contrite. 'Tobey, I'm so sorry. I shouldn't have just blurted it out like that. After all you and her were once an item.'

I shook my head. An item was overstating it. I took a moment, unsure what I was meant to be feeling. Surely more than this . . . nothingness? Misty was dead.

And she was the one who'd kidnapped my daughter in the first place? What the hell? What kind of mother would do that?

'How d'you know all this?'

'Troy told us in the video,' Callie said. 'Try watching it again and concentrate on what his hands are doing, not his mouth. I taught him one-handed sign language when he was younger as a way for the two of us to hold a conversation in front of Mum without her having a clue what we were saying. He got very good at it, better than me. He can sign different things with both hands simultaneously, something I was never able to master.'

I hadn't even noticed Troy's hands signalling. I thought they were just twitching with nerves or fright. Besides, watching the recording, I had eyes for nothing and no one but my daughter and the look of abject terror on her face. Someone was going to pay for that alone. I already had my own people working on finding Libby.

'Until I know they're safe, I'm going to give Dan's cronies exactly what they want. And so are you, Callie. Tell the judge you're no longer defending me.'

'No. Then the scumbags win. We give in, and then it's open season for anyone who thinks we lawyers can be blackmailed into capitulating.'

'It's not about winning or losing.' Didn't Callie see that? 'I don't want anything to happen to Libby and Troy – and neither do you.'

'I'm not dropping this case, Tobey.'

I sighed inwardly. Like this wasn't difficult enough already. From the speculative look on Callie's face, I knew my mask was beginning to slip. I was so tired. Tired of pretending. I was ever the politician, ever the diplomat, picking my words carefully so they couldn't be batted back at me to explode like grenades. It was hard to speak the truth in a world where lies were currency.

This was the fight of my life. I was about to go on trial for murder and someone was working overtime to see both me and Callie go down. That person didn't just want me out of a job, but locked up and disgraced. Out of a job, I'd still be hard to get at, protected. But in prison . . . In prison, I wouldn't last a day. Who hated me enough to feel that way? It wasn't a short list. Whether they had a personal grudge against Callie or she was just collateral damage, it was time for some damage limitation.

'Callie, please don't make me do this. Just recuse yourself from the case and let me find another lawyer.'

'And I've already told you that's not going to happen.' She was digging her heels in and she wasn't going to budge. There was only one thing left that I could do. And once I did it there'd be no turning back. Callie would never forgive me, but what choice did I have?

'Callie, you can't take this case because you're not allowed to deceive the court. Take this case and put me on the witness stand and you'll force me to tell the truth.'

Shocked realization crept into Callie's eyes, albeit with the wrong conclusion. 'Are you . . . are you telling me you did it? You killed Dan?'

'No.' I inhaled silently, bracing myself for the onslaught to come. 'Callie, I didn't kill Dan, your mum did – and, what's more, I can prove it. You can't defend me without putting your mum on the hook, which will never happen. That's why you need to tell the judge you're no longer my lawyer. That way you won't be forced to dissemble.'

Stricken, Callie stared at me, her mouth open. A storm was brewing. I didn't have to wait long for it to hit.

'That's a lie. You're a liar, Tobey Durbridge. No power on this earth could make my mum kill Dan or anyone,' she said with predictable fury.

'Wrong. There's one reason – love for you and your brother. Sephy would stop at nothing to protect both of you.'

'Protect us from what? Let's see this so-called proof of yours,' Callie demanded.

'I have the letter opener used to kill Dan. I carefully took it out of his back and plunged the ornamental knife into him to cover up any traces of the original weapon. That letter opener has Sephy's fingerprints all over it. That's my proof. I also have the disk and the files with the CCTV footage of Sephy committing the crime. I made sure to remove them before the police arrived. Both the letter opener and the disk containing the footage are in a safe place.'

'But the witnesses saw Mum leave while Dan was still alive—'

'She snuck back and hid in one of the bedrooms until Dan was alone.'

'I don't believe you. I want to see this so-called proof.'

I gave her a facsimile of a smile. 'You think I'm stupid? If I show it to you and all this comes out, you could be called as a witness against me or charged with perverting the course of justice. That way I still lose everything. I'm not bluffing, Callie. I do have proof of what I say. Up till now I've been trying to protect Sephy. I felt I owed her – and you – something. But not any more. That debt is paid in full. So I'll ask you once and once only. Are you my lawyer or not?'

The clerk popped his head inside the interview room to inform her, 'Miss Hadley, the court is now open.' He propped open the door, waiting for us to depart. Just beyond the door were two Cross police officers, ready to escort me to the dock. We both stood up.

'Callie, we're going to keep the customers satisfied. Right?'

She didn't reply.

'Right, Callie?' I insisted.

'Time to go. I'll see you up there.' And with that Callie turned and left the room.

I watched her walk away, my heart thumping. Would she back down? Her brother's life was on the line as well as my daughter's if she didn't. We both had to be smart about this.

The two police officers led the way to court number twelve. As we made our way up the stairs which led directly to the dock, it hit me that these were my last moments of freedom. Once I pleaded guilty, I would probably be remanded in custody until sentencing. And, if Dan's friends on the inside didn't get to me first, Owen Dowd's friends would. Either way, my hours were numbered. So it was up to me to make sure Callie didn't suffer the same fate. There wasn't a lot left that I could do to protect those I loved, but I could do that.

seventy-one. Callie

Court number twelve was packed with reporters. They'd take their notes and record every word said in the hope that the super-injunction would be lifted and they could report on one of the biggest stories of the decade. I sat next to Sol, my mind a hive full of angry bees. I could feel Tobey's eyes searing into my back from the dock.

Mum . . .

Was Tobey telling the truth about Mum? I didn't know, and that alone was killing me. In spite of all my bravado in front of Tobey, I wasn't at all sure what I was going to do. If anything happened to Troy and Libby, I'd never forgive myself. But if I were to capitulate now, once word got out about what had happened, justice would become a commodity to be bought, sold, exploited or bullied. And, if Tobey was right about Mum, how could I defend him and not implicate her?

Everything I thought I knew about myself was way up in the air. I'd always prided myself on my integrity. So much for that. I'd slept with my client, who was holding that fact and my mum's supposed guilt over my neck like a guillotine blade. The phone call I'd received this morning made it very clear that, if I represented Tobey, my brother was dead. What guarantee did I have that Troy's kidnappers would keep their word and let Troy go, even if I refused to defend Tobey? The answer was: none. Was Troy even still alive? Uncertainty brought tears to my eyes. The bees in my head were buzzing and stinging and swarming till I could hardly think straight. The judge entered the room. We all stood up. I groaned softly. The moment of truth had arrived.

'Callie?' Sol said quietly. 'Are you OK?'

I shook my head.

'Have you made a final decision yet? Am I taking over this case or is it still yours?'

I couldn't answer. This was the hardest decision of my entire life. I held my brother's life in one hand, Tobey's future in the other. How could I represent Tobey, knowing that, if I did, Troy was dead for sure? And, if I stayed on the case, wasn't I also putting my mum's head on the chopping block? Maybe Tobey was lying. But that unwavering look in his eyes as he told me he had proof of Mum's guilt . . . If he was bluffing, he had it down to a fine art. What should I do? I was heartsick and heartsore and the hearing was about to start.

A tap on my shoulder.

I turned to see Aaron, one of the Cross court clerks, behind me. He was a man in his fifties with silver hair at his temples and a ready, twinkling smile in his eyes – except he wasn't smiling now.

'The defendant in the dock wants a word with you,' he told me.

'Now?'

'Yes. He said it was urgent.'

Frowning, I looked across at Tobey. He beckoned to me, his expression serious, anxious.

The judge was approaching her chair. I could get into trouble for this as it was a breach of court protocol, but Tobey looked desperate to speak to me. I slid past Solomon and headed to the back of the court.

'What? And make it fast,' I hissed at Tobey.

At any moment, Judge Okafor was going to take my head off. All those in the court took their seats.

'Drop this case, Callie,' said Tobey quietly. 'It's not worth your brother's life. Just walk away. No hard feelings. And, if you're worried about any repercussions from me, there won't be any. No more threats, I promise.'

I realized what Tobey was saying. He was giving me a clear way out.

'Miss Hadley, is there a problem?' asked Judge Okafor.

I turned to face her. 'No, your honour. And my apologies for my rudeness. The defendant had some last-minute instructions for me.'

'Then perhaps, if your conversation has concluded, you'd like to sit down?' said Judge Okafor, looking daggers at me.

Not a good way to start this trial.

I headed back to my seat. The bees in my head weren't any calmer.

'Well?' said Sol softly.

I shook my head. Far from clarifying and ordering my thoughts, Tobey had just confused me further.

seventy-two. Tobey

Libby . . .

Was she dead? Alive? If alive, she had to be so scared. And here I was in this dock, unable to go to her or help her. The warning I'd received had been quite explicit – plead guilty or have my daughter's blood on my hands. So I'd plead guilty. But, even if I did do that, why would Libby's kidnappers let her go? So that they could be identified by her? To have a witness against them? No way. Once they'd got what they wanted, I'd be signing my daughter's death warrant.

But if there was a chance, no matter how slim, that the kidnappers would keep their word? Was that even likely though? Surely Libby's greatest chance was for me to *not* do as I was told. That way I could buy some time. Or was I just deluding myself?

And round and round. My thoughts fizzed and burned like fireworks. My head was about to explode.

Wait . . . What?

My name was being called.

'Will Tobias Durbridge, the defendant, please rise?'

I got to my feet, tugging at my dark blue tie, which was strangling me.

'Tobias Durbridge, you have been charged with the murder of Daniel Jeavons. How do you plead? Guilty or not guilty?'

I glanced at Callie. I couldn't help it. She was looking at me, her gaze intense. She knew as well as I did what was at stake.

The question was repeated. 'Tobias Durbridge, how do you plead?'

Libby . . .

I straightened up and replied, 'Not guilty.'

seventy-three. Callie

'Let the record reflect that Gabriel Moreland, QC, is the prosecution barrister, with Leanne Grant as his co-counsel,' said Adele Dupres, the head court clerk. She frowned down at the electronic tablet in her hand. 'Who stands as the defence barrister?'

Adele looked from me to Sol impatiently, her lips pursed in irritation. The announcement of the defending barrister should've been a formality at this stage, but that part of the form on her tablet was blank – and she wasn't happy. Adele liked her court to run like clockwork and she could make life pretty tough for those who didn't toe her line.

Sol placed an understanding hand on my shoulder as he stood up. I pulled at his sleeve, and he gave me a quizzical look. I shook my head at him and stood in his place. A quick glance behind to look at Tobey. Our eyes met for only a second or two, but it was enough. I turned back to face Judge Okafor.

'If it please the court, I'll be acting as the defence barrister in this trial,' I said. 'Solomon Camden will be my co-counsel.'

'So noted,' said Adele.

She sat back down, as did I.

'Are you sure about this?' asked Sol.

I shook my head. Sure? Was he kidding? I turned to look at Tobey again. His eyes were trained on me, clinging to faint hope while drowning in despair. I didn't doubt that my expression was a reflection of his own. *Troy* . . .

The trial had begun.

seventy-four. Libby

It's hard to gauge the passing of time when there are no windows to see the sky and no devices to count for you. My phone and smart watch had been taken, as had Troy's, so we were both in the dark — or as good as. How long have Troy and I been sitting on this crate? A few hours? A day? Longer? Troy says he managed to pass on some info about our kidnappers using sign language when they were filming us. I didn't even notice him doing it. That's a good sign, right?

What have they done with Mum's body?

Is she still up there, lying on the floor, eyes closed against the world. Is all this because I threatened to visit a solicitor on my eighteenth birthday? Did Mum do all this out of desperation? Or was it love? A profound and enduring love for lots of money and the lifestyle it afforded her. Slowly, I rub my arm along the corner of the crate, feeling the welcome bite of the metal strip along its edge scraping my skin. Not ideal but I'm having to improvise.

'Libby, stop it.'

'Stop what?'

'Stop thinking all this is your fault. It isn't,' says Troy. 'Your mum's mistakes were hers to make and own, not yours.'

'How did you know I was thinking that?' I ask, too astounded to deny it.

'You have a shit poker face,' he replies with a faint smile. 'And stop scraping your skin off. We've enough problems without you getting sepsis on top of everything else.'

I stop rasping my skin and look at him. Really look at him the way I haven't in years. The short locks styled at the top of his head, his large honey-brown eyes framed by some of the longest lashes I've ever seen, that ready smile of his.

'What?' Troy's smile fades.

'Thank you.'

'For what?' he asks.

'For seeing me. For saving my life.'

Troy shrugs. If I didn't know any better, I'd say he was embarrassed. I slip my hand into his.

'I mean it. If it wasn't for you, my chest would be home to a number of bullets right about now.'

'You're welcome.' Troy tries to pull back his hand, but I hold on to it tighter. 'I'll have my hand back now,' he says, but not unkindly.

Reluctantly, I let go. 'I'm glad it's you down here with me.'

Troy's smile vanishes. His eyes grow cold. 'Yeah, you said.' He starts to shift along the crate to put more room between us.

'No, I don't mean it like that,' I rush to explain. 'I don't mean it in a bad way. It's just that all my other friends would've blamed me for what my mum did if they were here instead of you. But you haven't thrown it in my face. Not once. You . . . you're more than I deserve.'

Frowning, Troy opens his mouth to speak, only the sound of hammering gets in first.

Troy jumps to his feet and races up the wooden steps to the door on the ground floor. I slowly stand, staring in horror after him. The hammering continues, the sound filling the basement and echoing round my head. Troy bangs on the door, rattling the doorknob.

'WHAT'RE YOU DOING? DON'T DO THIS! LET US OUT!'

I don't need to be on the other side of the door to know what's happening. We're being boarded in. The hammering comes from the top of the door, the bottom, the middle. Whoever is sealing us in the room isn't mucking about. I close my eyes, but I'm drowning in sounds – hammering, shouting, the door handle rattling, my blood roaring round my body. The noises are relentless. Ruthless.

But if the hammering is bad, the silence when it stops is worse. Troy must feel the same because he stops rattling the door handle and yelling. The quiet is shocking. Troy turns to me, despair dissolving his bones as his whole body sags and he falls to his knees. We've been boarded in. No one is getting into this room in a hurry and we won't be getting out.

Ever.

To be concluded . . .

AUTHOR'S NOTE

In 2010, during the Pan-Cafrique accords, it was unanimously agreed that the name of the continent should be changed to Zafrika in all official documentation to be used by each Zafrikan country. Where possible, all formal and legal documentation will be retrospectively amended. The unofficial name of Aprica for the continent is deemed acceptable for use during more informal settings.

Read all the books in the Noughts & Crosses series

'Unforgettable'
Independent

'Dramatic, moving and brave'
Guardian

Read more
by Malorie Blackman

Olivia and her twin brother, Aidan, are heading alone back to Earth following the virus that completely wiped out the rest of their crew and family.

Nathan is part of a community heading in the opposite direction, when their lives unexpectedly collide. Nathan and Olivia are instantly attracted to each other – like nothing they have ever experienced.

But surrounded by rumours, deception – even murder – is it possible to live out a happy-ever-after . . . ?

'A thrilling love story'
Mail on Sunday